THE ORDER OF THE SECRET CHIEFS

THE ORDER OF THE SECRET CHIEFS

SIMON SHERIDAN

Simon Sheridan

It was twelve hours to midnight. Nobody had ever closed a mark in twelve hours for the very simple reason that it couldn't be done. But Adam Sampson was going to do it. At least that's what he told himself as he strode up the bluestone stairs that led off Swanston Street and towards the coffee shop.

It was a Starbucks that was set well back from the street. The midday sun faded and was replaced by the harsh fluorescent light that filled the cavernous space and bounced off exposed concrete as he entered from the alleyway. His eyes slowly adjusted as he walked over and took the usual seat on the far wall.

The main advantage of meeting in a Starbucks was that you didn't need to buy coffee. You didn't need to buy anything. No cashier on minimum wage was going to take the trouble to kick out freeloaders. For that reason, there were usually a few undesirables around but they didn't cause much trouble and were far outnumbered by paying customers.

The disadvantage of Starbucks was that there weren't many left in Melbourne. The locals wouldn't touch the stuff. The stores that remained were filled mostly by international students and their visiting relatives. Occasionally an American tourist would come in. They were easily identifiable by the volume of their speech. There was one at the counter right now. He was having trouble understanding the cashier who was a young girl speaking with a heavy Indian accent.

Adam's mentor was an American. Not his direct mentor or even the mentor above that. The top guy. The head honcho. He'd never met him personally but late last year at a syndicate meeting they had him on video conference up on the big screen. He was from India originally but he spoke in a big, broad American accent. Part of the prize for this year's sales winner was a trip to New York for the international conference and the chance to meet the man himself. In a world that was all about contacts, that was the best contact you could have.

Adam checked his watch; a fake Rolex he'd picked up in Thailand. It was two minutes to twelve. He looked around the room but there was no sign of him. He should have been here ten minutes ago. He should have been here before Adam. Any protégé should know that. You don't keep the boss waiting.

Adam pulled out his phone and was about to call when he saw Cameron come through the door. He was wearing jeans and a t-shirt. Why was he wearing jeans and a t-shirt?

"Hey, man," said Cameron as he sat down beside Adam in the booth.

"You're late and you're not dressed properly," said Adam.

"Yeah, I wanted to…"

"Don't worry," said Adam waving his hand to dismiss Cameron's excuses. "How did you go with that lead?"

"No good."

"What happened?"

"She's a filcher."

In the argot of The Golden Vertex, a *filcher* is a time waster. A lonely person who just wants somebody to talk to.

"Just cos she's a filcher doesn't mean we can't convert her."

"Nah. She doesn't have any money."

"That not necessarily a problem. I've told you we can set up lines of credit. It's the latest product from the syndicate. Remember? You were there when Singh announced it a couple of months ago."

"Doesn't matter. She lives in a home. All the groceries are ordered for her."

Adam sank back in his chair. There weren't many deal breakers in this field but that was one. He'd tried it in the past, of course. No harm in trying. But it was a huge waste of time involving powers of attorney and all kinds of crap that you didn't want to know about.

"We need another mark," he said more to himself than to Cameron.

"I guess we're out of time."

"He's here."

Adam gave Cameron a wack on the arm and stood up. He smiled and waved to the middle-aged man who had just walked in. Neil Mitchell. He was tall, lanky and clumsy. His gait reminded Adam of a mildly drunk giraffe. Adam had never seen a mildly drunk giraffe but he supposed that was how one must look. A little bit ridiculous.

"G'day, Neil." He reached out and shook the man's hand.

"G'day, Neil," said Cameron also holding out his hand for the man to shake.

They sat down.

"So, this is it," said Adam. "Excited?"

"Yeah."

A casual observer would have deduced from the tone of his voice that Neil was about as excited as an overfed koala after half a packet of Valium. Adam knew different. The seven-stage initiation process for entry into The Golden Vertex meant that an associate got to know his marks very well. He'd learned that Neil operated in an emotional continuum that started at morose and ended somewhere around of taciturn.

"Excellent. Now, as we've already discussed, this is the seventh and final step in your journey to membership. And, you'll be pleased to know, it's also the shortest. All we need is your signature on the paperwork. Did you get a chance to read over everything?"

Neil nodded.

"Ok. Let's do it."

Adam opened his briefcase and pulled out some paperwork and a pen.

"Just a signature and date at the bottom of the last page is all we need."

Neil took the pen and scribbled in the appropriate places. Adam and Cameron both countersigned. Adam put the papers away and turned to face Neil.

"Neil Mitchell, with this signature you become the latest node in our sacred graph. The sacred graph runs all the way back to our founder, Varinder Singh. Like grandmaster Singh, you are about to embark on a path that leads to resplendence, riches and, above all, freedom. Cameron and I will be your mentors on this path and on behalf of both of us, I hereby wish you all success as you begin your journey as an associate. Welcome to The Golden Vertex."

"Thanks," said Neil.

"He's a talkative one, isn't he," said Adam looking over at Cameron with a forced laugh.

"We'll have to work on that. You'll need to be the one doing most of the talking when you convert your own marks."

"Have you got your first marks listed down yet?" asked Cameron.

Neil nodded.

"Get onto them quickly. You want to start building momentum as soon as possible. Get that network working for you."

Neil nodded again. Adam looked like he'd had an idea.

"While we're on the subject of marks, Neil. It is customary for a new protégé to give his mentors his highest probability mark when joining the syndicate. It's a gesture of, umm, respect and gratitude for the people who initiated him."

"It is?" said Cameron looking puzzled.

Adam and Cameron had been working together for almost twelve months now and had built up a range of non-verbal communicative signals in that time. The look that Adam now gave to Cameron meant "shut the fuck up". It was the most common non-verbal communication between the two. It was also rather high on the list of their most common verbal communications. Cameron got the message.

"I think Cameron has forgotten his own initiation which was only twelve months ago. Although it does feel like longer than that, doesn't it?"

"That sounds unfair," said Neil with newfound verbosity.

"Fair? It's perfectly fair, Neil. We've unlocked the door and set you on the pathway to wealth beyond your wildest dreams. Isn't it fair to reciprocate our generosity?"

"But I was hoping to start building my own network."

"And you will start building it, Neil."

Adam looked at Neil. He had underestimated the man's emotional range. Neil appeared quite capable of peevishness and querulousness alongside his base level of moroseness.

"Look, I'll tell you what. Even though it's highly irregular and frankly a little ungracious, I'll direct the commission to you. All you have to do is let me handle the conversion and sign the paperwork. That way I get the credit for the conversion and you get the money. What do you say to that?"

Neil gave the smallest possible shrug of the shoulders that was visible to the naked human eye. Adam whipped out his phone.

"Ok. So, who's your highest probability mark, Neil."

Neil looked down at the table.

"Neil?"

"My mum," he whispered.

"Say again. I didn't quite catch that."

"My *mum*."

Adam leaned back. Family members were, of course, prime candidates for marks but Neil was middle aged and his mother would have to be really getting on. The primary demographic for the syndicate was younger people. Adam knew that the probabilities of success with the elderly were very low.

"We can't do his mum," said Cameron turning to Adam and holding his hands up in a gesture of reluctance.

"Of course we can do his mum," said Adam.

He turned to Neil.

"We can do your mum, Neil."

"She doesn't live in a retirement home, does she?" asked Cameron.

Neil shook his head.

"What about your father? Will he need to be involved?" asked Adam.

"No. He died last week."

"Last week?" said Cameron.

"I'm really sorry to hear that," said Adam.

Cameron gave Adam another imploring look and this time Adam was inclined to agree.

"Ok, look. Let's forget about your mum. Who's your second highest probability mark? We can use that instead."

"Mum's all I've got on my list. I was going to convert her when I got home after work tonight."

"You still live with your mother?" asked Cameron his voice breaking halfway through the sentence and accidentally, but appropriately, conveying his incredulity at this fact.

Neil nodded.

Cameron looked at Adam again. It was one of the rarer non-verbal gestures between the two of them but Adam had no trouble picking up the meaning. It meant: *Fuck no. No fucking way. Don't fucking do this to me.*

Adam's response said simply: *sorry, bro.*

"Ok, Neil, just enter your mum's phone number right there and Cameron and I will be onto her in a flash."

Adam handed over his phone to Neil who slowly typed in the number. He handed it back to Adam who hit Save and then stood up sharply.

"Ok. Thanks a lot, Neil. Once again, welcome, and we'll be in touch next week to get you moving towards your hopes and dreams."

They all shook hands again and Neil hauled himself across the room and out the door.

"Fuck me, what a dead fish," said Adam sitting down again. "I don't think we're gonna get much action out of that guy."

"But we're gonna get some action out of his mum?" asked Cameron.

"You bet."

"What was that stuff about it being tradition for a new starter to give up his best mark?"

"Just something I made up."

"I don't think it's right to take a man's first mark. Especially if it's his bloody mum."

"Look, we need another conversion by the end of the day. I don't have any leads. Do you?"

"No."

"Then Neil's mum is our only chance of winning."

"We can't convert her by the end of the day anyway."

"Says who?"

"It's obvious. She has to attend a syndicate meeting and there's no syndicate meeting until next week. She has to meet with Mark. She has to meet with Trevor. There's no time."

"What's Varinder's first rule?"

"Huh?"

"His first rule. The first thing in The Golden Vertex handbook."

"I dunno. I can't remember."

"*If you think it, it shall be so.* In other words, you make your own destiny. Today, my friend, we're going to make our own destiny."

A single beep emanated from Adam and Cameron's phones simultaneously. They both grabbed their respective devices.

"Fuck," said Adam at a volume befitting an American tourist. Several patrons looked up nervously from their coffee flavoured milkshakes. He threw his phone down on the table.

"Well, that's it then," said Cameron closing his phone. "Kenneth has had another conversion certified. He wins."

Adam slumped into his seat and pushed back against the head rest.

"Kenneth fuckin Xu. Asshole."

"He's a smug bastard that's for sure," said Cameron in a conciliatory tone that barely hid the fact that he was glad he would no longer have to try and convert Neil's mum.

Adam sat up straight again and grabbed his phone. He pulled up The Golden Vertex app and went to the leader board. Kenneth Xu and his protégé, Malvin Liu, were now one conversion clear of Adam and Cameron.

"We can still tie it."

"What?"

"One more conversion and we tie for top place."

"What happens then?"

"I dunno. Maybe we all win."

Cameron turned to Adam.

"Just relax, man. We've had a great year. My income has more than doubled. I'm guessing yours must be even better. Let's just enjoy it. The holidays are coming up."

"I want to beat Xu and I want to be on that flight to New York in February. Just one last push. One last conversion. Are you in?"

Cameron sighed.

"You know I'm with you all the way."

Adam turned to his phone and pulled up the number for Neil's mum. He pressed Dial.

"Mrs Mitchell is it? Good afternoon, Mrs Mitchell. My name's Adam Sampson. I got your number from your son, Neil. Neil said you were the kind of person who loves to chase after your dreams and let no barrier stand in the way of..."

CHAPTER 2

"I don't think you're getting it, mate. It's the principle of the..."

Adam's mobile ringtone played back over the car stereo. He looked over at the phone sitting in its holder on the dashboard.

"Hang on, Cam. I've gotta get this. It's Jules."

Adam pressed the phone to accept the call.

"Hey, babe."

"I got your text," crackled a female voice through the car stereo speakers.

"Look I know you're..."

"No, no, no, Adam. I'm not interested in your excuses. It's your turn to listen to me for a change. Are you listening?"

Adam looked over at Cameron.

"Yeah, babe. But I've got Cameron in the car with me and I'm on speaker phone."

"Hi, Julie," said Cameron chirpily.

"Then pick up the phone, Adam."

"I can't. I'm driving."

"Fine. Then Cameron gets to hear it too."

"We could pull over or some...," started Cameron before Julie spoke over the top of him.

"Adam, we've been planning this dinner for three weeks. *Three. Weeks.* The same length of time since you last had to cancel because *something popped up at the syndicate.* And this time you promised. You said the year was over with. That things would be winding down and the final cut-off date for sales meant that everything would need to be sorted by now and there was no way you would be called away to do a meeting. And what happens? Another bloody meeting. So everything you said was a lie, wasn't it? And now I've got to cancel these reservations. And that costs money, honey. You can't cancel at Che Vue at the last minute. It doesn't work that way. There's consequences. And now I have to tell my parents that they still don't get to meet the man I've been dating for more than a year. And now I'm starting to think that maybe I shouldn't be dating him at all."

Adam took a moment to figure out if Julie was pausing to take a breath or whether she'd finished or whether she'd fainted from lack of oxygen. The speaker was silent. He inhaled carefully.

"I know you're upset. I get it. But we got this last-minute hot lead and we had to follow it up. Look, today *is* the last day of the sales year but the cut-off is at midnight. The guys we're competing against got an extra conversion so we're still one behind first place. If we can make this one we win."

"You mean you tie."

"Yeah, we tie for the winner's spot. And you know what that means?"

"What?"

"Don't you remember?"

"No."

"New York, baby. A free trip for two. You and I. I know you've always wanted to visit the States. Haven't you?"

"Yes," said Julie in reluctant agreement.

"That's right. I'm doing this as much for you as for me. We've got one chance to make this conversion and then that trip is ours. C'mon. Times Square. Madison Square Garden. That art gallery you were talking about. What was it called? The google-heim?"

"Guggenheim."

"Yeah, that one. You see? If we can make this conversion it's a trip to Big Apple. Don't you want that?"

A big sigh came through the car stereo speakers then another of the same length. It sounded like waves crashing onto the beach. Waves of perfectly formed excuses that Julie knew from experience would eventually erode into her anger and leave her damp and placated on the shore of frustration. She gave in.

"Fine. I'll cancel the reservations." You could hear the sagging of her shoulders and the drooping of her head through the speaker.

"Ok, babe. And look, tell your parents I really want to meet them soon. We've got the final syndicate meeting for the year tomorrow and then after that my calendar is free so we can meet any time."

Silence.

"Ok?"

"Ok."

"Alright. I'll speak to you later. Bye, honey."

Adam reached over and ended the call. Cameron turned to him with an angry look on his face.

"I thought you and I were going to New York."

"Umm, yeah. That was the plan."

"That's right. As your partner in the sales competition that ticket rightly belongs to me."

"I know, mate."

"But you just told your girlfriend that you're gonna give it to her."

Adam sighed.

"Look, let's not get ahead of ourselves. If we can't convert this old lady then it's all academic anyway, isn't it? We can talk about it tomorrow. I'll figure something out."

Adam cast a sideways glance at Cameron to see how this idea went down. It seemed to work. Or at least Cameron wasn't going to press the matter further for now.

He looked at the clock. They were about fifteen minutes away from Glen Waverly where Mrs Mitchell was waiting for them.

He glanced over again at Cameron who seemed deep in thought. Better make conversation to take his mind off the New York thing. That couldn't be good for morale in the lead up to a sales pitch.

"So, to go back to what I was saying before, once you've grasped the underlying principles, your whole approach changes, your whole way of seeing the world. You realise there's opportunities everywhere, all the time. There's never a situation where you can't make money."

"I'm sure there are some situations where you can't make money," said Cameron who wasn't in a mood to agree with Adam at the moment.

"Name one."

"I dunno. A funeral."

"Well, the funeral company makes money out of it."

"Yeah, but what about us?"

"I guarantee we could make sales at a funeral. Any time when people's emotions are running high is a time to make a sale. That's why the relatives of a deceased person are a common target for scam artists."

"So, we're just like scam artists?"

Adam looked over at Cameron.

"Is that what you think? That we're scam artists?"

"No."

"That's good. I think you're getting the point mixed up. I'm not talking about the morality of the sale, I'm just talking about the sale. And the fact is you can sell anything at any time. Shit, you can even sell death."

"What? Like euthanasia?"

"Yeah, that too. But I was thinking about the *idea* of death. I was reading an article about apocalypse cults the other day. Huge business opportunities there. People fork out serious cash. In many cases, they literally transfer their entire savings over to the cult."

"Makes sense. If you're about to join in a mass suicide you aren't gonna need your money anymore."

"Yeah, but everybody else in the cult is supposed to kill themselves too so why should *they* need the money?"

"But most of those groups don't go through with it, right? They don't actually kill themselves when the day comes."

"Doesn't matter. The point is that the sale was made. Money changed hands. And the product was your own death. I can even sell you your own death. How cool is that?"

Adam looked over at Cameron to see if the point was made.

"I don't know if *cool* is the word I would use," said Cameron. "And I don't know if I like the idea of everything being for sale. There's things in life beyond money."

Adam let this remark hang in the air for a few seconds.

"Listen, mate. Let me tell you something as mentor to protégé. You need to show more initiative if you're going to rise through the ranks of the syndicate. A bit more hunger. The people at the top don't care about the things in life beyond money. They care about money. Money makes the world go round, mate. You need to keep that in mind when you're doing work for the syndicate."

"Well, maybe I'm not cut out for the syndicate after all."

"Woah, hang on. That's not what I'm saying, Cameron. You've got what it takes. You're friendly, personable, you know how to get along with people. I just think you need to apply yourself more. Be more proactive. More aggressive."

There was no response. Adam looked over at Cameron.

"When I first approached you to join the syndicate, what was the reason you gave me for wanting to join?"

Cameron thought about for a second.

"To meet new people."

"And?"

"I dunno. I think that was all."

"To take more control of your destiny."

"Actually, I think you said that to me."

"Well, it's true."

Adam's GPS droned over the car stereo informing him to exit the freeway in five hundred metres.

"Ok, mate. We're almost there. I'm gonna give you the chance to show some of that initiative now. To take control of our destiny in this sales competition. Alright? I want you to take the lead with Mrs Mitchell. This is our last conversion for the year. I want you to show me everything you've learned with me in the last twelve months. What do you think? Are you ready?"

"Yeah," said Cameron unconvincingly.

"C'mon. You just told me you wanted to go to New York. Do you really want to go?"

"Of course."

"Well now's your chance to make it happen. Do you want it?"

"Yes."

"I'm not feeling it, mate. DO. YOU. WANT. IT?"

"YEAH!"

"Alright, let's do this old woman."

CHAPTER 3

Adam and Cameron got out of the car and walked up the driveway of 23 Wattle Street, Glen Waverly, a leafy street in a leafy suburb that had started off wealthy and become even wealthier in recent years. The house was a classic old school Melbourne weatherboard that had been kept in pristine condition. An array of roses stretched the length of the front picket fence and were in full early summer bloom. The front yard itself was dominated by an imperious elm tree which formed a canopy beneath which a densely planted cottage garden burst forth in colour. The shade beneath it was pleasantly cool blocking out the early afternoon sun of a beautiful blue-sky day.

Adam in his three-piece suit (no tie) and Cameron in his jeans and a t-shirt made a somewhat odd-looking couple as they approached the front door. There was a flick on the edge of the curtain at the front window as they stepped onto the porch. Adam rang the bell and a second later the door opened. Between the deep shade cast by the elm tree and the dark black grill of the wire security door they couldn't make out who was on the other side. Adam took a guess.

"Mrs Mitchell?"

"That's right," came a voice from the other side of the grill. Its tone was about as welcoming as a vegemite sandwich at a dinner party.

"I'm Adam Sampson and this is my associate, Cameron Wilkins. We spoke to you on the phone a couple of hours ago."

"Yes. Something about my son, Neil, wasn't it? What nonsense has he got himself tied up in this time?"

"We're from The Golden Vertex, an association that offers people like yourself…"

"The Golden what?" snapped Mrs Mitchell. "Have you roped my son into a bloody religious group?"

"No, no, no, ma'am. Nothing like that. Neil has just recently become a member and he suggested you might also be interested in joining. We offer people the opportunity to achieve the wealth and success they deserve."

"Well, that good-for-nothing boy doesn't deserve anything."

"May we come in and we can tell you more about what we can offer?"

"Alright. But you're wasting your time. I don't go in for these gimmicks."

There was a click from the lock of the screen door and the sound of footsteps leading back down the hall. Adam opened the door and saw a small and slender old lady in a white dressing gown with brown hair up in curlers walking away from the door and towards what looked like the kitchen.

"Close the doors behind you when you come in," said Mrs Mitchell over her shoulder.

Adam and Cameron stepped inside. Cameron ensured both the screen and the front door were properly closed. The small front entrance hall featured a beautiful old wooden grandfather clock that was about six feet tall. Its stainless-steel pendulum rocked back and forth giving a loud click on each rotation. To the right was the lounge room with a lavishly upholstered three-piece lounge suite that was drowning in frilled cushions and quilted throw rugs.

They followed Mrs Mitchell down the tiled hallway which ended, as Adam had initially guessed, in the kitchen. It was a wood-panelled affair that featured a long breakfast bar down one side. Straight ahead they could see into the separate dining room that had a large wooden dining table laid over with a tablecloth that was equally as frilly as the lounge room cushions. The place was immaculately tidy. Adam might have guessed that, given her age, Mrs Mitchell paid for extra help to keep it that way but the sprightly fashion in which she moved around led him to believe that it was all her own doing.

"One sugar or two," said Mrs Mitchell who had already inserted teabags into three cups that were sitting on the kitchen counter and had her teaspoon at the ready inside a pot of sugar.

"Do you have coffee, Mrs Mitchell?" asked Cameron.

"No, it's tea or nothing."

"Ok. One sugar for me, please."

"No sugar or milk for me, Mrs Mitchell," said Adam.

Mrs Mitchell proceeded to dole out the required sugar and fetch the milk from the fridge. The kettle began to bubble.

Adam made eye contact with Cameron and gave a gesture for him to start the proceedings. Cameron wracked his brain. It had been about a month since he'd had to do this. How do you start these things again?

Step One: *Establish rapport*

That was the first step, wasn't it? Adam raised an eyebrow in Cameron's direction.

Yes. Establish rapport. Let's try that.

"Right. Umm, Mrs Mitchell. This is a, ahh, nice place. Do you rent it or own it?" said Cameron.

"Does this look like a rental house, Mr...what was your name again?"

"Wilkins. Cameron Wilkins."

"Does this look like a rental house, Mr Wilkins?"

"I don't know."

"Of course it isn't. I own it. And once my recently deceased husband's will is executed, I will own it outright."

"Recently, de....umm, recently deceased," stammered Cameron. "I'm sorry to, umm, hear... When did he die?"

Adam raised both his eyebrows in Cameron's direction and gave a quick shake of his head.

"Last Friday. We had the funeral this morning."

"This morning. Right. So, Neil had to....ummm..."

"Yes. Neil had to rush off early. Said he had a meeting to go to."

"Rush off early for a meeting. About midday was it?"

"Yes. You know about it, Mr Wilkins?"

"No. Nothing about it. Nothing."

Cameron's head swirled with the new information. He knew this was not a good topic. He needed to change the topic. Maybe the new topic could be:

Step Two: *Find out the mark's motivations*

"So, Mrs Mitchell. What are you enthusiastic about in life at the moment?"

Adam's eyebrows were in danger of removing themselves from the top of his head and flying over to box Cameron in the ears.

"Death, Mr Wilkins," said Mrs Mitchell as if the question had been a perfectly logical next phase of the conversation.

"I'm sorry?" said Cameron who was now well and truly in over his head.

Mrs Mitchell handed Adam and Cameron their cups of tea and walked back to the kitchen counter to retrieve hers.

"I'm looking forward to the day when I'm the one lying in the casket and somebody else can take care of the catering and the eulogy and the silly questions from young fools who still haven't told me what they are doing in my house."

Adam decided he needed to take control of the encounter. He took a step towards Mrs Mitchell.

"Mrs Mitchell, you seem like a no-nonsense woman who knows what she wants. So, let me explain very clearly why we are here. We are from an organisation called The Golden Vertex. We offer people such as yourself the chance to take control of their financial situation and begin building real wealth. We seek out independent go-getters who like to get their hands dirty with all aspects of running a business and don't mind..."

"And what business is that, Mr Sampson?"

"Well, first of all, let me just say that the business side of things is only the mechanism by which our system works. More important are the learnings to be had, the social connections to be made, the mentorship at each stage of the journey, the sense of community that comes with..."

"Cut the crap, Mr Sampson. You've got until the end of that cup of tea before you can leave this house and never come back. What in blazes are you blathering about?"

If Adam had been wearing a tie, he would have straightened it.

"Network marketing, Mrs Mitchell."

"And what is network marketing?"

"That will all become clear in time, Mrs Mitchell. We have a seven-step process by which we gradually reveal the true nature of our system."

"A seven-step process, is it? How delightful. I also have seven steps. They lead from my front door to my front gate. I suggest you make use of them right now."

Mrs Mitchell held up her arm pointing firmly in the direction of the front door.

"Mrs Mitchell, if you just let me..."

"Mr Sampson, unlike my son, I have zero tolerance for bullshit. Either tell me straight what your scam is or leave my house."

"It's not a scam, ma'am."

"There's no need to sugar coat it, my dear. I like a good scam. When I was a young woman my best friend and I used to make a very good living pretending to be spirit mediums for rich and respectable ladies with too much time and money on their hands. These days I content myself with running the occasional airplane game down at the lawn bowls club. You might even say I scammed my way into this house. Neil's father wasn't very bright. The apple doesn't fall far from the tree, I'm afraid. So, tell me, how does this network marketing work?"

"Network marketing is all about connections, Mrs Mitchell. The more you build your network, the more reward you get."

"Yes, yes. But what products are you selling?"

"We don't sell products. Like I say, it's all about conn...."

"Mr Sampson, you really are an incredible bore. Tell me, at what point does money change hands?"

This piece of information was not normally revealed until the sixth stage of the process but Adam figured he was going to have to lay it out today anyway so he might as well get it over with.

"New members are required to pay a small fee. Very minor. Just for administrative costs. After that, you are required to purchase a minimum number of groceries per month from the syndicate's supplier. That counts as revenue for the new business that you will set up. You get a small percentage of the sales from each new member you convert and each new member they convert and so on."

Mrs Mitchell burst into laughter.

"Groceries? How utterly boring!"

The laughter grew. In fact, Mrs Mitchell was laughing so hard she had to grasp the kitchen benchtop for support. There was something in the tone of the laughter. Adam didn't know why, but it made him blush.

Finally, the laughter died down and Mrs Mitchell caught her breath. She straightened up and wiped the tears from her eyes.

"Oh, my word. No wonder you conned my son into getting involved, Mr Sampson. Groceries. Of all things."

Mrs Mitchell rubbed her left ribcage. The sudden outburst of merriment had given her a stitch.

Adam reached into his briefcase, pulled out a booklet and started leafing through looking for a page.

"Mrs Mitchell, there's nothing boring about this. If you'll look here you'll see that the returns from the network you will build are exponential. Which means there is the possibility of explosive revenue growth over time."

Mrs Mitchell waved Adam and his booklet away.

"Yes, yes, yes, Mr Sampson. It's a Ponzi scheme dressed up to look respectful and boring so that suckers join up rather than die from the sheer tedium of listening to you waffle on. There's no way I'm sitting through your seven-stage process."

Adam stepped back and flicked the booklet shut before putting it back in his briefcase. In a year and half of doing network marketing, he'd been accused of greed, stupidity and gullibility. He'd faced anger, elation and joy. He'd had several people break down crying in front of him. He'd been called very rude words. But this was the first time anybody had laughed in his face. He didn't know how to take it. He felt wounded. How dare this old lady judge him. She didn't deserve to be a network marketer. He snapped shut the briefcase and turned around.

"Well, Mrs Mitchell, we won't waste any more of your time. Thank you for the tea. Cameron, let's leave Mrs Mitchell in peace."

Cameron looked like he was still trying to process the information about Neil's father's funeral. Adam gave him a wack on the arm and motioned towards the front door. Cameron put his cup of tea down and the two began to leave.

"Aren't you going to sign me up before you go?" asked Mrs Mitchell.

Adam stopped dead in the kitchen doorway. Cameron bumped into him from behind.

"I'm sorry?" said Adam looking over at the old lady.

"I want to join."

"You just said you didn't."

"No, I said I didn't want to sit through your seven circles of hell."

"But....But, why?"

Mrs Mitchell gave a somewhat evil smile. Her eyes gleamed.

"I can have all kinds of fun with this. Starting with my idiot son. You know he still lives here, don't you?"

"He did mention that, yes."

"I've been trying to get that good-for-nothing to leave this house for two bloody decades. Now he wants to get into selling groceries on the side, does he? Well, I'll give him groceries. More groceries than any man could want. Does your syndicate sell baked beans?"

"Sure does."

"Well, it'll be Golden Vortex brand baked beans for breakfast, lunch and dinner from now on. My son will be eating so many baked beans he's going to have baked beans coming out his ears. When I'm done with him he'll be flying out of this house on a Golden Vortex."

"Actually, it's called Golden *Ver*-tex," said Cameron.

"Shut up, Mr Wilkins. Can you sign me up now, Mr Sampson?"

Adam smiled. He turned around and walked back into the kitchen. He put his briefcase down on the kitchen bench and opened it.

"Now, Mrs Mitchell. As I mentioned, normally there is a seven stage process every new member must go through. That process takes seven weeks to complete. However, I understand that you are interested in a shorter onboarding process and, as it happens, so are we. So, we can do this but it will require some creative paperwork on both our parts. What do you think?"

Adam gave her a cheeky smile. Mrs Mitchell reached out and patted him on both cheeks.

"Mr Sampson, that's the first interesting thing you've said since you got here."

CHAPTER 4

Although the syndicate's office was not far from Mrs Mitchell's house and although they had converted her far earlier than he had anticipated or even thought possible, Adam decided to wait until evening to submit the paperwork. The syndicate would be open to midnight to allow all conversions to be registered before the cut off time so there was no particular hurry. He liked the idea of dramatically walking in at the last minute with a conversion. And he figured that whoever was on the desk would be less alert and less inclined to ask questions if it was nearer to knock off time.

The syndicate's offices were in Collingwood, so Adam and Cameron took the opportunity to eat at one of their favourite Vietnamese restaurants on Victoria St, Richmond which was on the way. They dropped in for a couple of beers at The Wombat's Paw pub to kill a bit more time after the meal. It was about 9.30pm when they finally parked the car on Johnston St just on the west side of Hoddle Street.

Gentrification hadn't quite arrived in this little corner of Collingwood as yet. But one could see it oozing slowly down the hill from Smith St like green slime. The syndicate's offices were in an old office building that was hard to place in either a chronological era or an architectural style. It could best be described as "cheap". Although, of course, there was nowhere in Collingwood that was actually cheap anymore.

According to the gossip, the building was on permanent loan to the syndicate from an old lady who owned half of Collingwood but was no longer of sound mind. Her daughter lived overseas and, as long as the rent cheques kept rolling in, she was happy to allow tenants free reign to do what they wanted. This attitude showed in the condition of the buildings, which hadn't had a cent spent on them in decades. It also allowed for some variety in the various "business" activities that took place in the area. Within a five-minute walk of the syndicate's office you could perform about ten different types of yoga while having your Italian scooter repaired and waiting for your extra-large organic chemical-free kombucha drink to be gently nudged below room temperature so that the friendly bacteria contained therein would be at their friendliest when making friends with your digestive tract.

Adam and Cameron got out of the car and walked up the brown brick steps through an old 80s style brown aluminium framed door and into the foyer. They took the elevator to the second floor and pressed the buzzer for entry. A click indicated that the door had been unlocked. Adam swung it open.

At the reception desk was a twenty-something woman. She was wearing a loose-fitting suit with a white shirt featuring an extra-large collar that was turned up. It flattered her slender neck and face. She looked up from the computer she was working on as Adam and Cameron approached.

"Good evening, gentlemen."

"Evening, Natalie," said Adam with a big smile on his face. "I've got something for you."

"I hope it's a donut or something, I need some sugar to get me through to midnight."

"Nothing sugary I'm afraid, but this should at least ease the boredom a little bit. We've got a last-minute conversion to be processed if you don't mind."

Adam put his briefcase on the counter, flicked it open and handed over the papers to Natalie who sat back in her chair and gave them a quick browse. She looked up with a surprised and somewhat suspicious expression on her face.

"I didn't know you guys had any marks in the pipeline."

"Yeah, we didn't really hold out much hope for this one. It's an elderly lady that is not exactly in our target demographic but we got her over the line just in time. Bit of a surprise, wasn't it, Cam?"

"You bet it was," said Cameron.

"Mrs Mitchell," said Natalie looking through the papers in more detail. "How did you meet her?"

"She's the mother of the other guy we converted today," said Adam trying to hold his voice as steady and confident as possible.

"Mmm-hmmm. And she's gone through the seven stages, of course?"

"Absolutely, you'll find the signatures and dates all in order on the paperwork."

"It's funny, I don't remember seeing any old ladies at a syndicate meeting. According to Step 3's details, she was there on November 3rd."

"She came in late and had to leave a bit early. She was sitting up the back so you might not have seen her. She's quite short."

"And skinny," added Cameron.

"And she's met with Trevor?" said Natalie without looking up from the paperwork that she was slowly leafing through.

"Yep."

Adam was getting a little tired of this. It wasn't part of the administrator's job to confirm details. They were just meant to process the conversion. Natalie was stepping beyond her pay grade.

"November 10th? I thought Trevor was overseas that week?"

"They did it over videoconference."

"Is that allowed?"

"Look, Natalie, we could stand here all night going over every little detail. Can we just get on with the processing?"

Natalie looked up from the paperwork and pulled her glasses down.

"You haven't got anything to hide, have you, Adam?"

"Not at all. In fact, why don't you give Trevor a call. It's still early in the evening and I've heard he only sleeps four hours a night. I'm sure he'll be happy for you to interrupt whatever he's doing to confirm a minor administrative detail."

Natalie held Adam's gaze for several seconds. Eventually she broke away and put her glasses back on. There was several seconds of silence while she leafed through the rest of the papers. Eventually she put the booklet down on her desk and turned back to the computer.

"Ok. I'm sure the two of you wouldn't do anything devious at the last minute in order to get a conversion. Hey, looking at the leader board, this puts you level with Kenneth and Malvin. Well done."

"Do you know what happens when there's a tie for first place?" asked Cameron.

"I believe it's a fist fight to the death conducted naked in front a leering mob," said Natalie while typing into the computer.

"Oh," said Cameron in a tone of voice that indicated that he wasn't sure whether this was a joke or not.

"All done," said Natalie hitting the enter key on the computer in theatrical style and looking up at Adam and Cameron.

"Great. Thanks, Natalie," said Adam. "We'll see you tomorrow night at the awards."

"I can't wait to see the result," said Natalie with a big smile on her face.

Adam and Cameron's phones beeped simultaneously as they walked out of the office. They pulled them out. It was the confirmation that their conversion had been successfully registered.

"What do you think she meant by she can't wait to see the result?" asked Cameron as they left the building and walked out onto Johnston Street. "She already knows the result."

"I think it was just something to say," replied Adam.

"I dunno. I got a weird vibe. I didn't like all those questions she asked."

"Mate, it's all in the system now," said Adam holding up his phone and slapping Cameron on the shoulder. "We got it! Let's go and have one more drink to celebrate."

***

A couple of suburbs away, two mobile phones were sitting on a lounge room table. They beeped simultaneously. Kenneth Xu and Malvin Liu leaned forward to retrieve their respective devices.

"What the fuck?" said Kenneth.

"Adam and Cameron," said Malvin in a shrill tone. "How the hell did they get another conversion? They didn't have anybody else in the pipeline."

Kenneth's phone began to ring. He answered.

"Hi, Natalie."

"Yeah, we just got the notification. What's the story?"

Kenneth sat back in his chair and looked over at his protégé.

"Alright, we'll be there in about fifteen minutes."

CHAPTER 5

Adam slammed the door of his apartment shut and turned around to lock it.

"How far away is the car?"

"One minute," said Cameron peering at his phone.

"What time is it now?"

"7.49."

"Alright, we should just make it."

They hurried down the concrete walkway that ran along the second floor of the apartment complex and skipped down the steps to ground level. Straight ahead an archway led out to the narrow Richmond street where a set of headlights indicated that their driver had just arrived.

They were late. Late for the awards night. The plan had been to meet at Cameron's house. Adam had shown up to find his protégé dressed in grey chinos and a dress shirt. Although borderline suitable for a meeting with a mark, this was unacceptable for even a normal syndicate meeting and absolutely out of the question for the awards night. It turned out that Cameron had stained his suit several weeks ago and had been making up excuses about it ever since. They had rushed back to Adam's apartment and inserted Cameron into one of Adam's other suits. It was about a size and a half too big.

Adam was a little pissed off. More than a little. They were going to have to get up on stage to accept their award and there would be meetings with the top mentors and photos for social media. Cameron was about to be known to posterity as the guy who couldn't even get his suit right. This was the only fashion faux pas a man could make at the syndicate (other than not wearing a suit at all). The whole point of a suit was that you didn't have to think about it. If you couldn't get that right, what could you get right?

They tumbled into the car which began a slow amble down the street which was already narrow and was made narrower by the parked cars which filled all available spots on the left. Adam looked anxiously at his phone to check the time and then leaned forward to speak to the driver.

"Hey, mate. We're in a real hurry. We running late and we need to get to our destination by 8.20 at the latest. If you get us there by then we'll give you a five-star rating and a $10 tip. How's that sound?"

"No worries," said the driver in a tone that failed to convey whether this offer was of the slightest bit of interest to him.

Adam thought about pressing him on the point but sat back instead. It was in the hands of the traffic gods now.

"How'd you go with Julie last night?" asked Cameron.

"I didn't see her. Well, she didn't want to see me. But we caught up for lunch today and it's all good."

"Did you talk about New York?"

"Yeah, she's really excit...," Adam started and then realised that his matter was still not resolved. He and Cameron hadn't talked about it since the argument in the car on the way to Mrs Mitchell's house the preceding day. He turned to Cameron.

"Look, I've been thinking about what to do about that. It's going to be really important for Julie and I to claim the tickets from the award. I'd already promised her that we would take the trip together and go to the conference and all that. So, here's what I'm gonna do. I'll ask Trevor or maybe Mark if we can get an extra ticket to the conference and then you and I can work out your plane fare."

"By *work out* I assume you mean that you'll pay?" said Cameron.

"We'll sort something out. I'm sure there's a deal we can make."

Cameron sighed.

"Everything's gotta be a deal with you, doesn't it? This is a pretty cut and dried case of me being owed what's mine, I would have thought."

"Come on, mate. If we want to get into the nitty gritty we'd have to look at the sales record to see who's owed what."

Cameron felt a tightening in his chest. He hadn't expected this card to get played. They sat there in silence. He felt the wave of anger rise up from his boots like he was an empty vessel being filled with a hot liquid. It stopped in his throat and sat there pressing against his Adam's apple. He swallowed hard as if trying to push it back down into his shoes.

"You know what? You're right. You got most of the sales and you got the last sale that got us over the line and won us the award. So, obviously the ticket is yours."

"Yeah, but you still have to come, mate. It won't be the same without you."

"Nah, nah, don't worry about it. I don't want be a third wheel to you and Julie anyway. And I think that Rebecca has something in mind for that weekend. Something about a trip to the Prom."

"Oh yeah, how's she doing?

"She's good."

"Well, that's great, mate. Look, have a think about it. I'm happy to speak to Trevor and Mark and see if we can't get you a ticket to the conference. It's a once in a lifetime opportunity, you know. It's not every day you get to meet with Singh."

"I'm sure you'll enjoy it."

Cameron tugged on his tie and turned to look out the window. A drizzly rain had started to fall and the soft street lights of East Melbourne ebbed and flowed in a fuzzy warmth against the car window. They were almost there.

***

At 8.18pm, Adam and Cameron jumped out of the car and ran up the stairs of the Masonic hall, one of the many art deco style buildings in the leafy inner-city suburb of East Melbourne. This was not the usual meeting place for the syndicate but it had been the venue for the awards night for the last three years.

At the top of the stairs, a petite black-haired woman in a full-length black ball gown was waiting.

"Where the hell have you two been?"

"Sorry, Theresa, our ride got cancelled and then we got stuck in traffic," lied Adam.

Theresa ushered them through the foyer and into the main hall which was an expansive space with a second tier that stretched around the back offering views to a very large stage that took up almost the entire width of the building. Dinner tables were scattered about in the usual fashion.

"All the introductory speeches have been completed. We've just got the awards ceremony to go," said Theresa as she showed Adam and Cameron to their seats at a table right in front of the stage. She hurried off in the direction of a door that led backstage.

Kenneth Xu, Malvin Liu and two other syndicate members were already seated at the table. Adam and Cameron sat down.

"Nice of you two to make it," said Kenneth turning around to face Adam.

"We thought you might not show up," added Malvin.

"Just keeping you on your toes," said Adam.

"That's a good idea," said Kenneth smiling. "We should always remain vigilant and alert. Even up to the last minute. Don't let anything slip past us."

Adam looked at the two smiling faces. They reminded him of the laughing clown heads at a circus or fete. He opened his mouth to speak but applause began to break out from the audience. He looked up to see Theresa in her black ball gown leading three men onto the stage.

The men were all in their 40s. The first was a short man dressed in a black suit and red tie. That was Mark: head mentor of the Melbourne branch. The second was a tall and skinny blonde man who was dressed sharply, but quite provocatively, in a tan suit with no tie. That was Trevor. Head of the Asia Pacific segment of the syndicate. The big kahuna. Third was Marco. A larger man, though not in height. This characteristic apparently making it hard for him to find a well-fitting suit but he was making do with a navy number matched with a red tie. Balding and with round glasses that didn't suit the shape of his face he seemed to trail just a little too far behind Trevor as if he was trying to avoid comparison. The four of them walked over to a dais that was in the middle of the stage. Theresa stepped forward to speak.

"Thank you, ladies and gentlemen. As some of you may know, there have been some changes to the awards section of our evening this year. With instruction from Mr Singh himself in New York, we have gotten rid of the various award categories that have been used in the past. There remains only the single category of award for the best conversion team for the year. Mr Singh felt that this would add new focus to our efforts and promote an increase in sales, which is, after all, the primary, indeed, the only goal of our organisation. So, with that in mind, I would like to hand over to Mark for the award presentation."

Theresa stepped away from the microphone and shook hands with Mark as he approached the dais.

"Thank you, Theresa. It is indeed true that our organisation is obsessed with sales. As Trevor reminded us in his speech earlier on, we are fanatics and we make no bones about it. Everything we do, everything we strive for, everything we live for is the pursuit of conversions. In doing so, we add to the strength of the syndicate. As I look around the room I see the many new faces that our conversion efforts have introduced to us this year. The many new links in the chain by which our network becomes stronger. Tonight, we honour those who have done the most to help us grow and thrive: our top converters. As you know, each new link benefits not just those who made the conversion but every one of us. Therefore, I invite you to give hearty thanks and applause to those who have helped themselves and all of us to prosper. So, without further ado. I'm pleased to announce that, for the first time in the history of the Melbourne branch of the syndicate, we have joint winners this year. Please give a round of applause to the two sales teams who tied for the prize of top converters of the year: Adam Sampson and Cameron Wilkins. And Kenneth Xu and Malvin Liu."

The audience burst out in a loud applause as the four men got up from their table and walked up the stairs to the right of the stage. They walked over to shake hands with Marco, then Mark and finally Trevor who handed each a certificate. Mark gestured towards the dais to indicate that they should give a speech. Kenneth took a step back and motioned for Adam to go first. Adam stepped forward to the microphone.

"Thanks everybody. And thank you especially to Trevor for coming down from Sydney to bestow this honour up us. Cameron and I set our sights on this goal right from the start of the year and we're delighted to have achieved it. It's been a long year full of ups and downs. I'm sure we all know of the difficulties we face in this business. But this award just proves that tenacity, hard work and perseverance do pay off in the end. Thank you again and thanks to everybody in the syndicate who supported us this year."

Adam held up his certificate. The crowd applauded as he and Cameron stepped back and allowed Kenneth and Malvin to come up to the dais. Kenneth began to speak.

"Malvin and I would like to thank everybody for another great year. Like everybody here, we have worked our asses off this year and we are so happy to have received reward for our efforts. Unfortunately, it is my duty to report to you all that our competitors in this year's prize have been cheating."

A murmur rose forth from the audience. Kenneth allowed it to build. He cast a conspicuous disapproving look in the direction of Adam and Cameron.

"Adam Sampson and Cameron Wilkins submitted a conversion yesterday evening at the last minute. We believe they were attempting to get it through while nobody was looking. That conversion was invalid by the rules of the syndicate. Therefore, we ask the mentors to revoke the award from Adam and Cameron."

Kenneth stood back from the microphone as the murmur from the audience turned into something of an uproar. Everybody on stage looked around confused as to what should happen now. Mark and Marco were looking at Trevor as the host of a dinner party might look at a member of the royal family who has been given the desert spoon instead of the soup spoon. Mark said something quickly to Trevor before scurrying over to talk to Kenneth and Malvin. Adam and Cameron stood off to the side. Cameron gave Adam a nervous glance.

After what seemed like an eternity but was in reality about one minute, Mark approached the dais.

"Ladies and gentlemen, apologies for this unexpected turn of events. We will need to take a little time to discuss this matter in more detail. In the meantime, please be sure to avail yourselves of the bar. We hope to conclude the formalities very shortly and get on to the official drinks reception as soon as possible."

The uproar returned as Mark and Marco rounded up the four award winners and with Trevor and Theresa in tow exited via a door at the rear of the stage.

***

The backstage area was a large room that was split into two. There was a row of mirrors and tables along the left wall for doing makeup. Behind these there were a number of individual dressing rooms. Over to the right was open floor space that had been filled by props and racks of costumes.

The group wandered into the middle of the space. Mark closed the door behind them and turned around. He cast an anxious glance in the direction of Trevor who had not shown a single facial expression that might give an indication as to his opinion of the developments.

"What the hell is going on, Kenneth?" said Mark. "What's the meaning of pulling a stunt like this in the middle of the awards ceremony?"

Kenneth, whose face had until now wore a smug smirk, was visibly taken aback by this attack.

"But, it's, the...It's not our fault Adam and Cameron broke the rules," he stammered.

"And you couldn't have raised this earlier so the matter could be dealt with prior to the ceremony?" continued Mark.

"We only just found out," said Malvin.

"Exactly," said Kenneth. "The dodgy conversion wasn't lodged until late yesterday evening."

"So, you had all day to bring the matter up," said Mark. "I have a good mind to revoke your award. You've brought the whole ceremony and the whole night into disrepute."

Kenneth and Malvin were shocked by this charge. Adam was trying to hold back a smile when Mark turned to him and Cameron.

"What have you two got to say to all this?"

"This is the first we've heard about it, Mark," said Adam innocently. "We're still not sure what all this is about."

"Don't lie," shouted Kenneth who was going red in the face.

"We can't answer a charge if we don't know what it is," said Adam.

"We're wasting time," said Marco. "Kenneth, either explain to us clearly what the alleged wrongdoing is or we get back out there and finish the ceremony."

"Adam and Cameron falsified the paperwork for the conversion they submitted yesterday evening. They claimed their mark had gone through the seven stages when in fact she had only gone through the first. That conversion is therefore invalid and they should have their award revoked and whatever other disciplinary action the syndicate sees fit should be handed out."

"How do you respond, Adam?" asked Marco.

"Where is the evidence?" said Adam trying to buy some time.

"It's not here. It's back at the syndicate's office," said Kenneth.

"I think we need to review the evidence," said Adam.

"No, we don't," said Mark who could see what game Adam was playing. "There'll be time to review any evidence later. Adam, tell us now, did you or did you not falsify documents to convert a mark early?"

Adam wracked his brain but couldn't think of any more delaying tactics. He figured it was better to move to step two of his hastily constructed plan: *Try to worm your way out of it.*

"Ok, we did. But in our defence, this was no ordinary mark. She has years of experience in similar, ummm, similar industries. She knew all about the network marketing concept before we even started to brief her on it. She was a highly motivated mark. In fact, she immediately ordered over $500 worth of baked beans right after signing up. She told us that she would not join the syndicate if she had to go through the seven stages so we had no option except to rush her through or otherwise miss the conversion. For all these reasons, we believe we should be given an exemption in this case."

"That may be so, but you should have applied for an exemption using the normal and official channels," said Mark sounding like the headmaster of a school.

Adam stepped forward to address the mentors.

"Sirs, if I have learned anything in my time at the syndicate, it's that the decisive thing, the thing the separates the achievers of this world from the non-achievers, the winners from the losers, is speed. I recall the rousing speech that Trevor blessed us with several weeks ago at the syndicate meeting where he noted that time waits for no man. It was with that in mind that Cameron and I decided to push ahead with yesterday's conversion ahead of time. As Grandmaster Singh noted in his eighth commandment, we should Always Be Converting. That's what we were doing yesterday. And we did convert. Therefore, I believe we acted in the true spirit of the syndicate and its teachings and I again ask that we be give an exemption."

Adam stood back to see how this went down. Mark and Marco looked unimpressed. Trevor's face was still expressionless. Kenneth Xu looked like he was about to blow a fuse.

"What nonsense! This had everything to do with getting a conversion in so that they could win the award. It's just, it's cheating. That's all it is."

"Ok, Kenneth," said Mark stepping forward and holding up his hand to signal the he'd heard enough. "I think this is a pretty open and shut case."

Mark looked over at Marco to check that he had agreement. Marco gave him a small nod.

"As this invalid conversion did alter the standings of the leader board and therefore the result of the award, it cannot be allowed to stand. Adam and Cameron, your award will be revoked and Kenneth and Malvin will be named as winners for this year."

"Yes!" shouted Kenneth giving Malvin a fist bump.

"Adam and Cameron, you can go back to your seats and we'll wrap up the ceremony with Kenneth and Malvin's speeches."

"Just a minute."

The voice seemed to come to them in stereo surround sound. It was a deep and resonant voice spoken with a mild but clearly distinguishable southern US accent. It came from Trevor.

They all turned to look at him. Mark bowed his head and stepped away like a male gorilla acquiescing to a silverback.

"Let me tell you a little story. When I was a boy growing up Texas, there was this guy called David Koresh. David Koresh was a funny fellow with a lot of funny ideas. He had this compound out in Waco. Now, I don't want to bore you with all the details. But when the Feds finally decided to take this guy out they laid siege to that compound. Koresh and his followers held on for almost two months in the face of federal law enforcement. A siege they must have known they could never beat. You might say they were stupid and deluded. But one thing they had was determination and belief and perseverance. I remember thinking at that time what would happen if that determination and belief and perseverance could be put to productive ends.

"Now, I'm not up-to-date on the personalities or the interpersonal dynamics involved in this case. But I sure would hate to see a sales team punished for being too determined, too faithful and too hungry for success. A little bit of rivalry is healthy and normal and is to be encouraged if it works in the interests of the syndicate. It has to be channelled to productive ends. In this case, we have a sales pair that went the extra yard and worked late into the night to get a result. And they got it. They got the sale. That's the lesson I see in this story. So, Mark and Marco, I encourage you to reconsider your decision."

Mark and Marco didn't need to be told twice. They flipped faster than an endorphinated dolphin.

"Absolutely," said Mark smiling with profusive obsequiousness. "Absolutely, correct, Trevor. That is indeed the message we need to send to our colleagues outside. Thank you for clarifying this matter for us all."

He clapped his hands together and turned back to the rest of the group.

"Ok, then. Let's get back out on stage and put this business behind us. Adam, you have already given your speech, Kenneth and Malvin would you like the opportunity to finish yours?"

Kenneth had a look on his face that suggested Mark was not wise to have made this offer.

"Yes, we would," he said darkly.

***

Back in the auditorium of the Masonic Hall, the audience was still buzzing. The syndicate's meetings were normally very tame affairs. They were run much like the board meeting of a corporation. Somebody read out the schedule, somebody kept the minutes and somebody made sure the biscuits didn't run out. Like the conversion of a mark, everything went to script. They were now well and truly off script and the audience was eager to find out what came next.

The door opened at the rear of the stage. A silence quickly fell on the hall as all eyes were turned to the front. Mark strode forward with a big smile on his face.

"Ladies and gentlemen, thank you for your patience. We have just finished discussing the accusation levelled by Kenneth and Malvin earlier on. Adam and Cameron have admitted to pushing through a conversion that had not been executed in the usual fashion."

A murmur rose up from the audience. Mark held up his hands to try to quell it and waited for silence.

"However, the syndicate has ruled that the conversion will stand."

The murmur rose up again. Louder. Mark tried the silence gesture again but without success. He decided to talk over the top of the noise.

"It is important for every one of you to understand why this decision was made. It was made because Adam and Cameron were found to have acted within the spirit of the syndicate. They showed perseverance, determination and hard work. Most important of all, they got the mark. They made the conversion. And that, ladies and gentlemen, is what we are all here to do."

The audience was still buzzing. Mark again waited for a silence that was clearly not going to come. He ploughed on.

"To conclude tonight's formalities, I will now hand over to the joint winners of the sales award, Kenneth and Malvin, to give their victory speech."

Mark stepped back and gestured towards the dais. Kenneth slowly walked over to it. He had a look of determination mixed with consternation and indignation. Whatever it was, it hooked the attention of the audience. A razor-sharp silence came over the hall as he stepped up to the microphone.

"Thank you, Mark. Tonight, we have indeed learned a lesson. Malvin and I fully accept the decision of the mentors and we agree with the wisdom they have shown. We have re-learned what we already knew. Our syndicate values hard work. It values competitiveness. It values perseverance. It values winners.

"It is because of these values that I hereby challenge Adam Sampson and Cameron Wilkins to a contest to determine the true winner of this year's sales competition. Malvin and I will meet you in a sales contest of your choosing and we will beat you fair and square. There can only be one winner in life. Let us find out who it is!"

Kenneth shot a glance towards Adam as he strode from the stage. Malvin trailed behind him like a puppy dog following its master. General uproar prevailed among the audience and, for the first time that evening, Trevor's face showed an expression. It was a big smile.

CHAPTER 6

The minutes following Kenneth's public challenge were a blur for Adam. There was no formal conclusion to the awards presentation. Kenneth and Malvin had stormed off stage. The three mentors and Theresa just seemed to disappear. Cameron hung around for a minute or so wandering around in a small circle like a caged animal. Every now and then he would turn to Adam as if to say something and then think the better of it and go back to pacing. Eventually, he just turned and walked off muttering to himself as he went.

Adam stood there for a while. He looked out into the auditorium. Strangely enough given the circumstances, nobody seemed to be paying him the slightest bit of attention. They were busy talking amongst themselves. Although, every now and then he would catch somebody from a group of people turn and gesture towards him on stage as if to make a point.

All kinds of thoughts flooded through his mind. Random replays of the events that just happened, the consequences of those events, ideas about what to do next. Nothing stuck for more than a second or two before the next thought would muscle its way in.

He thought a drink might help calm his nerves. He walked off stage and over to a table on the right of the auditorium which had been set up as a bar for the evening.

On the way there, he tried to read the faces of his colleagues.

In a network marketing organisation, anybody you bring into the organisation is pre-disposed to be your ally. By the same logic, when you are in disagreement with another individual, the people they brought into the organisation were likely to be against you. Accounting for these facts, Adam concluded that the general sentiment was not favourable. The best he got were some forced smiles from his own converts and proteges. In some cases, he did not even get that.

He got to the bar and ordered himself a beer. While he was waiting a man came up beside him and ordered from one of the other bartenders. Out of the corner of his eye, Adam saw the man turn to face him. He kept his eyes fixed forward trying to avoid a conversation. The man waited for Adam to engage and, when he didn't, decided to talk anyway.

"Tough night."

Adam gave him a quick glance.

"Not really."

"No? Looked pretty tough to me."

"Really? We won the award."

"Wasn't the, shall we say, *cleanest* victory though, was it?"

"A victory's a victory."

Both bartenders returned with the drinks for Adam and his conversation partner.

"General consensus is that you're a cheater," said the man picking up his drink and getting to the point. "If I was you, I'd take Kenneth up on his bet or life might get quite difficult for you around here."

Adam had turned to face the man who gave him a smile and offered his glass up to give a toast. When Adam didn't reciprocate he clinked his glass against his anyway then turned and left. Before Adam could process the conversation, Cameron rushed towards him.

"I need to talk to you now."

Cameron grabbed Adam by the arm and dragged him past the end of the bar and over to the wall behind it where there as nobody around.

"Nobody's buying it," said Cameron.

"Buying what?"

"The story. They all think we cheated. Kenneth and Malvin have been telling anybody who'll listen and Natalie has been backing them up."

"Natalie? Shit, it must have been her who tipped them off."

"I told you there was something fishy about her. I think we should renounce our victory. Our name is going to be mud around here if we don't."

"Hang on, mate. Just calm down. We shouldn't be hasty. Things are a little heated right now but it'll all die down in time. Come next year, nobody will even remember this."

"Are you kidding? It's all anybody's talking about. It's all anybody will be talking about for ages. Nobody will forget this. It's the most interesting thing that's ever happened at the syndicate."

"I doubt that."

"Name one more interesting thing."

Adam couldn't.

"Look, mate," said Adam, "We've got the award and we've got the all-expenses paid trip to New York. That's in the bag. So, we don't need to do anything. We don't need to renounce and we don't need to take this bet."

Cameron looked, for the first time since Adam had known him, genuinely angry. His face flushed a deep red.

"You mean the all-expenses paid trip that you and your girlfriend will be going on? The one where you I will have to *work something out*."

Oh, yes. Adam had forgotten about that little detail.

"I want to renounce. I don't care about going to New York. I care about my reputation."

Cameron waited. Adam didn't know what to say. He just shook his head. When Cameron saw that he wasn't going to get agreement, he turned and stormed off.

Adam saw movement out of the corner of his eye and looked over to his right. Kenneth and Malvin were standing about ten metres away with a couple of other colleagues. Kenneth had a big grin on his face. He raised his glass to Adam.

"Ready for that bet yet?"

Adam didn't respond. He went to take a drink of his beer but realised his glass was empty. In spite of all the goings on he'd somehow managed to finish it. He needed some time to think. He headed back to the bar.

Kenneth. Fucking. Xu. Disapproving looks from colleagues didn't matter to Adam. But having to see Kenneth Xu's smug face at every syndicate meet, that was another thing. And now Cameron was a problem as well.

He started to think about accepting the bet. Kenneth had given him the option to name the terms. *A sales contest of your choosing* he had said. That was useful. He could choose a battleground where he had an advantage. But what battleground would that be? Truth be told, Adam didn't have much history in sales. Before the syndicate, he had worked behind the counter at an academic bookstore. That was the only other job he'd ever had in his life. He signed up to the syndicate during the school holidays before starting university. Alongside a small allowance from his parents, he brought in enough money to keep him going through his first year at uni. These days, he didn't need the allowance anymore.

He knew how to sell network marketing. But what else could he sell? He'd need to find a product. He'd need to get some inventory. They would need a system. It wasn't so easy to set up a sales contest. It would take work and he was looking forward to easing off over summer. Looking forward to New York.

For reasons that he couldn't explain, the idea of an apocalypse cult came into his mind. It had been a kind of joke when he first explained it to Cameron but events of the last couple of days made him think again. Mrs Mitchell had talked about wanting death. And then Trevor had talked about that thing in Waco. The cult that had ended in certain death. The good thing about selling death was you didn't need to keep a physical inventory so it could be set up without too many logistical issues. And there was no way Kenneth or Malvin would have thought of this. They'd be totally taken off guard. He could catch them by surprise and get a head start. If he kept the timeframe for the bet short, he could grab a quick victory before they even knew what had happened.

Adam was staring absently at the wall with these thoughts in his mind when Marco came over and tapped him on the shoulder.

"Adam, we need you over at our table for some quick photographs."

They walked towards the front of the stage where the mentors were seated.

"We thought it would be better to do separate photos with each conversion team given the, umm, developments of the evening," said Marco over his shoulder.

"No worries," said Adam airily, still thinking about the apocalypse cult idea.

They arrived at the table. Trevor and Mark were sitting next to each other having a conversation. Theresa was standing and talking to a woman who was holding a large camera in her left hand.

"Well, well, if it isn't the man of the hour," said Mark turning to look at Adam.

"Certainly seems that way," said Adam. He looked around for Cameron.

"Anybody seen my partner in crime. No pun intended."

Mark and Marco laughed at the joke.

"I sent somebody off to fetch him," said Marco.

"Have you given any thought to Kenneth's challenge?" asked Mark.

"A little."

"Are you going to take him up on it?"

"I haven't decided yet."

"I wouldn't take too long to decide if I was you. Remember, speed is of the essence in the business world. And in this case, I would give some thought to your reputation. At the syndicate, as in all enterprise, reputation is the most important thing you have."

"I'll keep that in mind," said Adam.

Paul Rosenthorn, an associate that Adam had converted to the syndicate about a year ago, came rushing over to the table.

"Adam, you need to come with me. Cameron's refusing to have his photo taken. I think you need to speak to him."

"Ok," said Adam who excused himself and followed Paul to the foyer. Cameron was sitting on the plush red carpeted steps that led up to the second-floor gallery. He had a drink in his hand. The look on his face suggested it was a strong drink.

"What's going on, mate?" said Adam.

"I'm out," said Cameron waving his hand in a manner that was both theatrical and drunken at the same time.

"Out of what?"

"Our thing. Our partnership or mentorship or whatever it's called. I'm renouncing my part in the whole affair."

"C'mon, mate. You don't have to do that."

"You just want me to tag along so you can claim your trip to New York. Well, I'm not gonna do it. I've had to spend all evening defending you to everybody here. I'm sick of it. It was your idea to cheat. It was your idea to convert Mrs Mitchell even though we didn't have time. So, you can live with the consequences."

"Look, Cam. What would you say if I told you I had a way to get you a ticket to New York?"

"One that I don't have to pay for?"

"Yes. One that you don't have to pay for. In fact, what would you say if I got Rebecca a ticket as well? Then the four of us, you, me, Julie and Rebecca could take the trip together. How does that sound."

"Sounds alright," said Cameron slurring his voice a little.

"Alright, come with me."

Adam began to reach down to help Cameron get up when he realised that the drinks he had consumed for the evening were catching up with him. He looked over and saw the men's toilet just a few metres away.

"Ok, just give me one minute. Don't go anywhere. I'll be right back," he said starting for the toilet. "Paul, you keep Cameron there," he yelled over his shoulder.

Adam rushed inside the toilet and strode over to the urinal. Trevor was making use of the facilities at the right-hand side. Adam veered left. He made sure to keep his gaze straight ahead while he did his business.

Trevor was drying his hands with the air dryer as Adam walked over the taps.

"Trevor, do you think it's possible to sell death?" said Adam.

If Trevor thought this was an unusual question, he didn't show it. His expressionless expression didn't change.

"Sure can. You can sell pretty much anything. With one proviso."

"What's that?" asked Adam flicking the water off his hands and grabbing a paper towel from the dispenser.

"*You* have to believe in it."

"Like those people at Waco?"

"Absolutely. Say what you want about David Koresh, he was a true believer."

"But if you can sell death then you can sell anything. Or nothing. You can sell nothingness."

"We sell the sizzle, not the steak. If the sizzle's good enough, you can make people forget all about the steak."

"And if there's no steak, that makes inventory management a lot easier," said Adam half to himself.

"That's one way of looking at it."

"Thanks, Trevor."

Adam turned and ran out of the toilet and over to Cameron.

"Ok, let's go," he said.

They helped Cameron to his feet. This turned out to a fairly difficult task. Adam sent Peter off to get Kenneth and Malvin and bring them to the mentors' table. He guided Cameron back into the hall.

"Ok, mate. You've had a few so just let me do the talking and we'll be fine."

They arrived at the table to find the three mentors standing around talking.

"Finally, ready for the photo?" said Mark as Adam and Cameron approached.

"Not quite," said Adam.

"What's going on?"

Adam saw Kenneth, Malvin and Paul approaching. He waited for them to arrive then addressed the whole gathering.

"I would like to accept Kenneth's challenge of a sales competition to decide the winner of the award. However, I would like to add one condition that will require the syndicate's consent."

"What's that?" asked Marco.

"I would like the contest to be winner take all. That means, the winner gets the other party's tickets and expenses for the New York trip. If we win, we get Kenneth and Malvin's tickets to New York as well as our own. If they win, they get four tickets too."

Mark and Marco looked at each other. Mark gave a nod.

"Fine by us," said Marco.

"Ok. Kenneth was gracious enough to give us the option to name the terms of the contest. So, I propose the following."

Adam realised what he was about to say was going to sound a little crazy. He took a deep breath.

"The winner is whoever can get more people to join an apocalypse cult within the next two weeks."

There was a silence. It wasn't really a stunned silence. It was a silence of incomprehension. Looked at another way, it was the sound of attempted comprehension. The kind of silence that occurs when a learner of a foreign language hears something in that language and has to take some time to translate it into their own language in order to understand it.

Eventually, Mark spoke.

"How will we verify that people have joined the cult?"

Adam thought about it for a second.

"I think a simple membership form should suffice."

"It's too easy," said Kenneth. "Anybody can sign a form saying they are a member of a cult."

"Ok. Then there has to be a membership fee. What about $50?"

The group thought this over.

"That sounds fine," said Marco cautiously.

Kenneth nodded his consent.

"What are you going to tell your marks at the end of the two weeks?" asked Mark.

To his surprise, Adam already had an answer to this question.

"That's easy. We make the date for the end of the world two weeks from now. When that day comes and goes and the world doesn't end, the cults will naturally cease to exist."

"Mmm-hmmm," hummed Mark in a tone that indicated he was surprised how logical this answer seemed.

There was another silence as everybody thought the matter over. It was a ridiculous idea but somehow nobody could think of an open and shut reason to reject it.

Mark clasped his hands together.

"It seems like we're all in agreement?"

He looked around the group.

Kenneth had a look of confusion and frustration like a tourist at a foreign flea market who has been talked into buying something he didn't really want but doesn't have the language skills to get out of it. He nodded his head in reluctant agreement. Adam smiled. This was exactly the response he had hoped for. He had caught his opponent off guard.

"Ok," said Mark shrugging his shoulders. "Good luck to all. May the best team win."

CHAPTER 7

Every good network marketer knows that to snooze is to lose. Every good cult leader knows that the story is everything. For these reasons, Adam and Kenneth were up bright and early the next morning scouring the internet for ideas to create a plausible backstory for why the world was going to end in two weeks.

Adam's intuition had been right. There *was* something to this cult business. In fact, there was too much. It seemed you could start a cult about anything at all and there would be somebody somewhere that would join it. The two men trawled through accounts of groups of faithful praying to a teapot or worshipping a drawer of cutlery. There were stories of fantastic ceremonies, enormous buildings and strange rituals. Money, sex, power. The amount of information available was all a bit overwhelming.

Fortunately, both Adam and Kenneth had been trained in avoiding analysis paralysis. They weren't going to let a little thing like not knowing what they were talking about stop them. They knew that success was based on action. Their approach was to start off light on the details and figure it out as they went. By lunchtime, they had ceased their information gathering and turned to the practicalities of getting their cults launched.

The primary constraint they faced was time. Most cults start off small. Just a messiah or two in a garage tinkering around with the metaphysical foundations of the universe. After a time, some make it out of the garage and into a room at a local library or beer hall. Over a period of years, things slowly build until, next thing you know, somebody's running for president and somebody else is running from the law. This path was not viable for Adam and Cameron. They had to get people hooked quickly.

Faced with excessive amounts of information and not enough domain knowledge to make a rational decision, Adam decided to do the equivalent of flipping a coin. He would do one more internet search and would base his cult on whatever was the first result returned.

A typing error saw him search for "ccult" instead of "cult". The first response returned was about the "occult". He followed the link and quickly realised that this was, in fact, a perfectly viable option. Secret societies, hidden knowledge, the supernatural, magic. Adam couldn't find any specific examples of occult apocalypse cults. It seemed he had found a niche. An untapped market that was based on stuff nobody could understand. He was free to make up anything he wanted and nobody would prove him wrong. He got to work concocting the story of his occult cult.

Kenneth reasoned differently. He figured that to get results in a short time span he needed to piggyback on an existing issue. Something with proven market appeal. He would then take that issue and "turn it up to eleven" by linking it to the end of the world.

Unlike Adam, who had decided to try to make his story about the end of the world faithful to its origin in the occult, Kenneth elected to go for exaggeration and hyperbole. Standard marketing techniques he had honed to a fine degree in what had so far been a highly successful network marketing career. He shortlisted a number of current issues that he thought would fit the bill.

The first was atheism. Atheists seemed to be a sizable demographic these days. The story would be that all religious believers on earth would simultaneously die in two weeks' time. There was no reason for this. It was just random chance. In some parallel universe it would have to happen and ours just happened to be the right universe at the right time. Everybody who renounced religion before then would survive to live happily on earth guided by the light of pure reason.

Another idea he had was an environmentalist cult. It would be called Sol Salvation. The sun god, Sol, and the wind god, Ventus, angry at humans for not installing enough solar panels and wind turbines, would come down to smite carbon burners in a combination heat wave and hurricane. It would be the solarpocalypse.

However, after careful consideration, Kenneth decided on a more niche demographic but one that he figured was highly motivated: vegans. He named the cult "The Früit Family". In the Chinese year of the Ox (this year), the cow god, Vitula, would come down to the earth on the full moon before the summer solstice (two weeks from now) to wreak a terrible vengeance on meat eaters and restore vegetative justice to the world. Everybody would live: *happily ever after*.

So it was that by mid-afternoon two new cults had taken form. Social media accounts were created, internet posts posted and the inaugural meetings organised for the evening of the following day. Kenneth and Adam briefed their proteges and prepared to step into their brand-new role of cult leader.

CHAPTER 8

What if I told you there was a secret knowledge? An occult knowledge? What if that occult knowledge predicted that the modern world would end in two weeks' time? Would you be interested? Would you want to know more?

Come to Office V at 17 Johnston Street, Collingwood (offices of The Golden Vertex) tomorrow at 6pm for the inaugural meeting of our new occult group. Find out about the thrice great Hermes and the hidden knowledge of the ancients that foretells of the great and the terrible. Free admission for all. Be there!

"Sounds weird, man," said Cameron sitting back from the computer where he was reading Adam's announcement for the first meeting of their cult which was due to start in fifteen minutes.

He and Adam were at their usual desks. The mentors had agreed to allow the two teams to use the syndicate's offices and meeting rooms to run their cults. This would make adjudicating the competition easier and was no great burden as the network marketing business was now in its Christmas slowdown period.

"It's supposed to sound weird," replied Adam from the other side of the desk. He was making some final notes for the presentation he would give attendees. "An apocalypse cult *is* weird."

"Yeah, but this tells me nothing at all. It could be about anything. Anybody could show up to this meeting."

"That's the point. Fail fast and pivot. Just like Singh said in his last webinar. We throw out the bait and let the people tell us what they're looking for."

"I dunno, man. We don't have much time to be experimenting."

"It'll be fine."

"What do you want me to do?"

"Nothing much. Just observe. Try and see if anything I say resonates with people. You might pick up some things that I can't see. And have the clipboard and the money box ready in case we get any membership."

"How many attendees have confirmed?"

"Four."

"Is that all?"

"It's a start, mate. Be positive."

"Look," said Cameron giving Adam an earnest look, "I don't know if I've got time for this. I need to put in some hours at the supermarket. Unlike you, I don't earn enough from the syndicate to live on. I need to make some money for Christmas. And I need to spend some time with Rebecca. Now that the network marketing work has eased off she's expecting me to be around more."

"No worries, Cam. I'm happy to do the lion share of the work. Take whatever time you need. This is my way of making it up to you. I still feel bad about what happened with the sales comp. I'm gonna get you those New York tickets, mate."

"Have you heard anything about Kenneth and Malvin's cult?"

"No. But they'll be using the meeting room right after us so stick around afterwards if you want. Should be fun to watch."

Adam checked his watch.

"Alright, mate. It's go-time. I'll set up in the meeting room. You go downstairs and keep an eye out for attendees."

***

Cameron checked his watch one last time and headed back into the syndicate's office building. He passed the elevator and skipped up the single flight of stairs that brought him to the second level. The syndicate's office was directly next to the stairwell on the right. The door gave a beep as he scanned his key card on the sensor. He pulled it open and walked down the hallway that led to the right of the reception desk. Kenneth and Malvin were loitering at the end smiling away to each other.

"Bit of a tough start, eh?" said Kenneth as Cameron approached.

"What you got there? Five people?" said Malvin.

"Six," answered Cameron brusquely as he brushed past them, turned right and headed towards the meeting room door.

"My mistake. One day I'll learn to count with *both* hands," said Malvin. He and Kenneth broke out into over the top laughter. Cameron turned around.

"Count these," he said giving them a middle finger with each hand before turning and opening the meeting room door.

Adam was addressing the group.

"So, before I begin I'd like to get a quick idea of what drew each of you here today. Let's go around the room and just say your name and why you came. We'll start with you."

Adam pointed to the man who was sitting immediately to his right at the end of the table. He looked to be in his early forties. An overweight man, he was wearing an Iron Maiden t-shirt that was simultaneously too lose in the chest and too tight in the gut. His mouse brown hair was cut short but still managed to stick out in multiple directions at the same time. He wore black glasses that were small and round making his eyes appear far larger than what they were and giving everything he said a kind of default exclamation like somebody whose eyebrows were permanently raised.

"I'm Fritz. I came because I seek the truth. The truth about how this world really works. The truth about the cabal that sits behind all illusion and pulls the strings of government. The secret society. That's what this is about, isn't it? I want to join. I want to know your secrets and learn the reality that is behind the reality. I am sick of living in the shadows. Bring me into the light. Show me the truth. Take me for I am worthy."

Fritz's voice broke halfway through the last sentence and the high-pitched squeak of his final syllables reverberated around the meeting room like a rubber duck at the end of a toddler's bath time.

Adam opened his mouth to speak but didn't know where to start. He closed it again. The next person along the table took this as an invitation to talk.

"Well, I'm with Fritz. They're keeping something from us. *They* are. Those in power. Oh, yeah, my name's Robert. I work in television. Are we supposed to say our jobs?"

Adam shook his head. Then nodded. Then shrugged.

"No? Ok. Yeah? Too late, then, right? Ha-ha. So, like I was saying, the little thing nobody wants to talk about in public. Peak Oil. Right? That's what we're here for? That's the thing that's gonna put an end to it all. This so-called modern world. What's so modern about it? It's ancient. Ancient history, man. It's all going up in smoke the second the supplies of petroleum hit their peak. Then we'll see what's modern. That's when the knives come out. That's when the real government steps forward and we'll see what's what. Is that enough? Should I keep going?"

"No, no, that's, ummm, fine. Fine. Thank you, Robert," said Adam.

He took a deep breath and looked to the next person along the table. It was another man. His age was difficult to tell as his face was covered in a giant beard that got wider as it got longer. It hung down in curls which billowed outwards like the hem of a Bavarian beer maid's dress. The follicular frenzy of his face was not replicated on his head where only a few wisps remained around his crown while a handful of short black curls clung to the lower regions of his scalp like clams on a white rock.

"I am Pavlos. At least I think I am. Because what do I really know? What do we know? We think we have answers but how do we know we are even asking the right questions? I know only that I know nothing and therefore I am certain of my uncertainty. And yet of this certainty I am also uncertain. Who here is not? You claim to have knowledge?"

Pavlos pointed at Adam in an almost accusatory fashion.

"Ummm, yes."

"Let us hear your knowledge."

"Yes. We'll get to that, Pavlov."

"Pavlos."

"Right. Thank you, Pav-*los*. Let's just continue around the room."

Adam motioned to the next person: a skinny young man about the same age as himself and Cameron.

"I'm Francis. You mentioned the end of the world in your post. We all know the end of the world is the end of capitalism and the dawning of communism as all history comes to an end. You claim to have special knowledge of this. Like this bloke, I want to hear about this knowledge."

"Good. Thank you," said Adam. "Next."

"I'm Darrell. To be honest, I'm not sure I'm at the right meeting. I thought this was about the occult."

"It is," said Adam then thought he should hedge his bets. "Sort of."

"Sort of? Is it or isn't it? I'm not interested in any of this other stuff."

"You should be, mate," said Robert from two seats away. "Peak oil will affect us all."

"They'll never let it happen," said Fritz.

"Who?"

"The illuminati."

"The what?"

"Are you with the illuminati?" Fritz asked Darrell.

"What? No."

"You said you were into the occult."

"Actually, the illuminati were against the occult," interrupted Pavlos.

"But they were secretive."

"Yes, but they were against magic."

"What's magic got to do with it?"

"Nothing if you're illuminati. They don't believe in it."

"I'm not illuminati."

"And I'm not secretive. The whole point is to bring things into the open."

"It's all in the open. Capitalism is out there for all to see. Are you blind?"

"And capitalism runs on oil."

"So does communism."

The noise in the room had gradually risen to a dull roar. Adam held his hands up to signal silence.

"Ok, everybody. It's great to see such enthusiasm but we've just got one more person to get to and we can start to discuss what we're all doing here."

Adam turned to the final person at the table and took half a step back. His breath seemed to evacuate his lungs as if he'd been elbowed in the ribs. He wasn't sure how he hadn't noticed her before. But he was noticing her now. He was noticing her full lips made red by a deep shade of lipstick. Her soft, smooth, milk white skin that looked as though it wouldn't last five seconds in the Australian sun. Her high cheekbones framed a perfectly shaped slender nose that led up to a voluminous head of jet black hair that seemed to crack like a fire that fell down well past her shoulders. And then there were her eyes. Shining blue. Like a blue diamond but paler, colder. With her thick black eyebrows framing them they seemed accusative, dangerous.

Adam realised that his throat had become dry. He swallowed in a fruitless attempt to moisten it and then croaked at the woman to introduce herself.

"I am Nastashya," she said in a heavy Russian accent. "I am new to Melbourne. In Russia, I was member of occult. I look for similar group here."

Nastashya had finished speaking but the men in the room had not finished looking at her. There was a silence. She looked around and just the smallest hint of a smile showed at the corners of her mouth.

"Should I say more?" she asked.

"No. No, that's enough," said Adam sounding out of breath. He took a moment to compose himself and refer to the notes he had made for his introductory speech.

"Well, thank you all for coming. I can see there are a lot of diverse ideas in the group but I think that we are all united in an enthusiasm to advance our understanding of the world. It is said that knowledge is power and truth is beauty. I want everybody here to be powerful and beautiful. That is why I started this group. That is what I hope for each and every one of you and for all future members. Together we are strong. Together we can achieve anything at all. I hope you will join me and we can strive for a brighter future together."

"What bloody future? I thought you said the world was going to end," blurted out Darrell.

"I'm not interested in working with communists," said Fritz looking over at Francis.

"And what are you then, fatso? Capitalist pig?"

"I'm a libertarian," said Fritz smugly.

Francis laughed.

"Even worse."

"Please," said Adam holding up his hands yet again. "Let me speak. Yes. This group is about the end of the world. The world will end. It will end soon. I am here to be your guide towards that end."

Adam attempted to make this sound as grave as he could but his rising inflection made it sound both upbeat and uncertain at the same time.

"And when will it end?" asked Fritz.

"Two weeks," said Adam again managing to sound upbeat despite his intentions. "Technically, it's one week and six days."

"By what mechanism will this occur?" asked Pavlos.

"It's, umm, it's unclear," said Adam.

"Then how do you know it will happen?"

"I have received a message."

"From who?"

"The Secret Chiefs."

"You're in the touch with the Secret Chiefs?" said Darrell.

"Who are the Secret Chiefs?" asked Robert.

Darrell answered.

"Supernatural beings. Many occultists claim to be in touch with them. They operate on a higher plane than the everyday world."

"Jesus Christ," said Fritz turning away in disgust.

"Yeah, like that," said Darrell.

"No, I mean, what bullshit."

"So, let me get this straight," said Francis. "You heard a little voice in your head and now you think the world is going to end in two weeks?"

"The voice told of a passage in an ancient text written by the thrice great Hermes," said Adam.

"Who?" asked Robert again, this time turning straight to Darrell who was becoming a kind of interpreter.

"Hermes was a Greek god."

"Oh, God," said Fritz.

"Yeah, like that," said Darrell.

"No, I mean, fuck, I came all the way to Collingwood to hear a bunch of religious gobbledy-gook."

'Hermes Trismegistus was a man. Probably."

"Probably, eh? Well, I'm probably leaving. Probably right now."

Fritz got up from his chair.

"Me too," said Francis.

"Hang on, hang on," said Adam imploringly. "Just give me one more minute."

He motioned for the two to sit down. They reluctantly complied.

"Look, I understand this all sounds a bit wacky but I encourage you all to hold your doubts and join up. The journey is more important than the destination and the destination is only two weeks away. What have you got to lose?"

"What are we joining up to?" asked Pavlos.

"Well, that's something we can decide as we go. There's a number of things we could do such as group ceremonies or readings from texts. And it's only $50 which is far…"

"What?" said Robert incredulously.

"Fifty bucks?" exclaimed Fritz. "You're taking the piss, aren't you?"

"Ok, that's me out," said Darrell getting up.

"Me too."

"Me three."

Fritz, Robert, Francis and Darrell were all on their feet and grabbing their jackets and bags. Only Pavlos remained seated although this appeared to be more out of indecision than any particular desire to remain. The four others were at the door when a voice rang out from the end of the room in a heavy Russian accent.

"Are you men?" it said.

They all turned to face in the direction of the voice. It came from Nastashya. She was sitting at the end of the table with her hands folded in front of her. She had the bearing of a judge sitting at the bench during a trial.

Nobody said anything. There were several seconds of tense silence.

"Sit," commanded Nastashya as if instructing a pet dog.

Fritz took an instinctive step towards his chair before his conscious mind intervened. Like the other minds in the room, it was confused as to what was happening.

Nobody else moved. They just stared as if transfixed.

Nastashya leaned back slowly in her seat and smiled.

"Sit down. If you are a man."

If her previous statement had been a stick, this one was a carrot. A carrot dipped in honey and spread over a piece of golden-brown toast at 11am on a Sunday morning. It seemed to promise something. It seemed to say: "I want you to be a man."

The men wanted to be men too. Fritz showed a sprightliness that belied his physical condition as he sprang back to his chair. One by one the others took their seats. Pavlos straightened his back and lifted his chin as if his decision to remain seated had been a demonstration of the virility of his own masculinity. Even Cameron felt the desire to sit down. He perched himself on the seat closest to the door. Adam alone remained standing. He wasn't sure what was happening but he sensed it was a time to pay close attention.

"Adam is correct. The world will end in two weeks. This prophecy was well known to our group in Russia and comes from occult tradition. You doubt because you try to use reason."

Nastashya tapped her head with her right hand.

"You must learn to use heart."

Nastashya moved her right hand to her chest and rested it over her heart. Seven sets of eyes eagerly followed it.

"You must learn to use whole of body. Whole of being."

Nastashya now held both hands over her chest and ever so slowly slid them down the length of her torso shutting her eyes as she did so. Adam noticed for the first time what she was wearing. A black leather jumpsuit. To say it was tight would not be quite accurate. It did not seem to fit at all. It just followed the contours of her body quite naturally. So did the eyes of the men.

Nastashya stood up. Fritz's bottom jaw dropped a little.

"Let us try easy occult exercise."

Nastashya held out her arms on both sides signalling the men to join hands. Darrell, the lucky man standing directly to her left was first on his feet. The other men quickly followed. Cameron was a few seats away on Nastashya's right. He eagerly shuffled over to take her left hand. Everybody was now holding hands except Adam who was still standing at the front of the room.

"Adam. You join us?" asked Nastashya.

"No, it's ok. I'll just watch," said Adam.

"C'mon, man," said Cameron waving his right hand for add to join. "It'll be better with you in it."

"What will be better?"

"I dunno. Whatever it is we're about to do."

"The power of a man who communicates with Secret Chiefs will be most valuable to the exercise," said Nastashya.

Adam didn't like the fact that he was being called on his own lie. But he appreciated that four people who were walking out the door a minute ago were now interested again and he figured he should play along. Perhaps there was a chance of getting some memberships after all.

He stepped forward and took Cameron's hand in his left and reached across the table to grab Fritz's in his right.

"We begin with simple exercise. Hum the same note as each other and hold for as long as we can. Like this. Ooooohhhhhhmmmmm."

Nastashya closed her eyes and held the sound for about ten seconds.

"Ok? Now everybody together. Join with me."

"Ooooohhhhhhmmmmm."

To the rational observer, the task of humming in unison with others in a group seems a straightforward one. Most of the group managed to achieve it to an acceptable standard. Their efforts, however, were drowned out by the dissonance coming from the vocal chords of Cameron and Fritz. Fritz, in particular, was problematic. He was apparently unable to hold a tone for more than about a second without losing his breath. His efforts to re-join the group saw him veering wildly over the frequency spectrum as he attempted but never managed to find the correct pitch. Cameron had no trouble with holding the sound. He was simply out of pitch from start to finish. The note he held was a slightly flat version of the devil's interval. The combined sound created by the group resembled a bee hive on LSD.

Nastashya smiled.

"Cameron and Fritz. Let us try just the three of us. Ooooohhhhhh-mmmmm."

Without the extra reinforcement of the other voices, this attempt sounded far worse than the first. Robert grimaced. Pavlos rubbed his head as if trying to remove the memory of the sound.

Nastashya dropped Darrell's hand, turned to Cameron and grabbed his right hand so that she was now holding both hands.

"Ok, Cameron. Just you and me. Copy me. Mmmmmmm. No. Lower pitch. Mmmmmm. Almost there. Mmmmmmmm."

Finally Cameron hit the note. Nastashya squeezed his hands.

"There. Good boy."

Cameron beamed like a fourth grader who had just been given a gold star.

Nastashya walked past Cameron and headed towards Fritz. This gave the men on the other side of the room the chance to view the black leather jumpsuit in more detail. Theirs heads turned in unison as she walked to the other end of the table.

Fritz had the look of a bunny caught in the headlights. Nastashya grabbed both of his hands as she had done with Cameron.

"Oooohhhhmmmmmm."

Fritz attempted to copy but this new proximity to Nastashya had further reduced the amount of air he was able to expel for any length of time. He gave a short "Mmmh" that was high pitched and cut off at the end. It sounded like a lonely puppy dog crying for its master and was followed by a kind of wheeze as he desperately attempted to refill lungs which weren't really empty.

"Ready, Fritz. Oooohhhhmmmmmm."

"Mmmh. Mmmh. Mmmh."

"Gooooood," said Nastashya. "Try again."

"Mmmh. Mmmh. Mmmh."

Nastashya gave Fritz a smile and put his hands down. A couple of beads of sweat rolled down his forehead as she returned to her position at the back of the room. The heads of the men followed.

"Let's try one more time," she said as she linked hands with Darrell and Cameron. The others followed suit.

"Oooooohhhhhhhmmmmmmmmmmmmmmmm."

"Mmmh."

"Very good," said Nastashya as she led the others in putting their arms back down. "That is example of simple occult ceremony."

"That was awesome!" exclaimed Darrell.

"Yeah, very cool," added Robert

"I totally felt something," said Francis. "In my chest, I mean."

"Maybe I was a little too hasty about this occult stuff," said Fritz.

Adam stepped back to the front of the room. He checked his watch. They had some time left but the salesman in him sensed that it would be better to end now and press for memberships.

"So, we're almost out of time, folks. Cameron has membership forms at the ready. Can I get an idea of who is interested in joining?"

There was no immediate reaction among the group. Several of them looked at each other. In particular, Nastashya was the focus of some furtive glances. Eventually, Fritz asked the question that was on everybody's mind.

"Will, ummm, will Nastashya be involved in the ceremonies?"

"Yeah, it seems she has occult knowledge that we can learn from," said Darrell.

"It would be good to have an international flavour to the group," added Francis.

"We'd be really happy to have some help with the ceremonial work," said Cameron enthusiastically looking over at Adam as if desperately hoping he wouldn't contradict this statement. "Right, Adam?"

"Yeah, I think that would be fine," said Adam who could see which way the wind was blowing and was happy to play along. "Nastashya, what do you think?"

"Well, if everybody is serious about learning occult I will help," said Nastashya looking around at the others.

"Dead serious."

"One hundred percent serious. One hundred and ten percent!"

The others nodded eagerly.

"Ok, I join," said Nastashya.

Fritz gave a little jump for joy. The others beamed.

Cameron opened the folder containing the membership forms. The men flocked around him like seagulls around a fish and chip wrapper. Suddenly, the $50 did not seem like a large amount. The meeting wrapped up with six brand new members. They were just getting ready to leave when Fritz asked a final question.

"By the way, what is the group called?"

"The Order of the Secret Chiefs," answered Adam. "In recognition of the powers that are greater than man."

Everybody seemed happy with this name and the meeting came to an end. They made plans to convene again in two days and Cameron escorted the new members from the building.

CHAPTER 9

Adam turned off the bathroom tap, gave his hands a shake and stuck them underneath the dryer. Satisfied that they were dry, he gave himself a quick once over in the mirror before heading back down the hallway to his desk. Cameron was leaning back in his chair with his arms behind his head.

"Did you see her eyes, man? That blue. I've never seen eyes that colour before. It was like frozen ice."

"As opposed to unfrozen ice?" said Adam sitting down.

"Like a clear blue. Like the water in the Caribbean," continued Cameron not registering Adam's sarcasm.

"Have you been to the Caribbean?"

"No. But I've seen photos."

Adam picked up the membership form that Nastashya had filled out.

"Nastashya Orlova."

"Such a beautiful name," said Cameron.

Adam looked up from the form.

"What are you in love with her or something?"

"No," said Cameron sitting up straight as though he'd been told off by the teacher in school.

Adam dropped Nastashya's form on top of the others and picked up the pile.

"I'm a little uncomfortable about having her in the group to be honest. She said she's been a part of occult groups in the past. That means she's quite likely to realise that we don't know what the hell we're talking about."

"Nah, it's perfect, man. We can just let her run the meetings. It seems like she'd be happy to do that. It gives you one less thing to worry about."

"I suppose so. What was that ohm business? Is that even an occult thing? Seems a bit cliched to me."

"Can I tell you a secret?"

"What?"

"I got a boner while she was doing that."

"I'm pretty sure Fritz did too. Wouldn't be surprised if he blew his load on that last ohm."

Cameron laughed. Adam picked up the papers and stood up.

"Alright, mate. I'm gonna head off and put these memberships in the database."

"What database?"

"I agreed with Kenneth and the mentors that memberships would be kept in a shared database so we can all keep track of the competition results."

"Kenneth and Malvin are doing their first session in the meeting room right now."

"Oh, yeah. That's right."

"Did you see how many people they've got?"

"A lot?"

Cameron stood up and gestured for Adam to follow him. They walked down the corridor to a point where they could see into the meeting room. It was packed with people. Kenneth was writing on the whiteboard.

"Shit. How many people are in there?" asked Adam.

"I counted thirty-three," said Cameron.

"I didn't know you could fit that many."

"I asked a couple of the people who arrived for the meeting why they were here. They said it was some kind of vegan meetup."

"Vegan? What's that got to do with anything?"

"Their cult is called The Früit Family. It's based around veganism."

"It's supposed to be based around the apocalypse."

"I know."

"That's bullshit. What's it called again, The Früit Family? Bloody dumb name. We might need to take this to the syndicate. This prick's supposed to be a running an apocalypse cult not a vegetable cult. Alright, I'm gonna go home and check out their website. I'll see you tomorrow, mate."

"See ya."

***

"Brassicas have to be out."

"What do you mean, *out*?"

"Prohibited. Prescribed. Verboten."

"Why?"

"The last group I was in allowed brassicas. It was an outrage. That's why I quit."

"I'm with her. No brassicas and absolutely no lilies."

"Woah, hang on a minute."

"No lilies?"

"Yeah, no lilies. Got a problem with that?"

"That does sound a bit extreme."

"Can we all at least agree that umbelliferous are acceptable?"

"What!? Celery? Parsley? Surely, you're joking. I mean, carrots. Bloody carrots."

"What's wrong with carrots?"

"I knew it. A carrot lover."

"The question is who or what is eating the carrots?"

"Huh?"

"Well, humans shouldn't eat them, but what about pigs?"

"Exactly. And is it ethical to eat a carrot when you could have given it to a pig?"

"I don't follow."

"Well, here you are stuffing your face with a carrot and over there a pig is thinking *I would have liked that carrot.*"

"Is it?"

"I'm not."

"Somebody is."

"Yeah, ol' carrothead over here. That's who."

"All I said was I liked carrots."

"Who cares about carrots? We still haven't resolved the asparagus issue."

"We already said lilies were out."

"No, we didn't."

"He did."

"We haven't agreed on it, though."

"I thought we had."

"I like lilies."

"Me too."

A huge thump came from the front of the room. Thirty-three vegans jumped in their seats and turned to see Kenneth, normally a cool and unflappable picture of serenity, bent over the meeting room table that he had just pounded with his fist. From this hunchback position he twisted his neck upward towards the group. His face was bright red and contorted into a shape that resembled a breakfast cereal box that had been run over by a truck. His eyes bulged out of his sockets and the vein on his left temple was threatening to remove itself from his head and throttle the nearest member of the emerging anti-carrot faction of The Früit Family.

He slowly raised his torso back to a vertical position, straightened his tie and ran his hand through his hair. This latter gesture proved surprisingly ineffective at restoring order to what was normally a perfectly maintained coiffure.

"Thank you, everybody. There'll be plenty of time to work out our *manifesto* in the coming weeks," said Kenneth. His tone of voice was about an octave lower than normal and seemed to emanate entirely from his stomach. Some attendees noted a distinctive percussive sound that was not, as they surmised, roadworks on the street outside but was in fact the grinding of Kenneth's teeth as he spoke. The grinding started again.

"Malvin will hand out the membership forms."

There was an eerie silence as Malvin scurried around the room handing each person a paper and pen. A couple of people glanced up from their form as if they were having second thoughts about joining or wanted to ask a question but a slight movement of Kenneth's head in their direction sufficed to resolve any doubts they might have had. Each person dutifully handed in their form and their $50 and The Früit Family took an early lead in the race for the prize.

CHAPTER 10

Rather than heading for his apartment in Richmond, Adam turned left as he headed out the door of the syndicate's office and started to walk towards Brunswick St before running to jump on a bus that was headed west and that had conveniently pulled up at the stop just ahead of him. He'd got a text as he was walking down the stairs: Liam Love was back in town for Christmas and was loitering around on Brunswick St if Adam wanted to catch up for a drink. A drink was just what he needed right now and he figured Liam could give him some useful guidance on the cult competition.

He got off the bus at Brunswick St and headed south to 'the first bar on he left' as Liam had described, which turned out to be only a few shops from the corner. It was an uber-gaudy affair that couldn't figure out if it wanted to be a speakeasy or a disco. A couple of unicycles stuck to the wall did nothing to swing the balance either way. Nevertheless, it was packed with the usual Fitzroy mix of young professionals, artistes and weirdos. Adam spotted Liam chatting to one of the girls behind the bar. He walked over at sat down next to him.

"Mr Love, I presume."

Liam turned and gave him a gregarious smile.

"Sampson," he said shaking Adam's hand then turning to barmaid, "Shazza, this is Sampson. Sampson, this is Shazza."

The girl, a pretty young blonde who would have been Adam's age, gave him a quick wave and a smile.

"Don't get any ideas, Shazz. Our Sampson has already met his Delilah. Hence the short back and sides and the suit."

"Her name's Julie," said Adam frowning.

"What are you drinking, mate?"

"I'll have a pint of Two Moons."

Sharon smiled and began pouring Adam's beer.

"Long time no see, bro," said Liam warmly. "How's life treating you?"

"Good, mate, good. It's been a good year at the syndicate. I'm now making enough from my network to live off."

"That's good, mate. I know that was important for you."

"It's a stepping stone. Just one of many on the path."

Sharon put Adam's beer in front of him on the bar and he whipped out his wallet and scanned his credit card on the machine. Liam took the opportunity to give her a wink and a cheeky grin. Her coy smile indicated she was enjoying the attention from the man who was at least a decade older than her.

"So, what brings you back to Melbourne?" asked Adam.

"I'm running a course early in January. I figured I should probably take the opportunity to catch up with my father and meet up with old friends. Cheers."

They clinked glasses and took a drink each.

"How are the courses going?" asked Adam.

"Good. Can I tempt you to join? There's still a couple of spots left for the January one. I'll give you mates rates."

"What is it?"

"The standard deal. Three-day course. Three sessions of day game and one of night."

"What's day game again?"

"It's what you do during the day. And night game is, get this, what you do at night."

Liam gave Adam a jab in the ribs.

"It's all game, mate," he continued. "It's all game. And game is what *you* need."

"I don't need it," said Adam looking down into his beer frowning again.

"I reckon you do."

Adam didn't respond. He took a drink of his beer.

"So, you're still with that same girl. What's her name again?"

"*Jul-ie*," said Adam accentually the two syllables to emphasise the fact that he'd told Liam her name only a minute earlier.

"And you've been together more than a year now?"

"Fourteen months."

"Do you love her?"

The question caught Adam unawares. He glanced over at Liam to see if it was a joke. It wasn't.

He thought about it for a few seconds.

"I don't know."

"That means you don't."

"Maybe I don't."

"Then why are you with her?"

"I dunno."

Adam took another drink wishing he could change the subject.

"I'll tell you why. Cos you've got no other options. And you've got no other options cos you've got no game. That's why you should do my course."

Adam shook his head.

"Let me ask you this," said Liam turning to look directly at Adam, "did you choose *her* or did *she* choose you?"

Again, Adam had to think about the question.

"I can't remember."

"How did you connect with her?"

"Through mutual friends."

"Where did you meet?"

"At a party."

"Did you approach her?"

"We were introduced by one of her friends."

"That means she chose you."

"No. It was just luck."

"Luck? Was it luck that you got you into network marketing? Was it luck that you now make enough money from your business to live on?"

"No."

"Exactly. And it wasn't luck at the party. This Julie girl snapped you up."

"Maybe she did. What's wrong with that?"

"This is what I don't understand about you, Sampson. You're a smart guy. Driven, motivated, energetic. You set yourself the goal of financial freedom and you're achieving it because you work hard towards it. That's more than most men of your age can say. Shit, most guys your age are still jerking off and playing computer games. But when it comes to your relationships, you take the first thing that comes along and you tell yourself you're happy with that. But you're not."

"I am."

"Mate, this is what I do for a living. This is my job. I coach hundreds of guys every year. I know what makes a man happy when it comes to the female of the species and nothing you've told me about you and this Julie girl makes me think you're happy."

Adam didn't respond.

"All I'm saying is, you're leaving a lot on the table when it comes to your love life."

"I don't have time for all that pickup stuff. The reason I'm moving towards financial freedom is because I work my ass off for it. That's why I'm getting results."

"Does it make you happy?"

"It's not about happiness. It's about freedom. You do the work now and you get your freedom later."

"So, what's the plan? When do you become financially free?"

"It takes years. Maybe decades."

"Great. So, you spend the best years of your life working for this financial freedom and then at some unspecified time in the future you'll start doing what you really want to do."

"What's wrong with that?"

"You don't know what you want. That's what's wrong with it. The only point of having Fuck You money is that you get to stand for something and other people can't take it away from you. What do you stand for, Sampson?"

"Freedom."

"Freedom to do what?"

"Whatever I want to do."

"And what do you want to do?"

Adam was stumped. Try as he might, he couldn't actually think of anything to answer. Now he was confused. It was a simple question and he didn't have an answer. He picked up his beer and took a long drink.

"Look, mate, I'm just trying to help. Believe me, I wouldn't waste my time with most of the dropkicks around here."

Liam nodded in the direction of a group of young men in suits that were drinking and joking around in the corner.

"You're following someone else's script. That's fine. We all have to do that to start off with. But ultimately you have to come up with your own script. And it doesn't help to postpone that. I've seen men in their forties who throw away every last dollar they earned because they lived somebody else's life and woke up one day and realised it was all bullshit. I don't want that for you."

"Geez, you're starting to sound like an occult mage," said Adam clumsily changing the subject away from the one he wasn't enjoying to the one he'd been wanting to talk to Liam about.

"An occult mage? What do you know about that?"

"Actually, I wanted to get your opinion on it. I've started an apocalypse cult."

For the first time since Adam had known him, Liam looked surprised.

"Why?"

"It's a long story. There was a tie for first place in the syndicate's yearly sales competition. We needed a tie breaker and so I suggested we could each start an apocalypse cult and whoever got more people to join would win. Pretty funny, right?"

Adam's grin slowly disappeared as Liam gave him a disapproving look and then turned away and took a drink of his whisky.

"Well, I, umm, I just thought you might like the story," said Adam looking at Liam with a confused expression.

Liam said nothing. He was staring at something stuck on the wall behind the bar. Adam took a drink of his beer.

"Have you ever had anything to do with the occult?" Adam asked in as casual a manner as he could muster.

"I experimented with it at one point," said Liam.

He turned to face Adam.

"What's the occult got to do with an apocalypse cult?"

"Well, nothing. I just used it as a gimmick to get people to join."

"Do people think they're joining an occult group or an apocalypse group?"

"Both. I made up some story about how the occult predicts the apocalypse. I figured nobody would know enough to check the story."

Liam shook his head.

"Sounds bloody stupid to me."

"The competition only goes for two weeks so I doubt anybody will figure it out."

"That's not the point. It's stupid. And it's dangerous."

"How is it dangerous?"

"Ever heard the phrase *be careful what you wish for*?"

"What? You think we're gonna actually cause the end of the world?"

Adam gave a sarcastic laugh that petered out quickly as he realised that Liam was not going to laugh with him.

"You see, Sampson. This is exactly what I was telling you before. You don't know what you want. You're just fucking around. And because you're just fucking around, you'll probably be ok. Nothing will happen. But one day you'll wake up and realise that nothing happened because you were just fucking around."

At that Liam Love finished the rest of his whisky and got up out of his chair. He slapped Adam on the shoulder as he walked past.

"Good to talk to you, mate. Let's catch up again soon."

Adam turned and watched as Liam whispered something in Sharon's ear as he passed by the table she was clearing up. She giggled and Liam smiled back at her as he walked out the door.

CHAPTER 11

The next scheduled meeting of The Order of the Secret Chiefs was two days later. Cameron was already at his desk when Adam came down the hall from the elevator.

"You're keen, mate," said Adam smiling as he approached. "I don't think I've ever seen you show up early for anything."

"Just wanted to get a bit of work done," said Cameron.

"Oh, yes? Maybe I should invite Nastashya along to all our meetings. Then you might show up on time."

"Huh? Dunno what you mean."

Adam smiled as he sat down and connected his laptop to the monitor at his desk.

"Have you checked the meetup registrations?" asked Adam.

"Yeah, just checked 'em. No change. Looks like we'll have three newbies."

"Geez. That's not much. Did you remember to share the post with your social media accounts?"

"Nah, I decided not to."

Cameron looked a little embarrassed.

"What? Why not?"

"I just didn't feel comfortable with it. I don't want my family and friends worrying that I've joined some death cult."

"It's not a death cult."

"Apocalypse cult then. It's the same thing when you think about it."

"It's not serious, though."

"Yeah, but they don't know that. The post talks about how the world is going to end in two weeks."

"Just explain the situation to them."

"What am I gonna say? Come and join my pretend death cult. It's only fifty bucks."

"Well, we need to find a way to get some more numbers. We're currently twenty-seven behind The Früit Family."

"I think we should de-emphasise the apocalypse part and just focus on the occult part. It will be an easier sell."

"Yeah, but then it won't be a valid cult. The competition is about running an apocalypse cult. That reminds me, there's a meeting with the mentors straight after ours. You might wanna come along."

"What's it about?"

"I've lodged a formal challenge with the syndicate about how The Früit Family is not a proper apocalypse cult. The mentors will hear the case later on."

"Do you think we'll win?"

"We better. I had a look at their site. It's clearly a vegan cult they're running. There's some bullshit about a cow god ending the world but it's just one sentence buried down at the bottom. Everything else they have is just standard talking points. Wouldn't be surprised if Kenneth just copied it directly from another vegan website."

"I'm just looking at their next meetup now," said Cameron looking his computer screen. "It's on tomorrow but it looks like they don't have that many extra people coming along for this one. Maybe about fourty-five."

"That's still a lot more than what we've got. I'm gonna ask everybody in the meeting if they can share the group with their friends. We need to get some word of mouth happening. Looks like there's not a lot of interest online."

"What else have you got planned for the meeting?"

"We'll need to welcome any new members and explain the group to them. I'll do that at the start."

"And then Nastashya can do her thing?" asked Cameron trying to sound as disinterested as he could.

"I certainly hope so. I didn't organise anything else."

"Cool."

"Alright," Adam clapped his hands. "Fritz just sent us a message on the group chat. He's bringing a friend along. So, looks like we'll have at least four new people."

Adam stood up and unplugged his laptop.

"I'm gonna go and get set up. I'll see you in there."

***

Adam looked at his watch. It was just on four minutes past six. He looked around the room to see the familiar faces of Fritz, Darrell, Pavlos, Robert and Francis plus three new faces including Fritz's friend who, if you ignored the facial differences, could have been his twin brother. There was no sign of Nastashya.

"Well, I think we should make a start," said Adam.

"What about Nastashya?" asked Cameron with undisguised disappointment in his voice.

"She is coming, isn't she?" asked Fritz in a wavering tone.

"She responded to the invite," said Adam, "but we can't wait for her forever."

Cameron slumped a little in his seat and several other faces in the room registered a downward turn of mood. Adam decided to try and lift the energy. He began in an over the top bubbly tone.

"Welcome everybody and welcome in particular to our new prospective members. As you may or may not remember, this is The Order of the Secret Chiefs, a group dedicated to the fact that the world will be ending in a little under two weeks. I am your host, Adam Sampson. And over here is my co-founder Cameron Wilkins."

"Can we just clear something up," interrupted Darrell sounding a little grumpy from the news that Nastashya might not be coming. "Are we here to learn about the occult or to talk about the end of the world. Cos I got the impression from the last meeting that it was the former."

"Yeah, and we still haven't heard anything about the details of this so-called end of the world," added Robert.

"Good questions. Good questions," said Adam trying to stay positive. "The answer is that it's both. There is a perfectly good occult reason why the world is ending but in order to understand it we need to get to know a bit about the occult first. Make sense?"

There was no reply from the room.

"So, let's get straight into the occult stuff," said Adam remembering that he had not prepared anything. He had spent some time fleshing out the story about why the world was ending but had been counting on Nastashya for the rest. He would have to improvise.

"I know. Let's begin with the ohm exercise that we covered last week. Everybody take each other's hands."

The roomful of men looked warily at each other. What had seemed like a good idea a couple of days ago suddenly seemed really weird. There was a distinct lack of movement accompanied by an awkward silence.

"C'mon," said Adam reaching out to grab Cameron's hand which felt like a dead fish wrapped in a wet rag.

Fritz's friend turned to Fritz with an enquiring look.

"This is not how you described it to me," he said.

"Well, it wasn't like this last time," said Fritz.

"Ok. Let's forget the hand stuff and just do the ohm," said Adam desperately trying to keep the meeting on the rails.

"On the count of three. One, two, three, oooooh...."

There was a sound that resembled an incontinent bagpipe. It was the sound of the wind going out of the sails. Of the spark getting lost. Of the magic being gone. Even Adam's chest sank at the sheer patheticness of it. A couple of others had a surprised look on their face that such a sound was even possible.

Adam stood there and tried to think of what to do next. He figured it might be best to steer clear of the practical exercises. This might be the time to talk about the end of the world. The mood was certainly right for it. He was about to start explaining how the thrice great Hermes had foreseen a calamity involving a supercomputer, an electric car and a mechanical toothbrush when she opened the door.

Was there ever a sight more fair for a room of deflated males? As one they straightened in their seats, put their shoulders back, lifted their chins up and screwed their eyes towards the doorway where Nastashya stood. This time she was not in the leather jumpsuit. This time she was in a two piece outfit that revealed much more of the pale white skin that Adam had noticed previously.

To say her skirt was short would be to miss the point. It was where it led the eye that was the key. As a wise man once said, it is the journey and not the destination. With that skirt as the starting point, whichever way the journey took you was quite alright, perfectly satisfactory and, in fact, rather excellent.

For example, you could go down. That was a good way to go. Down led to the soft, smooth, impossibly milky white thighs. Thighs that promised all the things that any post pubescent heterosexual man in the world could want. From there the eye was led to calves which had been honed and chiselled to a fine point. If ever anything was slender, those calves were slender. Slender was their middle name. Slender was their matrilineage. The soft, sweet ankle was just visible above black suede boots that bookended the whole affair in such a way that you just wanted to go back to the top and start again like your favourite slide at the local swimming pool.

 If you journeyed north of the skirt you experienced a cavalcade of curves, a serpentine series of sinuous spirals, an inundation of delights such as no man could handle. Like the skirt and the boots, the top Nastashya was wearing was black. It was held in place by what could only be called strings and it would have taken an advanced course in string theory to find a set of calculations that could explain how the whole thing stopped from simply disintegrating under the force of gravity.

All this was bad enough. But then Nastashya had the nerve, the audacity, the reckless disregard to walk from the door to the front of the room. This walking set objects in motion before the eyes of the men that would fill their dreams for years to come. Or at least they would have if the world wasn't going to end in two weeks.

"How are my secret chiefs?" said Nastashya as she reached the front of the room. She was, in fact, right next to Adam but turned to face the others as if he wasn't there at all.

"We were just doing the ohm exercise from last week," said Adam trying to appear authoritative.

"Excellent," said Nastashya without looking at him. "Can anyone tell me what is purpose of ohm?"

"Focus," said Darrell so fast it seemed as if he had answered before she had finished the question.

"Meditation," said Robert.

"Intoxication," blurted out Fritz who appeared to have lost control of both his mind and his vocal chords.

"Very good," said Nastashya. "All correct answer. We train in occult to use energy. With energy we make things happen. But energy must be focused. Ohm exercise is to use sound energy. Now, we learn to use energy of body. We learn to rub. Follow me."

Nastashya held up the palms of both hands then lowered them down to her thighs where she began the simple act of rubbing up and down. For a brief period, the men forgot that they were supposed to copy her. For a brief period, the men forgot they existed as separate beings capable of independent action. Eventually, Pavlos moved his hands to his thighs and began rubbing and each man followed in turn until the whole room was rubbing in unison.

"Now move to chest," said Nastashya.

If the men were transfixed before, they were now positively catatonic. Surely, she couldn't. Not in that top. The strings. The strings wouldn't hold. They couldn't. It would all have to come off.

But the top remained in place as Nastashya merely mimed the rubbing and eventually the men were rubbing their chests while staring at hers.

"Now place hands like this."

Nastashya moved her hands together in front of her chest with the palms facing each other but not quite touching.

"You should feel the energy. Can you feel it?"

"Yes," said Darrell quicker than immediately.

"Yes," said the others only slightly after him.

"This is lesson in how to focus energy. We will continue to build on this as will be important for 16th December."

Nastashya finished speaking and looked at the group. It took some time for the men's brains to catch up to what she had said.

"What is the 16th December?" asked Pavlov.

"The end of the world," replied Nastashya matter-of-factly.

"So, that's what two weeks means," said Fritz's friend.

"One week and four days," corrected Darrell.

"Correct. Now, everybody must do rubbing exercise and ohm exercise for homework. We must begin to prepare for the 16th," said Nastashya.

Nine heads nodded their agreement to this.

Only Adam refrained. He had moved several steps away from Nastashya and had been quietly observing from the other side of the room. Something weird was going on but he couldn't really figure it out. Were these actual occult exercises? They seemed far too simple. And it sounded like Nastashya was serious about this end of the world stuff. He would need to ask her for her interpretation of the story so they didn't get crossed wires.

"We have three new members, correct?" asked Nastashya.

"Yes."

"Absolutely."

"Sign me up."

"Good. But we need more members."

For the first time that day, Nastashya looked at Adam.

Adam snapped to attention and addressed the group.

"That's right. Now, what I would like to ask is for each of you to spread the word about The Order of the Secret Chiefs to your friends. Word of mouth is the best form of advertising. Each of you has access to our social media accounts so you can share those or just tell your friends to come along to the next meeting."

"When is the next meeting?" asked Francis.

"Saturday," said Adam. "Now, that's a weekend so let's all make a big effort to bring as many people as we can. More people equals more energy. Right, Nastashya?" Adam looked over to gauge her response.

"More people is more power,' she said looking straight at him.

"Right," said Adam turning back to the group. "What I would like to aim for is that we get at least forty people to the meeting on Saturday. If everybody follows Fritz's lead and brings just three friends, we can make it."

Fritz's friend slapped him on the back.

"Let's do it, boys," he said in the loud, resonant voice that only a man of a certain girth can achieve.

The others in the room rallied behind the call and the difference in energy from just several minutes earlier was stark.

"Ok. I go now," said Nastashya. "On Saturday I have extra special exercise for everybody."

With that simple phrase and the act of leaving the room she gave the men yet more material to fill their dreams.

From there things wrapped up rather quickly as the men packed up and left. Adam was sure to get the membership forms and money from the three newbies before they went. Within several minutes it was just he and Cameron remaining.

Cameron was again slouched in his chair but this time more from what appeared to be exhaustion rather than disappointment. Adam checked his watch and picked up the membership forms and other papers from the table.

"I'm gonna go and take some time to review my argument before the syndicate meeting at seven," he said. "Are you gonna come along?"

"That skirt, man," mumbled Cameron. "Did you see it?" he said looking over at Adam.

"Of course, I did. A blind man wearing sunglasses in the middle of the night during a blizzard would have seen it."

"She's so beautiful," Cameron sighed.

"Alright, I've gotta go to this meeting, mate," said Adam as he started to walk towards the door.

"Why don't you go home and get started on your rubbing homework," he smiled hoping Cameron would respond to the joke but Cameron just sat there slumped over and staring into the middle distance.

CHAPTER 12

The syndicate's official meetings were held on the second floor of the building in an area that was reserved exclusively for mentors and their administrators. Access to the area was considered a special privilege and was only granted to top performers for special events. On the rare occasions where rank and file members needed to attend on governance-related matters they were ushered into a small waiting room just inside the door of the office from which you could access the boardroom directly.

It was in that room where Adam now sat. He was browsing through a small notebook where he had listed his main points of argument for the upcoming tribunal which would hear his case against The Früit Family. The door opened and Kenneth was ushered in by an administrator.

"Well, well, if it isn't Mr Sore Loser himself," said Kenneth sitting down directly opposite Adam. "I know you're a long way behind already, Sampson, but don't you think you should wait a few more days before lodging Hail Mary complaints to the mentors?"

"Nothing Hail Mary about it, mate. The competition is about the *a*-pocalypse not the *meat*-ocalypse."

"That's funny. Hey, we saw your witch leaving just before. Nice pickup, bro. Where'd you find her?"

"She's not a witch."

"Witch, wiccan, whatever the hell they call themselves."

"I think you're getting your schools of magic mixed up."

"Am I? I guess it doesn't matter when you've got a hot chick running the show for you, right? Y'know, while we're on the subject of bending the rules. Having a half-naked woman prancing around the room seems like a strange way to run an apocalypse cult."

The door at the end of the room opened and Marco stuck his head through.

"We're ready for you, gentlemen."

Adam and Kenneth got up and straightened their suits as they walked through the door into a large room that had a massive oak table in the middle. Marco took his seat on the opposite side of the table. Mark was seated directly in the middle and a third mentor, Tracey, was seated to his right. Adam and Kenneth took seats on the side of the table closest to the door.

"Thank you for your punctuality, gentlemen," said Mark. "As this matter is an unusual circumstance that is not covered by the standard code of the syndicate, we propose a very basic format to conduct this meeting. As the chair of the meeting I will have final say as to who has the call. Participants are to follow my instructions at all times. We will allow Adam no more than ten minutes to state his case at the beginning of the meeting, following which Kenneth will have the right of reply. Both the plaintiff and the defendant will be allowed to ask questions or seek clarification at any time but we ask that you be civil in doing so and allow each other to speak. Once everybody has had their say, the mentors will retire for deliberation. Vote will be majority wins and there will be no appeals allowed. Does everybody accept these terms?"

"Yes," said Adam.

"Yes," said Kenneth.

"Good. Let's begin. Adam, please present your case."

Adam stood up.

"Thank you, Mark. The terms of the competition that Kenneth and myself entered into state that the winner would be the one who got the greatest number of members to join an apocalypse cult. I believe these terms are clear and not in dispute. However, the cult that Kenneth has started is not an apocalypse cult. It appears to be a cult aimed at vegans. His cult is named The Früit Family. The cult's marketing materials are available for all to peruse on the internet but I took the liberty of printing out the main marketing page."

Adam handed everybody, including Kenneth, a printout of what was the front page of the website of The Früit Family.

"Please note the liberal, some might say excessive, use of fruit and vegetable images that adorn the page including the large banana and eggplant which are featured in the cult's logo. I draw the mentors' attention to the text of the website and note that the first four paragraphs on the page, including all the text that is above the call-to-action button, relate to veganism and not to the apocalypse. In fact, the first four paragraphs are dedicated entirely to a, in the phrasing of the website, *felicity to fruit* and a *veneration of vegetables*. I found only one sentence on the page which relates to the stated goal of our competition. In the bottom paragraph there is mention of the cow god, Vitula, reaping vengeance on so-called flesh-eaters in order to restore quote, *cosmic vegetative justice,* to the world. At no point on the main page of the site is a date for the apocalypse mentioned. In fact, the date of the 16th of December is only mentioned in passing on the FAQ page of the site.

"Although I have not had the privilege of attending of The Früit Family's meetings, I did get the chance to view the public discussion forum on their website. I found no evidence of any discussion about the apocalypse or the cow god, Vitula. There was, however, a lengthy back and forth on the benefits of non-vascular plants in the ongoing fight against the flesh-eaters as well as a, frankly quite vicious, flame war between pro and anti-carrot members of the group.

"In summary, I submit that The Früit Family is not an apocalypse cult. Its name does not sound like the name of an apocalypse cult, its marketing materials make essentially no mention of the apocalypse, its members do not appear to be at all concerned about the imminent end of the world and there is no explanation of how the cow god, Vitula, will bring about that end. I ask that the cult be deemed invalid and that its members not be counted for the purposes of this competition."

Adam sat down.

"Thank you, Adam. Kenneth, we will now hear your reply," said Mark.

Kenneth got to his feet.

"Ladies and gentlemen, what we have here is a classic case of the pot calling the kettle black. Every one of the accusations that Adam has levelled against The Früit Family can also be raised against his cult. Let us take them one by one.

"The name of Adam's cult is The Order of the Secret Chiefs. Far from signifying the apocalypse, this name sounds more like a reference, and a culturally insensitive one at that, to some kind of hunter gatherer social structure.

"Adam stated that our group's marketing materials do not mention the apocalypse prominently enough. Well, neither do this. Rather, the primary focus of the website of The Order of the Secret Chiefs is, and I quote, *learning about the occult*. For those in the room not well versed in the matter, the occult is a broad term meant to signify a group of practices based around what we might charitably call magic and what we could less charitably call superstitious nonsense.

"The Order of the Secret Chiefs does not have a public forum on its website but I did have the opportunity to talk directly to one of its members about the activities of the group. These activities appear to centre around what are childish and immature exercises more befitting a group of kindergartners. Although, I leave it for the mentors to decide whether this outfit would be appropriate for a kindergarten teacher."

Kenneth placed a grainy photograph printed on A4 paper of Nastashya in her all-black outfit from earlier that day on the table and slid it over to the mentors. It had clearly been taken from a distance through the glass of the meeting room on level one but was sufficiently clear to provide an accurate representation of Nastashya's clothing, or lack thereof. Mark picked it up and then put it back down again as if it were a burning hot piece of metal. Marco looked at it in the same way a man might steal a quick look at the sun. Tracey took a longer look before giving Adam an explicitly and thoroughly disapproving glare.

"That photo is of the woman who appears to be leading The Order of the Secret Chiefs. Although our competition was hastily put together and lacking in formal rules, I would put it to the mentors that it is not in the spirit of the competition that Adam has apparently outsourced the running of his cult to a third party. I can assure everybody that Malvin and I are leading our cult personally and have not acquired external assistance.

"As to the final accusation about an explanation for the apocalypse, The Order of the Secret Chiefs does have such an explanation on their website but it is frankly a quite preposterous story centred around a mechanical toothbrush and certainly nothing that any sane adult could likely believe would cause the end of life on this planet.

"In summary, I submit that if my cult is invalid then so is Adam's. I would point out that apocalypse cults do not just spring up overnight and are rarely focused solely on the end of the world. They are, in some way, social organisations where people just want to gather and have a bit of a good time. For this reason, I believe it would be inappropriate and implausible to enforce the level of categorical purity around the notion of the apocalypse that Mr Sampson seems to believe is warranted.

"I ask that the charge be rejected and that we be allowed to continue with our current cults and may the best team win."

Kenneth sat down and gave a triumphant glance over at Adam.

"Adam, would you like the chance to rebut anything that Kenneth has just said?" asked Mark.

Adam shoulders sagged as he realised he didn't have a leg to stand on.

"No, sir."

"Very well. Please be so kind as to retire to the waiting room while we deliberate on the matter."

***

It took less than three minutes for a verdict to be decided and for Adam and Kenneth to be asked back into the meeting room where Mark addressed them.

"We find that both cults appear not to be primarily concerned with the apocalypse and are, therefore, invalid under a strictly literal reading of the terms of this competition. However, as the spirit of this competition is about salesmanship, we believe both cults represent an adequate test of those skills and are therefore an adequate vehicle for deciding a winner. We rule that both cults should continue in their current form and that the higher membership number on the 16th December will stand as the deciding factor in this competition."

Mark banged a gavel on the table to indicate the end of the meeting. Adam and Kenneth bowed to the mentors as per the syndicate's custom and left through the small meeting room.

***

"Son of a bitch," said Adam slamming down his notebook and papers on his desk.

Cameron was sitting at his desk opposite. He had decided to wait around to hear the result of the tribunal.

"I take it we didn't win," he said.

"We're changing tack," said Adam apparently not hearing Cameron's question.

"You were right. The apocalypse stuff is a hard sell, so we're gonna drop it. We're gonna focus on the occult stuff and on Nastashya. What do you think?"

"Focusing on Nastashya is good."

"Right. From now on it's gonna be *The Order of the Secret Chiefs: Come and learn the secrets of the Russian occult from our head instructor Nastashya Orlova.* Have we got a picture of Nastashya?"

"I can ask her for one."

"Good. Do it. Do it now. We'll print up some flyers and stick them around the area. This is Collingwood for fuck's sake, there's heaps of weirdos around here who wanna get into weird shit."

"I'll put Nastashya's photo on the website too."

"Good. We'll plaster her photo everywhere we can. If Kenneth and Malvin are gonna sell vegetables, we're gonna sell meat."

CHAPTER 13

Kenneth was wearing his standard syndicate uniform of navy suit, white shirt and no tie. Malvin, in deference to his mentor, was wearing a tie with his suit. The two of them stood out like sore thumbs in the room of committed vegans where the style of dress could best be summarised as floppy and colourful, much like the average vegetable drawer in a household fridge.

It was midday on Friday. The day after Kenneth's victory in front of the mentors. He was feeling good. They had forty-one people in the room. This was more than could be comfortably accommodated. He would have to start looking around for a bigger venue. That was a nice problem to have.

The Früit Family had a lead of thirty-one members over The Order of the Secret Chiefs. What's more, the decision from the day before meant he was now free to pursue a purely vegan agenda. That would make the cult easier to run. Your average inner-city vegan is not the type to be either amused or enticed by ideas of cow gods reaping cosmic justice. That story had so far only been a source of confusion. He was relieved he could drop it.

"Ok, everybody. Let's make a start," said Kenneth. He reached out and took a sheet of paper from Malvin who was standing next to him at the front of the meeting room. It was the list of new members.

"First order of business is to welcome our newest members to the group. Malvin has kindly handled the paperwork prior to today's meeting. Here at The Früit Family we aim to provide a welcoming and friendly environment for all fruit and vegetable lovers, so I'm sure you'll all join me in extending the warmest of welcomes to the following people."

As Kenneth read the names a slight murmur started on the left side of the room as several people began whispering amongst themselves. Kenneth glanced briefly at them over the top of his piece of paper but continued reading the rest of the names til he got to the end of the list.

"How about a round of applause for our new members," said Kenneth putting the piece of paper down on the table. He and Malvin began clapping and several others started to follow before one of the whisperers on the left took to her feet. The clapping petered out quickly as the woman began to speak.

"It is my duty to inform the group that one of our prospective new members is known to several of us. Bert Lincoln."

The woman raised an accusative arm at the end of which was a finger that pointed to a young man sitting directly opposite her. He was dressed in corduroy jeans and a t-shirt. He had brown hair done up in a man bun and a thick beard that was well maintained.

"Please tell me this isn't about carrots," said Kenneth.

The woman ignored him.

"Several of us will remember that Bert was a prominent member of the Fitzroy branch of the erstwhile Vegetable Institute. In fact, he was a board member. During his time on the board it was discovered that he had failed to renounce a previous indiscretion involving dairy products. He was subsequently asked to leave the institute. To the best of our knowledge, Bert has still not apologised for his sinful behaviour and we would ask that his membership to this group be forbidden."

A loud murmur swirled around the room. Bert got to his feet to answer his accuser.

"Friends, I will only re-iterate what I have stated in the past. That accusation was never proven. There was never a shred of evidence for it. I never renounced because I committed no crime in the first place. I am deeply saddened that this issue persists several years later. I ask you to forget about it and let bygones begone."

"Liar!" shouted a man who was sitting next the woman who had just spoken.

The room broke out into open shouting as a couple of people on the other side of table leapt to Bert's defence. Kenneth held up his arms for silence. It took some time before he was able to speak.

"Ladies and gentlemen, please. As I mentioned earlier, our goal here is to be as inclusive as possible. As Bert has indicated, these issues have long since passed and certainly have nothing to do with the activities of our group. I see no reason why his membership cannot proceed."

"Let's put it to a vote," shouted the woman on the left. "All who oppose the membership of Bert Lincoln, please be upstanding."

The clique on the left rose to their feet. Others members in the room also got to their feet with varying degrees of speed and enthusiasm. A quick count was conducted by the woman who had started the commotion.

"We just need one more person for a majority. If anybody else doesn't want Bert to join, you have to move now."

Everybody eagerly scanned the room looking for one more agitator. Eventually, a small woman in her 20s who was seated at the back of the room slowly rose to her feet with her hand up.

"Maxine!" exclaimed Bert.

"I always knew you weren't one of us," said the woman turning to Bert with a solemn expression.

"That's it! We have a majority," said the woman on the left as the group around her started clapping.

There was patting of backs and shaking of hands. People began to resume their seats.

"Hang on," said Kenneth from the front of the room. "That's not how it works. You can't just kick people out arbitrarily."

"There was nothing arbitrary about it. It was a democratic vote," replied the woman.

"Bert's membership has already been processed."

"Then un-process it."

"I won't."

The woman's facial expression turned from triumphant to wrathful. She glared at Kenneth.

"It's him or me."

The woman took to her feet again.

"And me."

"And me."

Four others took to their feet followed by a fifth and then a sixth. Suddenly there were eleven people upstanding.

Kenneth's face reddened and his eyes narrowed. He was not used to insubordination. In the syndicate, you did what you were told. Obedience was mandatory. Obsequiousness was encouraged. You were obliged to be obliging. He decided it was time to draw the law of the land in the sand and to lay down the gauntlet of authority.

"Bert stays," he commanded.

A commotion ensued. A kerfuffle. A brouhaha. There were shouts of "Judas", cries of "traitor" and somewhere in the melee Kenneth could have sworn he heard somebody yell "fuck carrots!"

***

At exactly the same time The Früit Family was having *its* domestic dispute, Adam was having one of his own not too far away on the other side of Punt Road. He and his girlfriend, Julie, were at a fashionable Abbotsford café. The kind where the seats suck, the food is overpriced and you have to wait half an hour to get in. The perfect setting for an argument.

"I don't want to hear any more about the competition. I'm sick of hearing about the syndicate," said Julie as she scissored away at a piece of cold muffin.

"The syndicate will be paying for this lunch," said Adam.

"You want me to pay? I'll pay. I'll pay for both of us."

"Of course I don't want you to pay. I'm merely pointing out that the syndicate brings in money. It's not just some hobby."

"So what? You don't hear me talking about the pharmacy all the time."

"Really? You just finished telling me that story about the old woman and her dermatitis cream. Hardly fitting conversation over a meal."

"Oh, so now I'm not a good enough conversationalist?"

"That's not what I meant."

"Yes it was. And while we're on the subject of what's appropriate, I don't think it's appropriate for you to be getting around with some Russian stripper."

"She's not a stripper."

"Certainly sounds like she is."

"She's fine."

"I still can't figure out why you don't know anything about her. You've got some stranger running your group. Or maybe you just don't want to tell me?"

"It's just the way it's worked out. We've never really had the chance to talk properly. But I'll definitely make sure to talk to her at the meetup tomorrow."

Julie put her knife and fork down.

"There is something *you and I* need to talk about."

Famous last words. Adam braced himself.

"We still haven't agreed on what we're doing for Christmas."

"What do you mean?"

"I mean, who's having lunch where. And dinner."

"I kind of assumed we would each just do our own thing. See our own families, I mean."

"Did you? And it didn't occur to you to ask your girlfriend about it?"

"I thought we were on the same page."

"No, we're not on the same page, Adam. We're not reading the same book. We're not singing from the same hymn sheet. We're not in the same ballpark, watching the same tv show or humming the same tune."

"We aren't?"

"Adam, you still haven't met my parents."

"I know. That's why I think it's best to skip Christmas this year. It's a bit full on to just go from nothing to a Christmas lunch, don't you think?"

"What's the reason you haven't met my parents?"

"I know. I know."

"At this rate, the first time you'll meet is at our marriage."

"Marriage?"

Julie picked up her knife and fork and stabbed at her bacon in a way that seemed like it should be against some kind of RSPCA regulation.

Adam's phone beeped. He picked it up and read the message.

"No way! Babe, you're not gonna believe this. Cameron just messaged me to say The Früit Family just lost eleven members in some big argument."

Julie neither answered nor looked up from her eggs benedict.

"This means we can take the lead if everything goes well tomorrow."

Adam slapped the table top in excitement then looked up to see that Julie was not sharing in the emotion of the moment. He figured he might as well cut his losses.

"Look, it's nearly time for me to meet Cameron at the syndicate office, anyway. Let's talk about this Christmas thing tonight. Alright?"

Julie didn't respond. Adam got up and kissed her on the cheek.

"I'll pay the bill on the way out."

***

For the second time in a row, Cameron was early. He was at the printer looking over some sheets that were printing out. Adam walked straight over and gave him a high five.

"Mate. The tide is turning. I just checked the spreadsheet. The Früit Family is down to thirty members."

"I know. I was here when the whole thing blew up. It was crazy. There were people screaming. Pushing and shoving. It was like a soccer riot."

"How did Kenneth look?"

"Pissed off."

Adam laughed.

"Sucker."

"Malvin was running around like a sheep dog trying to keep the two groups separated."

Adam sat down at his desk still laughing.

"That is too good."

"Have you seen the numbers for tomorrow?" asked Cameron.

"Sure have. Looks like we're in for a bumper session."

"How'd you go with the venue?"

"Just got off the phone with that old lady. All sorted. So, we're at the Uniting Church hall just a couple of doors down. Maximum capacity there is two hundred so we should have no trouble fitting everybody in. I'll update the meeting invite now."

Adam opened up his laptop and began typing away. The printer finished doing its job and Cameron picked up a large stack of A4 sheets off the tray. He carried them over to his desk where he had a small paper guillotine at the ready to start cutting them in half.

Adam hit the enter key enthusiastically and closed his laptop.

"Alright, all done."

He got up and walked over to Cameron's side of the desk.

"Are those the flyers?"

"Yep," said Cameron bringing down the guillotine blade.

Adam picked up one of the uncut A4 sheets off the pile. He turned it sideways to have a look. Then turned it one eighty degrees. Then turned it back to where he started.

"What the hell is this?"

"Did I get something wrong?"

"The photo."

"I know. It's, oh my god, it's so good. I'll show you the original in a minute."

Adam held up the A4 sheet. Featured prominently was a grainy black and white image of Nastashya. More precisely, it was Nastashya dressed in lingerie. Well, the top half of her was. The photo cut off around her belly button leaving the beholder to use his imagination to fill in the rest.

Adam let out an exasperated sigh.

"I don't know if we can use this, mate."

Cameron looked up from his guillotining.

"What's wrong with it?"

"What do you think? She's half naked. It looks like an ad for an underwear shop. Or a brothel."

"I think the text makes it pretty clear that it's not about underwear."

Adam read the top of the flyer: *Come and learn the secrets of the occult with Madame Orlova.*

"*Madame Orlova.* Did you make that up?" asked Adam.

"No. Nastashya asked me to use that name."

"I think we should ask her for another photo."

"It's too late now. I've already printed out all the flyers.'

"We can always print more."

"What's the big deal? Dude, this is Collingwood. I've seen far worse than this up on lampposts. Shit, there's poster for an S&M dungeon up on the street just outside."

"I guess so."

Adam put the sheet back down on the stack and Cameron picked it up and put it through the guillotine.

"Besides, you said you wanted to feature Nastashya. That's what we're doing."

"Ok. I suppose it'll be fine."

Adam took one more look at the stack of flyers and decided to let it slide.

"Alright. Let's hit the streets and get this job done."

Cameron put the papers into a large backpack and shut the zipper.

"Got the sticky tape?"

"Yep. Rebecca and her friend are gonna meet us on Smith Street to give us a hand."

"Oh, nice one."

"You should have asked Julie to come along. Might have been fun."

Adam gave a satirical laugh as they walked towards the elevator.

"No chance of that. She was in a foul mood. She mentioned marriage for the first time today."

"What? You and her?"

"Yeah."

"That sounds serious."

"It's scary that's what it is. I'm starting to think it's time to part ways."

Adam pressed the going down button.

"Really? You gonna do it before Christmas?"

"I think I have to," said Adam as they got into the elevator. "If I don't, it'll be a new year and then we'll have the New York trip and then it'll be her birthday. There's never a good time for this kind of thing."

"It's funny," said Cameron. "If you broke up with her a week ago, there would never have been an argument between us about going to New York and we might never had got into this competition."

As Adam pondered this fact, the elevator doors closed and the two men went out and plastered the streets of Fitzroy and Collingwood with photos of Madame Orlova.

CHAPTER 14

The Uniting Church in Collingwood was a rather ugly medium-sized church done in brown brick with yellow highlighting. This gave it, in the words of one of Adam's mates, an *excremental* appearance. The church hall was right beside the church and had been built with the exact same materials in the exact same style.

The insides of both buildings were more impressive than the exterior. The hall was a large expanse. It must have been about ten metres tall and featured old Tasmanian oak floorboards that had been kept in top condition over the years. There was some Christian ornamentation lightly and unobtrusively scattered around but it was an otherwise undecorated space. It had no stage, but a piano and a small public address system at the front of the room indicated that it had seen some use as an entertainment facility. A single male and female toilet to the left of the entrance door and a small kitchen to the right, were the only rooms inside the building.

Adam and Cameron had arrived early to begin setting up. As with the day before, Cameron's girlfriend, Rebecca, had come along to help out. She was a short, thin and pretty girl, dressed in black yoga pants and a black ski jacket despite the warm weather. This was the third time Adam had met her but he still struggled to form an opinion of the girl. What conversation there had been between them had consisted entirely of pleasantries. He guessed that most of Rebecca's conversations were like that.

The three of them had set up chairs in two large squares facing the front of the hall. This created an aisle down the middle that led from the door to the front in a perfectly straight line. To the left of the front door, just after the entrance to the toilets, they had put a folding table with a stack of membership forms, pens and a metal cash box. Adam and Cameron were standing behind the table going over the plan.

"You know, I really think we should switch to electronic membership. It would be easy to set up a form online. These paper forms are getting to be a pain in the arse. We could process the membership fees online too," said Cameron neatening up the pile of forms on the table.

"Yeah, but then we'd have to set up a bank account and we'd have to give a cut to whoever is processing the transaction. Given that we're only running this for two weeks, it's easier to stick to paper," answered Adam.

"Only nine days left."

"Time flies when you're having fun."

Rebecca came around the corner from the kitchen and walked over to the table.

"Feeling confident, Rebecca?" asked Adam.

"Yeah, no worries," said Rebecca.

"Bec's got this. No problem," said Cameron putting his arm around her. She smiled but looked a little uncomfortable at this public show of affection.

"Just remember to give the form a quick once over after the person has finished filling it out. We don't need to be too picky but it would be nice to correct any obvious errors or handwriting that's hard to read or whatever," said Adam.

He looked at his watch.

"I think we can open the doors now. Everybody ready?"

Cameron and Rebecca gave a nod as Adam walked to the entrance. The doors of the hall were old fashioned heavy timber. Thankfully they were wide enough that you only needed to open one of them. Adam wrestled the door on the left open and latched it against the brick wall.

Fritz and his mate were already waiting outside. Adam realised he hadn't gotten to know them, or anybody else in the group for that matter. In the absence of anything better, he gave them a hearty greeting.

"Afternoon, gents. Come in."

Adam stepped back and the two rotund gentlemen entered.

"Looking forward to the meeting?" asked Adam.

"Certainly am. We just saw one of the new posters," said Fritz. "Frank decided to nick one."

Frank proudly held up a flyer that still had the sticky tape stuck to the top half but had been torn across the bottom. Fortunately for Frank, the tear had occurred low enough on the page to retain a full representation of Madame Orlova's bosom.

"Looks like we're in for some fun," said Frank.

"You'll be in for some fun with that when you get home, that's for sure," said Fritz giving the torn flyer in Frank's hand a flick.

The two began laughing like a couple of fourteen-year-old schoolboys.

Adam forced a smile.

"Well, grab a seat. We should be ready to start in about fifteen."

"Front row, if you don't mind," said Fritz and the two of them took two seats at the front on left side of room.

****

Once again, Nastashya was late. Adam had considered addressing the crowd but feared a repeat of the awkwardness of the failed ohm exercise from last time.

A similar failure this time would be much worse. Numbers had exceeded their expectations. Cameron had counted seventy-one people in the hall. It seemed the flyers had worked.

Adam stood at the folding table near the front door. He had vowed to grab Nastashya as soon as she came in the door so they could quickly go over the plan for the meeting. He would give a quick introduction, followed by her part and then a time for all the new people to sign their membership forms.

He surveyed the audience as he waited. Its outstanding feature was its maleness. Not counting Rebecca, there were only two women in the room: a couple of goth girls in black leather dresses and tattoos. They sat together in the back-row giggling with each other.

Other than that, it was a complete sausage fest. The average age would have been mid-twenties but there was significant variation around the mean including several teenage boys who must have been under eighteen. Adam decided he would let it go this time, but there would be an adults-only rule for subsequent meetings just to be on the safe side.

The variation in style of clothing among the attendees indicated a very broad cross section of socio-economic groupings. Metalheads in band t-shirts, rockers in tight denim, rappers in baggy shorts and t-shirts, preppy boys in chinos and shirts, even a couple of men in suits and ties. Adam pondered the meaning of it. Perhaps the occult really did have a wide cross section of interest? Or perhaps they were here for other reasons.

He checked his watch again. Now, it was really getting late. He was sick of this shit. He was going to make sure to bail up Nastashya afterwards so they could get organised for future meetings.

Some movement at the front door caught his eye. He started to walk in that direction but realised it was not Nastashya. It was a different woman who was about the same age as Nastashya. She was wearing the exact same outfit that Nastashya had worn last time. The string thing.

The woman did not look around. She did not take a seat. With chin up and head forward she walked slowly, deliberately, ceremoniously and downright sexily towards the front of the room.

She reached the back row of chairs just as a second woman came through the door. The second woman was wearing the same outfit, walking at the same pace with the same bearing. They stayed equidistant from each other as they moved towards the front.

It was about this time that the audience realised that something was happening. The loud hubbub of the room died as if somebody had switched it off from a power point. All heads snapped to the front door.

A third woman entered. Same outfit. Same deal.

The three of them continued their journey to the front. It was a like a fashion show where the designer had only one outfit to sell. But then a second outfit walked through the door. Inside it was Madame Orlova.

At first glance, her outfit was more conservative than the string thing. But that was just because it was more ornate, more complicated. It took longer to parse. There were frilly things and bits of lace and material attached to well-chosen places. Once the eye got beneath the busy exterior, you realised that she was as good as naked. Or was that just the imagination getting carried away with itself. It was hard to tell.

A fifth woman followed Nastashya through the door just as the first woman had reached the front of the room and had taken up a position on the far right. The second woman went to the far left. The third turned right and Nastashya and the other followed to complete a straight line with Nastashya directly in the centre. They were standing not far from the front wall, several metres in front of the front row of seats. They stayed in this position for several seconds. The silence in the room seemed to buzz with a hidden energy.

"We begin with ohm," announced Nastashya in a commanding voice that reverberated around the hall.

The five women raised their arms, lifted their eyes to the ceiling and began to vibrate a long ohm sound. The ten existing members of The Order of the Secret Chiefs, the ones who had seen this at the last meeting, took their cue, raised their arms and proceeded to ohm. The first timers did not need any further explanation for this simple exercise so that within a very short space of time all seventy-one people in the room were ohm-ing away.

Adam looked to his right to see that Rebecca was still behind the folding table but Cameron was nowhere to be seen. He scanned the room and eventually spotted Cameron right down the front in the first row with his arms in the air and his eyes, perhaps a little lower than the ceiling. Perhaps just low enough to get a view of Nastashya's first assistant who was standing about three metres in front of him. Adam glanced back over at Rebecca to see what she was making of the spectacle but her face displayed her usual equitable expression.

After a couple of minutes, Nastashya signalled the end of ohm time by lowering her arms and her gaze. It was now time to rub. Thighs first and then chest. It all proceeded in a way that was surreally effortless. The sight of so many men vigorously rubbing their chest got Adam thinking of King Kong. The girls at the front were miming the action as Nastashya had done previously no doubt conscious of the fragility of the string thing to excessive friction. Adam remembered the two goth girls at the back and couldn't resist a look in their direction. They were not miming. They were giving their black leather outfits a good working over. Adam decided it would not be prudent to spend too long appreciating this fact. He turned back to the front.

Eventually, the rubbing came to an end and Madame Orlova addressed the audience, her voice resonant and powerful in the cavernous enclosure.

"Welcome, my secret chiefs. Today we begin the next step in our preparations for glorious ending of the 16th December. In occult, we learn to generate energy and to focus energy. You, my secret chiefs, are the raw materials. You will focus your energy through me. In this way, we prepare for the glorious December 16th."

Once again, Adam had a feeling of discomfort at what was going on. His mind seemed to oscillate between finding the scene preposterous and then thinking that it wasn't that bad. After all, it wasn't that much different to what they had done last time. Maybe his feeling of unease was with the larger crowd and the larger venue. He decided to put it out of his mind. If they could convert even half of the new people that had shown up today they would gain a sizeable lead over The Früit Family.

"Final exercise for today. We combine sound energy and body energy. We will rub thighs. You may rub wherever you wish."

The five women began a simultaneous ohm and rub but with the difference that the ohm sound had been shorted. It was now a series of discrete vocalisations lasting less than a second with a frequency of two complete rubs per vocalisation. The rest of the room gradually joined in. Most copied the woman in electing to rub their thighs, some, like the two goth girls, were more comfortable with the chest. Thankfully, nobody appeared to be rubbing anywhere else.

For a good several minutes the hall of the Uniting Church of Collingwood heaved and hoed with energy. Adam had to admit he could feel it even though he was not partaking of the motions. Perhaps there really was something to this occult business.

Then it was over. The five women stopped their rubbing and their ohm-ing. There were several seconds of silence which featured the same buzzing energy that Adam had felt earlier only this time even more prominently.

Nastashya was the first to move. She began to walk at the same pace and in the same fashion as they had entered. The other women followed. They maintained an equal distance of about five metres just as they had previously. They walked slowly and deliberately and every eye in the room was glued to them.

As she reached the front door, Adam took a couple of steps towards Nastashya hoping to talk to her before she left. But he realised that all eyes were on the spectacle and he would look a fool to get in the way at that moment. He decided to wait.

Eventually, the fifth woman slowly made her way out the door. Adam waited for an opportunity to go after them. It was a good several seconds, perhaps longer, before the audience snapped out of the trance they appeared to be in, stopped staring at the front door and began to talk to each other.

He sprinted over to the door and looked out on the street. There was no sign of any of the women. He ran down the stairs and craned his neck in both directions. Nothing. He ran over to the nearest side street and had a look. No luck. They seemed to have vanished into thin air.

He sighed and made his way back into the hall. There was a crush around the folding table. Everybody that had watched the ceremony seemed to be crowding around. Cameron and Rebecca were handing out membership forms and pens as if they taking final bets before a boxing match.

Adam smiled as he realised they were about to take the lead in the competition.

"Adz, give us hand, can you?" shouted Cameron from behind the pack.

Adam grabbed a stack of membership forms and pens and began distributing them to the eager crowd of soon-to-be-members.

CHAPTER 15

For the first time in the competition, and for the first time since Malvin had known him, Kenneth looked dejected as they sat at their desks at the syndicate office. It was Monday morning. The Früit Family was now thirty-one members behind The Order of the Secret Chiefs. They were one week into the competition and they had one week to turn it around.

What made it worse was the ridiculous nonsense of last Friday where he had lost eleven perfectly good members. He and Malvin had had to keep them apart and try and remove the mutineers from the building like security guards at a nightclub. The cumbersome business of having to organise the refund of membership money and the avalanche of hate that had inundated their online forum over the weekend had robbed him of the time and mental space to think about what to do next.

They had organised a meeting for midday. RSVP numbers were way down, so they decided to host it at the syndicate's offices. Another backwards step. Adam and Cameron had already expanded to a larger venue and they were stuck in the same crappy office.

"We really should have called this off," said Kenneth. He was sitting with his feet up at his desk at the syndicate killing time before the meeting.

"I think it's still a useful exercise to keep the momentum going," said Malvin clicking away at his laptop.

"What momentum? We're going backwards at the moment. God knows what will happen today. A mass exodus because somebody put the wrong kind of turnip in a pea soup? Nothing would surprise me anymore."

"I've been thinking, maybe we should throw in some incentives," said Malvin looking up from his computer. "I mean, there's no rule in the competition to say what happens with the $50 membership fee, right? We can promise people "free" vegetables when they join. If we pool the membership fees and buy in bulk we can get a decent deal."

"That's a good idea," said Kenneth brightening up a little.

He put his feet down and sat up in this chair.

"Wait. I think I've got a better idea. We should introduce a referral bonus. $25 for every referral. We'll just take it out of the new person's membership fee."

"Great idea. That'll definitely work."

"Oh, man. We should have thought of this right at the start. In fact, let's make it a $40 referral bonus. We don't need the money anyway. Might as well go all out."

Kenneth was now on his feet and back to his old self pacing around the room in an animated fashion as he considered the possibilities of the idea.

"How many people are we expecting again?"

"About ten."

"Alright. I'll announce the referral bonus first thing. This is gonna change the game."

***

As per usual, Kenneth was preparing the meeting room while Malvin was downstairs meeting the attendees and letting them into the building. Several familiar faces walked in to the room, including the cause of last week's trouble, Bert Lincoln. Then several new faces appeared. Then several more new faces. Before Kenneth knew it, the room was packed almost beyond capacity. By the time Malvin closed the door behind himself, Kenneth had counted over forty people, most of whom were newbies.

"Wow, thanks for coming everybody. This is a far better turnout than we had anticipated."

"I bought a few friends along," said Bert smiling. He had taken the same chair to the right of Kenneth that he had sat in the preceding Friday.

"We heard about what happened last week and how you stood up to those bullies," said one of the new attendees, a girl in her early twenties who was seated to Kenneth's left.

"It's about time someone did," said another.

"How about three cheers for Kenneth," said Bert.

"Hip-hip. Hooray".

"Hip-hip. Hooray".

"Hip-hip. Hooray".

Kenneth smiled.

"Thank you, everybody. It was the least I could do."

Bert stood up and retrieved a large duffel bag that he had placed on the floor when he came in. He put it on the table and opened it.

"Now, before we get started, there is one matter I'd like to raise. The people I brought along today will remember this one from our last group. In that group, we all agreed that we should have a uniform to promote solidarity amongst the members. I've still got a heap of them left over. There's more than enough to go around. So, I thought I might as well bring them."

Bert started to lay out a number of clear plastic bags on the table. Each one contained some kind of yellow garment. The people nearest began passing them around the room. Eventually one reached Kenneth. He opened up the bag and removed its contents. Grasping the ends, he allowed it to fall down to full length. It was a bright yellow onesie complete with hoodie.

Kenneth looked up to see others in the room enthusiastically perusing their new piece of clothing. A couple of people were swapping to getting the right sizes. A couple of others had already put theirs on over the top of the clothes they were wearing. With the hoods pulled over their heads, Kenneth thought they looked like giant yellow condoms.

"Thank you, Bert. That's a really nice gesture," said Kenneth as he folded his up and began to put it back in the plastic bag.

"No, no. You've gotta wear it," said Bert. "Everybody does."

"I'll wear it at home," said Kenneth throwing his down on the table.

"I don't think you understand," said Bert, the tone of his voice effortlessly changing from friendly to threatening. "You have to wear it now. We *all* have to wear it."

The others in the room began to put on their onesies and, before they knew it, Kenneth and Malvin were the only ones who were out of uniform.

"Well?" said Bert with undisguised menace.

"Look, I can't," said Kenneth. "I'll get yellow fluff all over my suit."

Bert sat back and looked Kenneth up and down.

"Are you a vegan, Kenneth?" asked Bert his eyes narrowing.

"Of course, I am."

"I don't think I've ever seen a vegan who wears a suit. Has anybody else ever seen a vegan in a suit?"

A group of heads in yellow hoods moved slowly and ominously from side to side.

"I reckon this one's a faker."

"Fay-kah.

"Fay-kah.

"Fay-kah."

A couple of voices started to chant, then a couple more and soon every banana in the room had turned on its leader.

***

There was a banging on the door.

"Adam! Adam!"

Adam got up from the dining room table where he was finishing off his lunch and walked to the front door.

"Ad...," shouted Cameron as the door opened.

"He's out!"

"What?"

"Kenneth has pulled out of the competition!"

Adam looked around outside the front door of his apartment conscious that Cameron was creating quite a ruckus. He ushered Cameron inside closing the door behind them.

"What do you mean?"

"I tried calling you but there was no answer."

"My phone battery died this morning."

"That must be why they called me. I spoke to Mark about half an hour ago. He said Kenneth has officially withdrawn from the competition."

"What happened?"

"Apparently he got kicked out of his cult."

"The Früit Family?"

"Yeah. They kicked him out!"

"Why?"

"I dunno. There was some kind of mutiny."

"How do you get kicked out of your own cult?"

"Who knows? But that's it, man. We won!"

Cameron gave a still confused Adam a double high five.

"I can't believe it," said Adam walking around the room in a daze.

"This means we can all go to New York. You, me, Rebecca and Julie."

"Yeah. Julie," said Adam still deep in thought. He slowly sat down on the edge of the couch.

"That is, if the two of you are still an item."

"Well, I haven't called it off yet. Been too busy with the cult stuff."

"I know. I got some phone calls yesterday from people still wanting to join. Apparently, some of the new members on Saturday were raving about it to their friends."

"Well, it's all over now. I guess we'll have to close it down."

"We could keep it going," said Cameron with a cheeky grin.

Adam looked up at him.

"Maybe you could ask Madame Orlova for some private lessons."

"Oh, man. I still can't get over those outfits from Saturday."

"What did Rebecca think of the whole thing? She seemed pretty nonplussed about it."

"Yeah, she was cool with it. I think she was just happy to get out of the house and do something."

"Fair enough."

"*Start spreadin' the news...*"

Cameron began singing and badly ballroom dancing around the room. Adam was still on the couch processing the information.

"*I'm leavin' to-daaaay...*"

"How many people have accepted the invite for the meeting this afternoon?" asked Adam.

"More than a hundred."

"Shit. It's gonna be a pain in the arse to cancel it. Is it too late to send an email? We've got everybody's email, right?"

"Let's just go ahead with it. One last meeting. We'll have to explain to Nastashya what's happened. It would be better to do that in person. And we've already got the hall booked and everything."

"Yeah. You're right. Maybe Nastashya can take the members and go off and start her own thing. She's certainly got a growing fan base."

"That would be sweet. I wouldn't mind learning some more about the occult," said Cameron grinning.

"You're not buying that, are you?"

"What?"

"That what she's been doing are real occult practices."

"What do you think they are then?"

"I think she's just an exhibitionist who likes having men gawk at her. I tell you this, she's chosen the wrong line of work. She could be making a fortune in a strip club."

"Is Russia still communist? Maybe they don't believe in making money over there."

"Well, she's not in Russia anymore and I think she's wasting her talents."

"I dunno. I think there's something to this energy business. Even you admitted that you felt it on the weekend. There was definitely something going on in that hall. It wasn't just stripping."

"Maybe. Anyway, I'll be happy to watch one more performance this evening and then go back to life as normal. It's been a bloody strange week."

Adam sat back on the couch. He looked over at Cameron and smiled.

"New York, huh?"

Cameron threw his arms out theatrically.

"*Neeeewww Yooooooork.*"

Cameron's ability to hold pitch while singing was no better than it had been while ohm-ing but Adam didn't mind. His plan had worked. He'd beaten his rival. He'd made things right with Cameron. He still had the Julie problem to deal with but that could wait. Life was good.

CHAPTER 16

It was 6.05pm and there were more than one hundred people in the hall of the Uniting Church in Collingwood. This time there were no chairs laid out, no folding table with membership forms and pens, no Rebecca. In fact, there were no women at all in the room. The absence of the two goth girls was noted with some sadness by Adam. He'd always had a thing for black leather.

The men in the hall stood around in the typical way that a large group of strangers organise themselves in a space. Small group conversations combined to create a sound in the lower range of the audio spectrum and the natural reverb of the hall emphasised the bass tones to create a nice warm bubbling energy.

"Should we announce that this is the last meeting?" asked Cameron. He and Adam were standing together at the rear of the room near where the folding table would have been.

"I don't think it's necessary to announce it to the whole group. I was thinking we should get Nastashya, Fritz and the others together after the show. It would be nice to give them a proper explanation. I've already told Fritz, Darrell and Robert to hang around. If you see Pavlos and Francis, let them know."

"What are you gonna tell them? *Sorry folks, you've been the guinea pigs in our devious little experiment.*"

"Nah, nothing like that. I'll just make up something about the workload being too much and how you and I will be otherwise occupied planning a trip to *America*."

Adam gave Cameron a fist bump.

The volume in the room took a precipitous drop. Adam and Cameron turned to face the door.

"Here we go," said Cameron elbowing Adam playfully in the ribs.

The first woman was already inside. She was wearing the string thing but this time the colour had changed. It was a bold red. She was wearing lipstick and high heeled shoes in exactly the same shade. The sea of men who had been standing around parted down the middle to allow her to take the same passage she had taken two days earlier which led direct from the door to the front of the room.

The second woman was in blue. A light blue. It reminded Adam of the blue of Nastashya's eyes. Her lipstick and heels were also a matching colour. She proceeded on the same path as Saturday for about five metres and then suddenly, simultaneously, the two women turned ninety degrees to their right. From the centre line of the hall they walked forward about another five metes so that they had stopped an equal distance between the centre line and the wall. They turned around elegantly and faced back to the centre of the room. Around them the men on that side of the hall instinctively formed a semi-circular perimeter at a distance that seemed appropriate, although what was appropriate in this circumstance was anybody's guess. It ended up being about three metres from each woman.

The third woman was dressed in yellow and the fourth in green. They followed the same path as their companions but turned left when the time came. The final positions of the women formed a large square that would have been ten metres long on each of its sides.

It was into the middle of this square that Nastashya walked. Her outfit was unchanged from the previous Saturday. It was the black lace number. She reached the very centre of the room and turned one hundred and eighty degrees to face back towards the entrance door.

Adam and Cameron had been relocated in the shuffle to now be placed at the front of the straight line that formed the southernmost edge of the larger square of men that had formed around the square made by the four women. It was the edge closest to the front door. To their left was the green woman. To their right was the blue woman. Nastashya was directly ahead facing straight towards them.

If the hall had felt full before, it was now packed. In order to preserve the space around the women, the men had crammed themselves against the walls. Adam could feel the pressure pushing towards the centre of the room, pushing into his back. He realised he was leaning backwards as if to hold the men in their place. It was like being in the front row at a rock concert.

"Welcome, my secret chiefs. Today we begin our final preparation for the glorious 16th. There is only one week to go before we fulfil our destiny. There is much work to do. We begin with ohm."

Things proceeded as they had on Saturday. The entire room had their hands pointed to the sky and their chins raised upwards. Even Adam added his voice to the chorus, partly out of peer pressure caused by his prominent position at the front of the pack and partly out of curiosity. He had only observed up until now but he was in a good mood after his victory in the competition and felt like joining in this time. It would be the last chance he got.

The ohms continued on for longer. Several minutes. Adam had to admit there was something to it. He felt a little like he was swimming in a sea of energy. His own voice seemed to be both a unique contribution that he could readily distinguish but also just a small part of a more powerful whole. It gave him a feeling of connection.

The rubbing was less edifying. In fact, it was downright awkward. Adam, Cameron and the others at the front had unrestricted access to their thighs and chest. The same could not be said for those at the back. As the men behind rubbed their thighs they inevitably rubbed the hamstrings of those in front. Chests and backs were being simultaneously rubbed. Adam glanced around the room and was surprised to note that nobody seemed to find this odd and in fact all were happily participating despite the cramped conditions.

The rubbing also lasted longer this time and Adam was exceptionally glad when it came to an end. If he remembered correctly, the next thing was to simultaneously rub and ohm. He didn't like the thought of this.

The ohm-ing part was ok but this rubbing business was not his cup of tea. He looked around for a way to remove himself to an empty corner and realised there wasn't one. He would just have to stick it out til the end.

"We must generate energy in order to focus it," intoned Madame Orlova. "Where does this energy come from? It comes from most powerful force in universe: sex. This is root of all other energy. For most powerful energy, we must access sex energy. Every man take a place around woman nearest to you."

At this command, and with an efficiency and coordination that would have made a military marching band jealous, the men in the hall began to rearrange themselves. Adam seized the opportunity to escape. He ducked slightly and braced himself and with a bit of a nimbleness and a bit of force managed to fight his way to the back corner where the wall of the toilets met the western wall of the hall.

There was a small metal bin in the corner which was empty. Adam turned it upside down and stepped onto it. The boost in height gave him an unimpeded view of the hall.

The women were all placed as before but the men had formed full circles around each woman. They kept a distance of about two and a half metres making the diameter of the circles about five metres. Around these smaller inner circles, squares had formed. This made sense on the sides which butted up against a wall but the surprising part was the straight lines that backed onto where Nastashya was standing. These formed a perfect square made out of the backs of the men who were facing away from her and towards the nearest woman. It was as if there was some invisible force holding the men at a fixed distance from her.

"Today we access our strongest energy. Our sex energy.

"Stare at woman in front of you.

"Take her with your eyes.

"Rub your manhood.

"Say ohm."

As if these four commands made perfect sense and they had done it a million times before, every man in the room reached down to his crotch. They leant their upper bodies slightly back and extended their groins slightly forward. Their necks craned to allow their heads to point straight at whichever one of the four women was closest to them. They rubbed themselves and emitted simultaneous ohms that came in short bursts of less than a second.

Adam looked on in horror as he saw Cameron a couple of metres away from the woman in blue stroking himself like he was polishing a brass cup. Around the rest of the hall every other man was doing the same. The only redeeming feature of the scene was that the men seemed content to access their sexual energy from the outside of their clothing.

Adam was starting to feel nauseous. He thought of turning the bin over just in case he needed something to vomit into when the exercise finally came to an end. Nastashya had raised her arms. Without further instruction, without any noticeable signal whatsoever, the men straightened themselves out and returned to their original positions in the hall.

Adam figured that the ceremony must be coming to an end. This time he wasn't going to let Nastashya escape. Foregoing all pretence of civility, he pushed, clawed and even kicked his way to the front door. He fell out onto the street like a slice of toothpaste being squeezed out of its tube.

The early summer evening was still bright and sunny. His eyes slowly adjusted to the light and his breathing returned to normal. He shook his head and marvelled as he looked back at the hall. Thank god this was the last one. It was time to put this business to an end.

CHAPTER 17

Adam waited in front of the hall for several minutes. He wasn't exactly sure what he was going to say to Nastashya when she came out but he knew that he would lead her over to the side alley on the right-hand side of the hall. He wanted to get her out of sight and especially out of sight of the men exiting the hall. Otherwise, it might take hours to get rid of them.

This plan quickly became irrelevant. A man was the first person out of the hall, followed by another man and then a tidal wave of men as the attendees of the meeting left. Adam noted a dazed look on their faces. He figured this must be due to their eyes having to adjust to the light like his had earlier.

Among the mob he was able to pick out both Pavlos and Francis and ask them to stick around so they could join the others and he could give them all the news. The three of them waited till what felt like the main body of men had left then they re-entered the hall. There were still scattered groups around the place talking amongst themselves but the hall was mostly empty.

Cameron waved to Adam from the other end. He had Fritz, Frank, Richard and Darrell with him. Most importantly, he had Nastashya. She had acquired a long black overcoat to cover up her lace outfit. The other four women were nowhere to be seen. Adam, Pavlos and Francis walked over to where they were standing.

"Where are the other girls?" asked Adam.

"I let them out through the side door," said Cameron pointing over his left shoulder to an inconspicuous single door in the front corner of the hall which was still open.

Adam looked around the hall. There were now only about half a dozen groups of men present.

"Cam, give me a hand to get rid of these blokes so we can have a bit of privacy."

Adam and Cameron went around politely asking the men to leave. Once this was done, Adam wrestled the front door closed and re-joined the group at the front of the hall. The five men and Cameron were babbling away excitedly about the ceremony that had just taken place. Nastashya was standing a foot or so back from the circle they were standing in. It was as if they were unaware that she was even there. She was the woman who led the very thing they were talking about and yet they neither spoke nor even looked at her.

Adam waited for a break in the conversation then started to speak.

"Look, thanks for staying back everybody. Cameron and I just wanted to get together with our original group because we've got some news for you all. Unfortunately, we won't be able to continue with The Order of the Secret Chiefs. As you know, Christmas is fast approaching and there will be all the social commitments that entails. Also, we've both got our normal work to attend to. And early in the new year, Cameron and I will be going on a trip to the USA and we'll need to start organising that soon. So, the workload is just getting a bit much for us. We've had a great time, though. It's been great to meet you all. We'll continue to be around the area so we might see you on the street or something. And, yeah, good luck."

The six men gave each other confused looks.

"I don't understand," said Fritz. "We've been growing so quickly. Things have been working out perfectly and now you're ending it all. Just like that?"

"Well, yeah, it's partly because of that quick growth," said Adam. "Y'know there's a lot of work to process membership and put details in the databases and all that."

"We can help with that," said Frank. "Fritz and I work together in IT. Your systems are way out of date. The whole membership thing should be online and everything should be mobile based. You're wasting a heap of time with those forms. We can whip something up that will cut the workload down to nothing."

"Right. But there'll still be work though," said Adam.

"Let us help. I don't mind doing data entry or whatever," said Francis.

"Absolutely," said Darrell. "Now that uni is finished for the year, I've got heaps of free time."

"It's not really that," said Adam desperately racking his brain for more excuses.

"What is it then?" asked Pavlos.

"It's this occult stuff. I just, I think it's not really for me. Y'know, we've given it a go and I just don't think it works. For me. It might be different for you guys, of course."

"What about December 16th?" asked Robert.

"I think I was mistaken. I'd had a few too many drinks that night and I just saw and heard something that wasn't real."

There was silence. Adam looked from one face to the next trying to read whether he had satisfied them. It seemed he had. He was just about to wrap things up when a new voice entered the conversation.

"Is Judas?"

The voice was Nastashya's.

They turned to face her.

"Every Jesus has his Judas, no? Adam is Judas?"

Adam thought he heard a gentle mocking tone in Nastashya's voice that stung him in the chest.

"No, I'm not," said Adam. "I'm the one who started this group. So, if anything, I must be Jesus."

Adam had never had occasion to liken himself to Jesus before. But, then again, he'd never been accused of being Judas either.

"Is natural to doubt. But you must remain strong, Adam," said Nastashya in a detached manner.

"Yeah, bro. We're all here for you," said Fritz grasping Adam on the upper arm.

"That's right," said Francis grabbing the other arm.

Adam had the feeling that what were ostensibly hands of friendship could very quickly turn into hands of enmity.

"I don't think Cameron is doubter." Nastashya turned to face Cameron who was standing right beside her on the left.

"Are you doubter, Cameron?" She reached out and ever so gently rubbed the back of her hand against the back of his then took his hand in hers.

Cameron, staring into Nastashya's beautiful blue eyes, practically melted.

"N-n-n-no doubts from me," he managed to stammer.

"Good." She patted his hand and let it go.

Adam gave Cameron a quick wtf-look but dropped it as Nastashya turned back towards him.

"So, is no problem then?" said Nastashya.

Adam could read the mood. He knew the correct answer.

"No, no problem." he almost sighed.

Fritz and Francis let go of his arms and Nastashya addressed the group.

"We continue as planned. Next ceremony is on Wednesday. We meet tomorrow morning at Adam and Cameron's office to begin further preparations."

"What's that?" asked Adam.

"Cameron has agreed to allow us use of office."

This time Adam's wtf-look towards Cameron was explicit and prolonged. Cameron, looking like a dog that had displeased his master, gave a teeny shrug of the shoulders.

"Unfortunately, Cameron does not have the authority to do that," said Adam.

"Do you?" asked Fritz.

"No. It's a matter for the management."

"But you can ask management for us, right?" asked Darrell.

"I don't think it's appropriate."

The members of the group exchanged glances not, this time, of confusion but of suspicion.

"Maybe you are Judas, after all," said Fritz looking down at Adam.

Adam was standing right next to Fritz. He noted that, although girth was his defining feature, Fritz was also tall. And heavy.

Adam decided to cut his losses. He had tried to wind this up gracefully but it wasn't to be. Fifteen minutes ago, these blokes were rubbing their crotches in public, now they were trying to strong arm him. Better to just get out make a clean break.

"Look, I'll take it up with management tomorrow. How's that?" He faked a quick look at his watch.

"Now, I've gotta be somewhere. Cameron, you coming?"

Adam cast an imploring look at Cameron who seemed to be in a daze.

"Nah, I'll hang around here for a bit."

"Alright. Can you lock up then?"

"Yep. No worries."

"Ok. I'll see you all later."

Adam took one final look at the group, turned and walked out of the hall and into the evening.

CHAPTER 18

"Liam.

"What? Nah, it's Adam.

"Sampson.

"Yeah, yeah, good. Are you Collingwood by any chance?

"Oh, yeah? The same place?

"Yeah, sweet. I'll be there in five. I need a drink."

***

Liam Love was at the same seat at the same bar as he had been a week or so before. Sharon was behind the bar talking to him. Come to think of it, the whole damn place looked exactly the same. The same blokes in suits, the same hipsters, the same unicycles.

Adam ordered a pint.

"You're looking a bit rattled, son," said Liam taking a sip of whisky.

Sharon gave Adam a beer and a smile. He took a long drink, put the glass back down on the bar and turned to Liam.

"It's been a strange week. Very strange."

"Problems at the syndicate?"

"Nah. Well, sort of. It's that cult thing I told you about last time."

"Cult? Oh, that stupid apocalypse group?"

"Yeah. It's gotten really crazy now."

"No shit. Hey, I think I'm getting a vision. Yeah, it's coming down from a higher power. Holy shit. I think it's coming from God himself. It says. Uhhh, it's a bit hazy. It says: *I told you so*."

He nudged Adam hard in the ribs. Adam didn't take the joke and Liam's shit eating grin slowly faded.

"So, it's serious, is it?"

"Not really. I'm disbanding it today. I just got back from the last meeting."

"So, what's the problem?"

"I just don't understand what happened. At the meeting today, there were more than a hundred men rubbing their cocks in public."

Liam raised an eyebrow.

"Were they trying to summon God?"

"Sort of."

"What do you mean *sort of*?"

"They were trying to access their sex energy."

"Well, rubbing your cock *is* one way to do that. Why were they accessing their sex energy?"

"It was part of an exercise."

"That you gave them?"

Adam looked horrified.

"No. I didn't give it to them. Why would I get a bunch of men to do that?"

"You tell me. I don't know what lies behind that rigorously heterosexual exterior of yours."

"It wasn't my idea."

"I thought you were running the group?"

"I was. Sort of."

"Y'know, I'm sort of getting the feeling that you should sort of tell me the whole sort of story from the sort of start. Sort of."

Adam took a deep breath.

"Ok. So, you know that I started the cult because I was trying to win the competition at the syndicate. The cult was supposed to be based on the occult. So, I made up some story about an old text that predicted the end of the world in two weeks. Well, things were going pretty bad at the start. We didn't have many members and I didn't know anything about the occult. But then this girl showed up at the meeting. Nastashya Orlova. She's from Russia. And she said she knew stuff about the occult. She started to do some exercises for the group and everybody really enjoyed them. So, I figured I could let her run the meetings because she knew what she was talking about. Make sense so far?"

"She was the one who got the men to jerk off in public?" said Liam quickly filling in the blanks.

"No. I mean, they weren't jerking off. Just rubbing themselves from the outside of their pants."

"That's still jerking off in my book."

"That's not the point. It all started off fine. Simple. Then the next meeting she rocks up in this outfit. This short skirt and this top and....oh, man. This woman is beautiful. The most beautiful woman I've ever seen. So sexy. And everybody's just mesmerised. But she does the occult exercises like before. Same easy stuff but just a little more in depth this time.

"Then numbers started to grow. We had to move out of the office cos there wasn't enough space. We went to the Uniting Church just down the other end of Johnston St and rented the hall there for the next meeting. She brings along these four other women, each one as hot as her and they're all wearing that same ultra-sexy outfit. But this time the whole thing has more of a ceremonial vibe to it. They enter the hall in formation and take up fixed positions and everything. But it's still just these easy occult exercises. Really easy stuff. Like saying ohm and rubbing your chest."

"Rubbing your chest?"

"Yeah. And your thighs."

"So, prior to rubbing their cocks in public, she had the men rubbing their chests and thighs in public?"

"Yeah. Then today the numbers really exploded. The hall was almost full. And these girls, Nastashya and the four others, did another ceremony only this time instead of rubbing your thighs and your chest, you had to rub your cock. And everybody fuckin did it! A whole hall full of grown men just did it like it was nothing."

"There were no women?"

"No. A couple of girls showed up to one of the meetings but after that it was all dudes."

Liam let out a big sigh and leaned back on his stool. Adam looked over at him.

"What do you think?"

"I think it's a bloody good thing you're putting an end to it."

"Yeah, but what does it mean? How can that happen?"

"She conditioned you. She started off small and then gradually increased the pressure. It's a common technique when teaching anything."

"So, you think she was really teaching about the occult? I mean, surely rubbing yourself and saying ohm is not the occult?"

"What do you think the occult is, mate? Didn't you bother to research it at all before you started this group?"

"It's Merlin, isn't it. Magic spells. Secret potions and shit."

"Do you believe in it?"

"No," said Adam scoffing.

"That's why you don't understand what happened."

"So, you're saying what happened *was* magic?"

"Of course, it was."

"I don't believe that."

"That's because you don't even know what magic is. That's why I told you not to get involved with this shit in the first place."

"So, what is magic?"

"Technical definition? It's the change of consciousness in accordance with the will."

Adam spent a moment trying to make sense of this statement. Liam could see he was struggling so he repeated the sentence a little slower.

"It's the change of *consciousness* in accordance with *the will*. Which raises the question: whose consciousness is being changed and whose will is doing the changing. The thing I want to know is, what was this Nastashya Orlova trying to do with you all?"

"What do you mean?"

"Well, she changed your consciousnesses in accordance with her will. What is her will? What does she want?"

"I don't know. I never really got the chance to talk to her."

"What!? You just let some hot Russian woman come in and run your group without even asking what she was doing there?"

"It just kind of happened. I didn't plan it."

Liam finished what was left of his whisky and slammed the glass down on the bar.

"You're an idiot, Sampson."

There was something about the way he said it that stung Adam right in the chest. Liam had called him an idiot before but it was always in the light-hearted, playful way that men criticise each other. This time he meant it.

"You should be glad you've gotten out of it. Crazy shit can happen when people play with things they don't understand. You know, there was once a cult where all the men castrated themselves. A big group of men literally chopped their own fucking nuts off. Can you imagine that?"

Adam shook his head.

There was a long silence. Liam waited for Sharon to re-appear then ordered himself another whisky.

"I want to learn more about it," said Adam finally.

"What?"

"The occult."

"Why?"

"I want to understand."

"Fuck understanding. Understanding gets you nowhere. You have to do. Do first. Understanding comes later."

"What should I do then?"

"Come and do my course in January."

"I can't."

"What do you mean?"

"I can't afford it."

"I thought you were doing well? From your network."

"I am. But your courses are bloody expensive."

"Look, I'll let you join in for free. How's that? You're not gonna get that offer again by the way."

"That's great but what's a course on picking up girls got to do with the occult?"

"This is what I mean: you're not ready to understand. You have to take things slowly one step at a time. All this stuff is related. Sex, magic and the occult. It's will. Energy. Self-understanding."

"Funny. That's what Nastashya Orlova said: sex is energy."

"She's a step ahead of you then."

Liam took a drink of the new glass of whisky that Sharon had discreetly placed in front of him.

Adam looked up at the clock on the wall.

"Oh, shit. I gotta go. I'm late for dinner with Julie."

He got up out his chair and sculled the rest of his beer.

"Thanks for the chat, Mr Love."

Liam turned and shook Adam's hand.

"Come and do the course in January, mate. It's on me."

"Alright. I'll think about it."

CHAPTER 19

Adam's phone buzzed silently beneath the pillow. He was already awake and reached his right arm over his head to retrieve the phone and disable the alarm. His left arm was pinned beneath Julie who was still sleeping with her head on his chest. He checked the phone for messages. There were none.

It was 7.00am. First order of business for the day was to de-activate the website, mailing list, email accounts and other bits and pieces related to The Order of the Secret Chiefs. Unfortunately, he had left his laptop at the syndicate's office. He had intended to pick it up the preceding evening after the meeting at the Uniting Church but the craziness of the day had intervened and he forgot about it.

He put the phone on the bedside table and began the process of trying to dislodge himself without waking his girlfriend. He grabbed the two pillows that would have been her usual support and slid them in under her head as he simultaneously slid his chest and shoulder out. This seemed to work and he turned his attention to the rest of his body extricating his legs last of all. As slowly as he could he got up off the bed.

Mission accomplished. Julie was still asleep.

He grabbed his jocks and pants off the floor and put them on. They were at Julie's house in Clifton Hill. She had a whole townhouse to herself. It was paid for by her parents. The ones Adam had still not met. Her father was some kind of judge and her mother was high up in the state government bureaucracy. Neither occupation had filled Adam with the hope that a meeting with the two of them would be a lightweight, carefree affair and this was part of the reason he avoided that meeting.

He went into the ensuite to relieve himself and then returned to the bedroom to retrieve his shirt. He looked at Julie as he buttoned it up. Last night had been a mistake. He'd organised dinner with the firm intention of breaking up with her. But after the business with Nastashya and the others, then the meeting with Liam, he was not in the mood for more confrontation. And Julie had been in one of her playful moods. It was the side of her that had originally attracted him even though he had seen it so rarely since.

He grabbed his phone off the table and scanned the room one more time before quietly walking out.

"Adam. Come back to bed."

Julie's voice was deep and throaty and not just because she had just woken up. Adam turned around to see that playful look once more.

"I can't, babe. I've gotta get down to the syndicate to get my laptop."

Julie said nothing. She was lying on her right-hand side. She lifted the bedsheet and doona with her left hand and wiggled the index finger of her right hand to beckon him to her. Adam knew he shouldn't. But short of breaking up with her then and there he didn't have much choice and it was hardly the worst way to start the day. He went back to bed.

***

It was 9.43am when Adam finally arrived at the syndicate's office. It wasn't just the sex that had held him up but the breakfast afterwards which had to be taken at Julie's favourite café.

He walked into the foyer and took the stairs rather than the elevator. He was really hoping that Kenneth and Malvin would be around. Partly this was so he could gloat about his victory but he was also genuinely interested to know the full story behind them withdrawing. Adam knew

Kenneth was not a quitter. Whatever had convinced him to pull out it must have been pretty big.

The syndicate's offices were normally dead quiet at this time of year. The small core of administrative staff was based on level two and didn't have any reason to visit the first floor. Nevertheless, Adam could hear several voices as he walked down the hallway and towards the small, open-plan room where his and Cameron's desks were located.

He saw Fritz first. Then Frank. Then Darrell. Pavlos was sitting at Adam's desk. Francis and Cameron were seated together at the latter's desk talking about something or other. There were no other syndicate staff or associates around.

"Adz!" Cameron called out. "You made it."

"Yep," said Adam walking over. He saw his laptop. Pavlos had pushed it over the side along with his photo of Julie and his box of pens. Cameron noticed the look on his face.

"Sorry, bro. We didn't know what time you were getting here so I told Pavlos to sit there."

"Is this *your* desk?" asked Pavlos making as if to get out of the chair and cede the desk to Adam.

"No, mate. You're all good. Stay there. Cameron, can I speak to you, please?"

Adam and Cameron walked over to the closest meeting room. Adam shut the door behind them and swung around.

"What the fuck are is going on?" he whispered.

"What?"

"Why are *they* here?"

"We talked about it yesterday. The Order needed some office space and we both know that the syndicate is empty at this time of year."

"And you and I had already agreed we were gonna shut this thing down."

"Well, I've changed my mind. I want to keep it going. I want to stay involved."

"Why?"

"Because I'm enjoying it."

"Enjoying what? Perving on Nastashya?"

"It's not perving."

"No. I guess it's not. Perving would imply the girl wasn't in on the act. I don't even know what you call this. It's like a strip club without the money."

"Why do you always bring it back to stripping?"

"Cos that's what it is. Are you blind?"

"It's the occult. You started this bloody thing. You should know what it's about."

Adam sighed loudly.

"Look. I don't want to be a part of this anymore."

"Fine. Nobody's stopping you from leaving."

"Maybe not. But you've brought these people into our office, Cameron. For fuck's sake, there's somebody sitting in my chair, at my desk."

"So what? It's only for one more week. Not even that. Six days. You won't even be here this week. Nobody will."

"And what happens after that?"

"I dunno. Whatever happens on the 16th."

"Has Nastashya explained what's going to happen on the 16th?"

"No."

"I'll tell you what's going to happen. Nothing. Nothing will happen. *I* made up the date. Remember? Just like I made up the bullshit story about the occult. Have you forgotten how all this started, Cameron? Now you've gone and invited these people in. We'll never get rid of them. We'll have Fritz and his fat arsed mate, Frank, and the others hanging around here indefinitely."

"Well, that's my problem now, isn't it? You don't have to worry about it."

"Look, Cam, I'm a little bit worried about what's going on. This is not normal. Ok? I don't know what the deal is with Nastashya, but something is not right. I really don't want to see you involved."

"Too bad. I like it. I'm gonna keep doing it."

Adam could see he wasn't getting anywhere. One thing about Cameron was his stubbornness. Adam had never figured out how to get him to show up on time, how to get him to dress properly, how to get him to speak properly to marks. He started to wonder whether he'd been able to teach him anything at all.

"Alright, mate. I'm leaving. I'm going to remove myself from the accounts and I'll make it known that I don't have anything further to do with the group. It's all on you now. You're responsible. Deal?"

"No worries."

Adam sighed as he looked at his protégé. Cameron had been one of the easiest marks that Adam had ever converted. He was like a little child in some sense. He believed whatever you told him. And just like a little child, he didn't like being told what to do. But Adam was not his father. There wasn't much more he could do to get him to stop.

The two of them left the meeting room and walked back to their desks. Fritz and Frank were excitedly showing off something to the others.

"Adam, Cameron, come and look at this."

They walked over to Fritz's desk. There were about five computer monitors on it. Each was filled with different kinds of windows and applications that were running. Adam had enough experience with setting up websites and had picked up enough from a couple of his more nerdy mates to know that some fairly low level website development was taking place.

"Check this out," said Fritz pointing to one of the screens. It was the website that Adam and Cameron had created a week or so earlier. But it had changed significantly. Cameron must have given them access to the accounts.

"We've put the fields for the mailing list up here in the header so anybody can sign up instantly. Also, we've got social media integration over here including live feeds from the Secret Chief's social media accounts. And, best of all, the livestream will be displayed front and centre when you open the page."

"What livestream?" asked Adam.

"Oh, you haven't heard yet," said Francis. "We've gone international."

"International?" said Adam not liking the sound of this.

"We've already picked up more than five hundred people on the mailing list," said Frank.

"In more than twenty countries too," added Pavlos.

"What's going to be livestreamed?" asked Adam although he was pretty sure he already knew the answer.

"The ceremonies," answered Cameron. "The first one is going live in just over half an hour."

"From where?"

"From here. We've set up one of the meeting rooms with cameras and microphones. Robert's in there right now. He brought in a bunch of pro gear. It's gonna be awesome."

"They're doing a dress rehearsal right now," said Francis. "You should go and have a look."

Francis pointed in the direction of the meeting room they had originally used for the cult. As with the invitation to come back to bed that morning, Adam knew he probably shouldn't accept this one, but he couldn't resist the temptation to have a look. He walked down the familiar hallway and peeked around the corner.

Robert had indeed done a professional job of setting the room up. There were three cameras on tripods located on the right, centre and left of the room. Several large LED light pads looked down from the ceiling. They were held up by extra-large stands. The lighting had been set to a fairly mellow red kind of tone so that although the room was very well lit it wasn't harsh or glaring. Robert himself was monitoring the events from behind a desk where two large monitors sat with live feeds of what was coming through the cameras. There must have been a fourth camera somewhere as there were four windows open with video feeds. Adam surmised that there was a handheld camera somewhere around the place.

And then there were the girls.

They were lined up straight along the back wall. Nastashya was in the middle in her usual lace number. The others were coloured as before but the string things had been replaced by lingerie. Not your everyday lingerie. Not anything you could buy at a department store. In Adam's mind, and he had no particular experience with the genre, it was S&M lingerie. Bright leather with studs. The bras were fastened in the front by three smalls straps that buckled into position creating short horizontal lines that ran from one breast to the other. The panties featured a couple of leather strings that were tied together at the left hip although these were not load bearing strings but more for decoration.

They were currently in the ohm phase of the dress rehearsal of the ceremony. The girls had their arms raised and their heads lifted as they ohm-ed. This part came to an end. There was some discussion where Robert asked the girl in blue to slightly alter her position then they returned to their poses.

The rubbing commenced. This time, it was for real. There was no miming. The four women were all over their leather lingerie just like the two goth girls had been at the first meeting at the church hall. As usual, Nastashya was not taking part but standing motionless at the centre of it all.

Robert gave a thumbs up. The girls stopped. Nastashya began to speak again. It was time for the crotch rubbing and this time the girls were demonstrating the correct technique explicitly. Very explicitly.

It was probably because it reminded him of the roomful of men doing the same, but the sight of the girls leaning their shoulders back and pushing their crotches forward was not as alluring to Adam as it might have been. Not that the girls weren't doing their best to make it so but somehow Adam wasn't feeling it.

He turned away and took several steps back down the hallway before pausing to think.

This was deep. There were now half naked women gyrating in the meeting room in S&M costumes. Cameron was either too dumb to figure it out or he just didn't care. If one of the mentors walked in right now, Cameron would be out on his ear.

More importantly, so would Adam. He was still responsible for this mess. As far as the mentors were concerned, this was still his cult. He couldn't just walk away. He had to find a way to get them out of here. The only question was, how?

He walked back to his desk. Pavlos was still there. Adam told him to stay put, picked up his laptop and took up a position at an empty desk in the corner. Cameron walked past on the way back from the kitchen.

"You hanging around, after all?" he asked Adam.

"Just for a little while. I wanna check my syndicate accounts and stuff."

"Goddamnit," shouted Fritz in a loud booming voice that made everybody in the room jump.

"What's up?" asked Cameron walking over to the desk with five monitors.

"My code failed to upload again. The bloody Wi-Fi keeps dropping out."

"Yeah, it's dodgy as around here. It normally comes back pretty quickly though."

"Alright, it's back," said Fritz hammering away on the keys of his computer. "I don't know how you people work under these conditions."

This gave Adam an idea. He got up from his desk and made his way down the short hallway that led to the kitchen. To the right of the kitchen door, several inches above the door frame and just below the ceiling was a small ledge and on the small ledge was a small black box. It was the wi-fi router for the first floor. He shot a quick look back over his shoulder to check that nobody was watching then stretched upwards and pressed the button at the back of the unit. An ever-so-slight clicking sound and sudden blinking out of the lights on the front indicated that it was off.

He went into the kitchen and grabbed himself a glass of water. Over a fifteen-metre distance and through no less than three sets of walls he could hear the voices of Fritz and Frank swearing. Adam allowed himself to picture them both shaking their big fat fists at their tiny little computers. This brought a smile to his face.

He waited a minute or so then returned to the room.

"This is bullshit," said Fritz. "I can't work here. Let's just go back to my place. I've got proper fixed line, state of the art internet."

"You should do that," said Adam trying to suppress a grin at the fact that his plan was working perfectly.

"The internet here has always been shithouse."

Fritz started to pack up his things when Cameron came into the room with Joel.

Adam cursed under his breath.

Joel was the IT operations guy. Adam had no idea he would even be working at this time of year. He had a little cupboard sized room down near the men's toilets from where managed the core IT systems of the syndicate.

"Looks like the whole internet is down this time," said Joel poking around on Cameron's laptop. "Let me check the router."

Joel walked off down the hallway to the kitchen and returned about ten seconds later.

"The router lost power or something. It was switched off. I've turned it on again so the internet should come back any second."

"It's back!" said Cameron jumping up and down a couple of times like an excited schoolgirl.

"Thanks, Joel."

"No worries," said Joel walking off back towards his cupboard.

Adam watched him go before noticing that Frank was giving him a strange look. He turned to face him but Frank had turned away before Adam could make eye contact.

Adam turned back to his computer and started to formulate Plan B.

CHAPTER 20

For fifteen or so minutes, Adam had sat back and watched as the group worked away. He had to admit, they seemed to be coordinating very well together. Fritz and Frank obviously new their way around code. It seemed like every other minute they had some new feature uploaded to the web. Pavlos was handling social media. Francis was taking care of the mailing list. In addition, he was working various internet forums and whipping up interest in the group. Darrell was also active on some forums and the two of them were reading out some of the more notable exchanges that were going on. There seemed to be a lot of interest in the Secret Chiefs on whatever sites they were using. Cameron was coordinating back and forth between the two rooms and giving the guys updates on preparations for the livestream. They were all on track to go live any minute.

Cameron stuck his head through the doorway.

"The livestream is about to start. Anybody who wants to watch it in the flesh come down now."

The other five men eagerly got up from their seats and headed off down the hall.

"Not coming, Adam?" asked Francis on his way past.

"Nah, mate. I'm just in the middle of something here. I'll watch it online."

As soon as Francis was out of the room Adam leapt up and ran off down the hallway towards the men's toilets. On the left there was a door that looked like a cupboard door. He slid it open and almost unhinged it as it slammed back against the rail.

Joel swung around on his chair alarmed by the sound.

"Oh, it's just you, Adam."

"Yeah, sorry about that, mate. It was lighter than I thought it would be. I think this is the first time I've ever been in your office."

"Well, nobody really comes in here. Mainly it's because you can't fit two people in here."

"Oh, really. Let's try."

Adam squeezed through on Joel's right just far enough to close the door behind him. He tried to sit on the small table that was up against the wall but only succeeded in knocking a couple of pens and a wireless computer mouse onto the floor. Bending down to pick them up had the effect of knocking some things off the other side of the table. He started to bend down to try and get under the table.

"Don't worry," said Joel holding up his hand. "Leave them there. I'll get them later. Look, why don't we go outside where there's more space."

"I'd rather talk here," said Adam quietly.

He tried to crouch down but, that method not being geometrically possible, ended up leaning over the two tables with both arms extended giving him the appearance of standing over Joel who was still seated with this body facing towards his computer screen.

"There's something I need some help with."

"Mmm-hmm."

"Look, I know you and I haven't had a chance to get to know each other. I just want to say that I've always thought you've done a great job with the internet, and the other, umm, systems around here. I mean, I've always thought the commissions app was a really good choice on your part...."

"You don't have to butter me up, Adam. Just tell me what you want."

"I need you to disable the internet for a little while. But only for everybody else's computer on this floor. Not for yours or mine. Is that possible?"

"It's possible. But can I ask why?"

"It's a long story. But you've seen what's going on in the other room, right?"

"You mean your group?"

"Well, it's not really my group. I mean, it used to be my group but it's not anymore."

"Whose is it?"

"Ok. Yes. It's my group. Fine. I just. I'm playing a little prank on the rest of the guys. I tried it before with the router but you switched it back on. So, yeah, I want to disable the internet. Just for my guys."

"This isn't really within my job description, y'know."

"I'd consider it a huge, a massive favour."

"The problem is, I do you a favour now, then somebody else wants their email address changed, then somebody else wants me to fix their mother's old computer. It never ends. I've seen it before."

"Joel, just tell me what you want?"

"I don't want anything."

"Name your price, Joel. What can I do for you to make you disable the internet?"

Joel thought about it. Then thought about it some more. Adam checked his watch. Time was wasting. He thumped the table. Several more things fell to the ground.

"What do you want, Joel!?"

"I want to meet Madame Orlova."

"What?"

"Madame Orlova. I want to meet her."

"You can walk out there at any time and meet her. She's about fifteen metres away."

"I want a formal introduction."

"What's *formal*?"

"A proper one."

Adam had lost patience.

"Fine. I'll introduce you two. I'll do it later on. Easy peasey, mate. Now, can we just disable the internet please."

Joel reached for his mouse and clicked around for a few seconds.

"Everybody in your group except you, right?"

"Right."

"Done."

"Just like that?"

"Just like that."

"You sure?"

Before Joel could answer Adam heard the now familiar sound of swearing from three rooms away which confirmed that the deed was done. He opened the door and stepped out.

"Thanks, Joel. Come over in about fifteen and I'll introduce you to the Madame."

Adam started to walk away then turned back quickly.

"Oh, and by the way. They're gonna come and ask you to fix this any minute. You have to pretend you don't understand and you can't find the problem. Ok?"

"Ok."

Adam walked back to his desk. Cameron came rushing in from the direction of the meeting room and just as quickly rushed off in the direction of Joel. Adam sat down and opened his laptop.

Fritz and the others slowly wandered back into the room.

"This is why you need a hard-line connection that you control," said Frank. "It's the only way to be absolutely sure that you don't get dropouts."

"I think that's a bit of overkill," said Pavlos.

"Did you see the stream?" Francis asked Adam. "The part before it cut out."

"Nah, I missed it. Had to run to the toilet just when it was starting. Did I miss anything?"

"Not really. We only got up to the rubbing bit.

Cameron returned from his visit to Joel and addressed the room.

"Looks like we might be down for quite a while. Joel can't seem to figure out what the problem is."

"Oh, man. I was hoping to post the homework exercise straight to social media after the live stream," said Pavlos.

"Just tether your computer to your phone," said Fritz.

"What does tether mean?"

"Here, let me set it up for you."

Fritz went over and starting playing around with Pavlos computer.

"There's homework now?" asked Adam to nobody in particular.

"Yep. New addition starting today," answered Francis. "Come over here and I'll show you."

Adam walked over behind Francis and looked at his monitor. Francis dragged a picture over to the main screen. It had The Order of the Secret Chiefs logo at the top. A high-resolution photo of Madame Orlova filled the whole rest of the page. She was in the lace thing but something seemed different. Adam leaned forward and squinted his eyes.

"Do you see it yet?" asked Francis.

Finally, Adam saw it. Or rather, didn't see it. *It* wasn't there. She was naked underneath.

He took a moment to digest this development and another moment to appreciate it. In fact, he was starting to appreciate it too much. He straightened himself out, shook his head a couple of times and took a step back from the screen.

"How is this homework?" he asked.

"The homework part is on the second page," said Francis.

He scrolled down. The second page also had the logo at the top. Beneath it were five commands:

Stare at Madame Orlova

Take her with your eyes

Pull down your pants

Rub your manhood

Say ohm

Adam shook his head again and re-read it. His mind struggled to process the information even though the only addition to the existing formula was the third line.

"You're sending this to the social media accounts?"

"No. Only to the mailing list. It's for members only. But we'll be mentioning it on social media as a way to encourage membership. It was supposed to be part of today's ceremony but we got cut off so it'll have to wait for tomorrow. Madame Orlova wanted to send it out today. Apparently, it's an important part of the preparation for the 16th."

"The 16th?" mused Adam. "Has Madame Orlova said what's happening on the 16th yet?"

"Not yet. I think it will be announced in the next couple of days."

Adam nodded thoughtfully then walked back to his laptop.

"Ok. It's posted," said Pavlos from his computer.

"Sweet," answered Francis.

Adam looked over to see Fritz and his mate packing up their stuff.

"You blokes heading off?"

"Yeah. No point hanging around here if there's no internet. I can work better from home anyway."

The others signalled their agreement with this sentiment and began to get ready to leave.

"Hey, is Madame Orlova still here?" asked Adam.

"Nah, she left. She'll be back tomorrow for the next livestream," said Richard who had just come in from the meeting room.

"What time is the stream tomorrow?"

"Same time. 10.30am," said Francis.

"It's a weird time to do it, isn't it? In the morning?"

"It's a better time for the overseas members."

"There's overseas members now?"

"Yep. Fritz and Frank set up the payment system first thing this morning so anybody in the world can now join up and pay online. We've already got more overseas members than local ones."

"Welcome to the twenty-first century," said Frank cracking his knuckles.

Fritz and Frank packed up and left. The other men were gone shortly afterwards. Adam sat back in his chair. He realised he hadn't seen Cameron for a while. He got up and checked the meeting room. All the gear was set up and switched off but nobody was there. He checked the kitchen. No good. He walked to the men's toilet and had a look but nobody was there. It seemed that Cameron had left. Had he left with Nastashya?

As Adam was walking out of the toilet when he remembered his promise to Joel. He stuck his head through the door of the closet.

"Hey, Joel. Sorry, mate. Madame Orlova has already left so I can't introduce you today."

Joel turned around and on the screen behind him Adam could see the logo of The Order of the Secret Chiefs and below it the picture of Madame Orlova. It was the homework assignment.

"No worries. I can wait," said Joel.

"You've, ummm, you're..." Adam couldn't find the right words so he just pointed at Joel's monitor.

Joel turned to the screen and then quickly turned back.

"Yep. I'm a member. Can't wait to get home and do my homework."

"Right," said Adam trying desperately not to form the image of Joel doing his homework.

Adam tried to focus his mind. Things were moving so fast. He started to walk off but had an idea.

"Hey, Joel, there's one more thing I need."

"What's that?"

"I need you to disable Cameron's access card."

"His access card for the building?"

"Yeah. Can you do that?"

"Sure thing. But that would mean he won't be able to get into the office."

"That's the idea."

"Another practical joke?"

"Yeah, that's right. It'll be just for a couple of days."

CHAPTER 21

This time Adam spent the night at his own apartment so there were no interruptions. The previous day had been one of improvisation. Trial and error. That wasn't how Adam liked to work. He liked to be organised and work to a plan. This time, he had a plan. A plan to shut down The Order of the Secret Chiefs once and for all.

He had been up since 5am. There wasn't a lot of work required to disable the cult's web presence. There were the main website, the email accounts, the mailing list, the membership database and the social media accounts. He couldn't do anything about the forum posts that Darrell had been making but he could certainly disable the main channels. That should at least put a stop to the international side of the operation.

Before closing the accounts, he took the opportunity to catch up with the latest developments. The scale of what had happened was hard to fathom. Things had exploded. There were now more than ten thousand members. Most of them had joined in the last twenty-four hours. The mailing list was much bigger, measuring well over fifty thousand. The social media channels had more than one hundred thousand followers.

The operation was now truly global. The main source of interest was the video of yesterday's livestream. Adam didn't need to watch it. He knew what he would see. But he did check the analytics: it had more than half a million views.

Of course, there were new systems that Adam didn't have access to. The payment service was one. That was fine. He knew that shutting down the cult's web presence wasn't definitive. He was sure Fritz and

Frank could re-build the website in no time. They could start new social media accounts and find a way to communicate with existing members. The primary goal here was to get himself removed from culpability.

The secondary goal was to tell them the truth. He would meet them at the syndicate office this morning and lay it all out. The cold hard facts. That everything was a lie. That he had made it all up to win the sales competition at the syndicate. There would be no more pussy footing around. If Adam told them the whole story right from the beginning there was a good chance they would all just quit and the matter would be over with anyway.

By disabling Cameron's access pass the day before, he had ensured none of them would be able to get into the syndicate's office. He had packed up all the audio-visual gear that Robert had left in the meeting room and put it in a storage cupboard in the common area of the building. There would be no need for anybody to go inside the office again.

Adam knew this course of action was not without danger. Telling them the truth could lead to reprisals. He had lied to these people. Led them astray. They had a right to be angry.

He also remembered how quickly they had turned on him after the ceremony a few days earlier. Fritz and Frank between them had about four times his body weight on him and he was outnumbered six to one. In a physical altercation, he was not going to win.

He planned to have his back up against the door of the syndicate office just in case. If things got heavy he should have time to scan in and close the door behind him. He would be safe inside. In the absolute worst case, he knew the fire escape stairs would be directly to his right and he could make a run for it.

By 5.30 am the job was done. All the internet accounts were disabled. Adam felt that it was too early to go to the syndicate. He decided to grab a quick breakfast and then head off so he could prepare for the showdown.

***

It was just before seven when Adam arrived at the syndicate. He took the fire escape stairs up to the first floor to make sure everything was clear in case he needed to make use of them later.

The storage cupboard where he had left the audio-visual gear was directly opposite the stairs as he came out. He opened the door and confirmed that everything was still there.

There was now just the matter of the setup. Adam wanted to be waiting for them outside the office. The main reason for this was his plan to rush inside if things turned nasty. If he was inside when they came, he would have to open the door to confront them and that wouldn't work. They could easily muscle in.

He would have to wait for them outside the door. That could potentially get pretty boring but he had brought along his laptop which was in a backpack slung over his shoulder. All he needed was a chair. He walked over to the syndicate's door and was just about to pull out his access card when the bell for the elevator rang about six metres to his right. Shit. This might be them. They were here early.

It was game time. He turned around so he was facing away from the door. He unslung the backpack from his shoulder, started to throw it away and then changed his mind and swung back to its original position. He took a deep breath. At least, he tried to.

A dull clunk indicated the elevator doors had opened. Fritz and Frank were first out. They each had a take away coffee cup in hand. They smiled as they saw Adam standing there. These weren't the smiles of friends.

"Morning Adam, you're bright and early today," said Frank.

"Y-yeah," said Adam. Shit, he was stammering. He couldn't remember ever having stammered before. Even when addressing a big audience at the syndicate.

He noticed neither Fritz or Frank had their laptop bags.

"Did you forget your computers?"

"No. We've got them."

"Oh yeah? Are they downstairs?"

"Yeah."

"Is that where the others are?"

"Sure."

The two Fs stopped in front of Adam. A little bit closer than what would be considered socially acceptable. Close enough that Adam had to raise his head to meet their gaze. He was reminded again how tall they were.

"Do you mind letting us in, Adam?" asked Fritz. "We don't need to wait for Cameron to get here."

"Isn't he downstairs?" asked Adam.

"Why wait? We're all here."

Adam took a big gulp.

"I'm afraid I can't do that."

"Do what? Let us in?"

"No."

"Why on earth not?"

"You've gone a bit white, Adam. Are you feeling ok?"

"I can't let you in because The Order of the Secret Chiefs will no longer be operating from these premises," Adam spluttered managing to sound both overly formal and completely unconvincing at the same time.

"What do you mean?" Fritz's tone was excessively high pitched and he was speaking slowly like he was talking to a five-year-old.

"You can't use these premises and I've disabled the Order's accounts. If you want to continue operating you'll have to find somewhere else."

Fritz and Frank looked at each other but it wasn't a look of surprise or confusion. It was a look of...*agreement*?

They each took a step forward so that they were now right on Adam's chest. He realised he was surrounded and pinned against the door. Both of his escape plans had been rendered useless. He could neither get inside nor get to the fire escape. He froze.

"Madame Orlova was right. You are a traitor," said Fritz looking down his nose.

Fritz and Frank grabbed an arm each and, with the coordination of one man who just happened to be a heavyweight judo champion, flung Adam to the ground. He felt a rummaging in his pocket as if an angry Tasmanian Devil was trying to steal his car keys. His wallet removed, the two Fs picked him up just a little and threw him to the ground a metre or so away. His nose burned against the carpet. His pride just burned.

Adam slowly turned himself over and saw the two Fs looking at him as if they were waiting. Fritz had Adam's wallet. He raised it theatrically as if showing it to Adam then turned around and held it against the sensor next to the door. A red light flashed and querulous beep rang out. Fritz tried again. Then once more.

"What's going on here?" he said in his talking-to-a-five-year-old voice.

"Looks like somebody's card has been deactivated," said Frank mimicking.

"Who would do such a thing?" asked Fritz.

They both looked at Adam in mock seriousness for a couple of seconds before bursting out laughing. This went on for a while. Adam's cheeks burned red to match the burn on his nose. He realised he was being deliberately humiliated.

Fritz threw Adam's wallet at him with disdain. It hit him in the chest and bounced away to the left. Frank pulled out his own wallet and scanned it. A green light flashed.

"Good thing that this one works."

The two Fs opened the door and walked inside. Frank turned around holding the door open with his left hand. His cup of coffee was still in his right hand.

"Oh, by the way, Adam. Those accounts you disabled. They weren't real accounts. Little thing called mirror sites. Fritz and I whip those up all the time for our little side projects. So, the only thing that's been disabled around here is you."

Frank gave a girlish little giggle supremely amused at his show of wit. He had half shut the door when he opened it again. Fritz walked out and came straight towards Adam who instinctively lifted his right leg and arm to his chest as if to protect himself from a blow.

"Almost forgot," said Fritz walking straight past him. "Don't want to leave this stuff here where little troublemakers can get to it."

Fritz somehow picked up all the audio-visual gear that was in the storage room in one go and lugged it through the door of the office that Frank held open for him. Adam watched as Frank's shit-eating grin disappeared behind opaque glass as the door swung shut and clicked into its closed position.

CHAPTER 22

Adam was trying to digest his food and the morning's events at the same time. One or both of these tasks was giving him indigestion. He pushed the plate away and took another sip of coffee.

He wasn't hungry anyway. It was too early for lunch. He had wandered into the café in a daze and ordered food because it felt like the correct thing to do. Really, he just wanted to sit down.

After the events at the syndicate he had decided to take a walk to try and make sense of it all. He had walked and walked and, by the time he looked up to see where he was, he was almost in Richmond not far, in fact, from his apartment. He didn't want to go home so he had sought shelter in a café where he and Julie often ate when she stayed over.

The humiliation of his defeat stung. The sting was made worse by the pre-meditated and elongated nature of it. They must have known the day before. Adam remembered the look that Frank had given him after he had turned off the wi-fi router. It had to be that. Fritz and Frank, the fat-arsed IT nerds, must have figured it out.

And Joel. Joel must have been in on it too. Of course, it all made sense. He was a member. Those bastards must have sat around yesterday evening plotting the whole thing. Timing it out. Maybe they had someone watching him that morning as he came to the offices. They seemed to know exactly when he had arrived.

And then there were the fake accounts. He had checked the web on his phone. Nothing that he did that morning had made any impact. All of The Order's websites and social media accounts were still up and collecting new members. Fritz and Frank must have somehow routed his computer to fake websites. Again, it was the premeditation that stung. They had gone out of their way and taken extra trouble to make him look a fool.

There was also the fact that they were still operating from the syndicate's offices. This meant Adam could still be held responsible for them. He still needed a way to get them out. Thankfully, this was one problem where he still had a card left to play: the mentors. The mentors had the authority to kick the cult out of the building.

The problem with this was that he would need to explain to them what happened. That things had moved too quickly. That he had lost control. After the glory of his victory over Kenneth this would bring him down a few pegs in their eyes. His reputation would suffer. The mentors could also point out that the whole thing was his idea in the first place. Like Liam Love, they would probably tell him that he was an idiot to have started the whole thing and let it get away from him.

Yes, he would have to swallow his pride. But swallowing his pride was a small price to pay. Naked women. Lascivious dancing. Masturbation homework. The whole thing had gotten way out of control. Adam imagined a visiting dignitary, some high-ranking syndicate official from overseas, being led through level one by Mark or Marco only to walk directly into a virtual lap dance.

He decided to walk back to the syndicate and think up his explanation on the way. He would make his case to one of the mentors. He hoped it was Marco, who was usually a bit of a pushover. But that was in the fate of the gods now. One way or another, this would end it.

He finished the rest of his coffee and then set out for Collingwood.

***

Adam took the stairs up to level two making sure to keep an eye out for cult members as he went. He pressed the bell that was on the right-hand side of the syndicate's door. The door clicked open and he walked in to see a forty-something brown-haired woman in thick rimmed glasses at the reception desk.

"Morning, Adam. What can I do for you?"

"Hi, Janice. This is very unusual I know, but I was hoping to be able to have a very quick meeting with one of the mentors. Perhaps Marco?"

"You don't have an appointment?"

"No. It's a bit of a last-minute thing. But it shouldn't take long at all if they have just a few minutes."

"Oh. Well, Marco's not in but Mark is around. Let me go and see if he's free."

Janice ushered Adam into the usual waiting room that led to the boardroom. None of the associates ever met the mentors in their offices. It was a protocol of the syndicate that meetings with higher ups always took place in a meeting room.

After a minute or so, Janice stuck her head in the doorway.

"Mark has a meeting in about ten minutes but he can squeeze you in right now if you'd like, Adam."

"That's fine. Great. Thanks a lot, Janice."

Janice gave him another smile and went away. A minute later, another women opened the door on the other side of the waiting room and ushered Adam in before leaving through a door at the far end of the room.

Mark was seated in the middle of the boardroom table. He was working on his laptop but pushed it to the side and stood up as Adam approached.

"Adam," he said warmly holding out his hand to shake.

"Mate, first time we've seen each other since the big win. Just want to say congratulations and really well done. Beating Kenneth is no mean feat and, of course, you didn't just beat him, you embarrassed him. Withdrawing in shame. We couldn't believe it. Just between you and me, my money was on Kenneth. Not that I didn't think you were up to the challenge, of course. Kenneth's been our best for a long time. But that's all history now. We've got a new best, don't we? Anyway, you should know that this business has not gone unnoticed among the mentors. And not just the Melbourne crew. This little competition was being followed with interest interstate and even overseas. I think you're in for a very special trip to New York in February. You and Cameron can expect something a bit out of the ordinary. It's gonna be great. I'll be there, of course. And Marco and Trevor. What do you think? You excited?"

Adam was pretty sure that Mark had not taken a single breath since he started speaking. But he smiled, happy to take the praise.

"Yeah, really looking forward to it."

Mark looked down at his watch.

"Look, mate, I've got a meeting real soon. What did you want to see me about?"

Adam considered sitting down but decided to remain standing.

"It's a bit of a sensitive matter, Mark. I don't want to bore you with the details cos I know you're busy, so I'll just say that there's been some activities going on down on level one that I think are inappropriate and not befitting the integrity of the syndicate."

"This sounds serious, Adam. What kind of activities are we talking about?"

"Again, I don't want to get bogged down in too many details. It's to do with Joel Weiss."

"The IT operations guy?"

"Yes. I'm afraid I caught Joel with some, umm, sensitive material on his computer. Material not befitting the integrity of the syndicate."

"I see."

"I think it would be best if you suspend Joel immediately pending an investigation."

"Hold on, Adam. These are serious allegations you're making. I'm afraid I'm going to need some more information. Exactly what sort of material are we talking about?"

"Pictures. Pictures of naked women."

"Can you describe them?"

Adam looked closely at Mark trying to gauge the nature of this unexpected question.

"I don't think that's really appropriate."

"Just give me the gist," said Mark sitting back in his chair.

"Well. One was of a woman with long black hair, sitting on a table, leaning back on her hands with her legs apart."

"You mean this?"

Mark reached out with his left hand and spun his laptop so that it was facing Adam. The logo of The Order of the Secret chiefs was at the top and beneath it was the photo of Madame Orlova in all her glory. It was the exact same homework picture Adam had been shown the previous day.

Adam stepped back. He looked at Mark with barely hidden amazement.

"What's going on, Adam?" said Mark with a confused expression.

"Why do you have that picture?"

"Why wouldn't I have it?"

"Are you a member?"

"Of course not. We're the sponsor."

"Who's *we*?"

"The syndicate. We're hosting The Order of the Secret Chief's activities down on level one. You know that. Cameron came to see me about it two days ago. Are you feeling ok, Adam? You look a bit ill and you're acting weird."

Adam had to admit he wasn't feeling great all of a sudden. Perhaps there was something bad in the meal he had eaten earlier.

"Right. No. It's all good," he stammered.

"Look, Adam. I don't know what game you're playing here. Whether this is some kind of test or something. But I don't think it's cool that you come in and try to throw Joel under the bus."

"N-no," said Adam holding up his hands. "It was just a miscommunication, that's all. My mistake. I didn't mean anything by it."

"That's good, mate. Because as far as I can see, this thing is about ready to take off. I had a look at the numbers just this morning. Staggering growth. I've never seen anything like it. At $5 a pop, it's money for jam."

"You mean $50?"

"Well, $5 is the syndicate's cut, of course. You, on the other hand, mate, you're laughing. Your grocery revenues from the syndicate must pale into insignificance in comparison, am I right? Anyway, I've gotta get on the phone with Trev. We all good, Adam?"

"Yep."

Mark reached out to shake his hand and Adam obliged. He was feeling nauseous but whether it was his brunch or the conversation he didn't know.

He left the office and walked out into the street in a daze before turning and heading for Richmond. This time he felt like going home.

CHAPTER 23

Adam slept a long time. In fact, by the time he woke, it was Thursday morning. He felt a little hungover which was probably due to dehydration. More than anything, he was hungry.

He ate breakfast then cleaned the dishes and stood in the kitchen wondering what to do. Nothing moved him. He felt empty inside. Listless. Maybe he should just go back to bed. He walked over and slumped down on the couch.

The feeling of humiliation hung over him like mosquito repellent. It had been made worse, far, far worse by yesterday's meeting with Mark. Adam's head rang out in anger and frustration at the very thought of it. The syndicate. His business. His livelihood had now been compromised. At some point, Mark would learn the truth that Adam had also been kicked out of his cult. Just like Kenneth. And just like Kenneth, Adam's name would be mud. That was how it worked at the syndicate. Results were everything. If you got the results, you were a king. If you didn't, you were nothing.

In fact, he would be even worse off than Kenneth. Not only had he got kicked out of his cult, he had been kicked out right when things took off. Right when fortunes were being made. Everybody would know that he had been made a fool of. He would never hear the end of it. He didn't think that he'd be able to show his face at the syndicate again.

But there was something else in him. Something new that was welling up after yesterday's meeting with Mark. The syndicate was now getting a cut. Which meant that Mark was now getting credit. That was probably why he was on the phone to Trevor. He would have been bragging about how he made the deal.

It was how that deal must have gone down that really infuriated Adam. Mark said that Cameron came to him to ask to use the syndicate's offices. Adam pictured that meeting in his mind. There was no way Cameron went to Mark and offered him a cut. Adam knew Cameron and he knew that Cameron simply didn't think that way. Cameron would have asked to use the syndicate's offices. And Mark, the slimy bastard, would have extracted all the information out of him. All the sales figures. All the membership numbers. Then Mark would have offered Cameron the deal. And Cameron would have agreed instantly. Ten percent. In hindsight, it was amazing it was so low. Mark could have asked for fifty percent and Cameron would have rolled over and asked for his tummy to be rubbed.

It was Adam who had done all the work. He'd come up with the original concept, organised the meetings, booked the church hall, set up the original IT systems. Now Mark and the syndicate got paid for doing nothing. Just for being there. Just for existing. It wasn't right.

And what the hell was Nastashya's game? Had this been the plan all along? To make money? It seemed like a roundabout way to do it. How could she possibly have planned it? And yet, she was the only one who seemed to be in control. She was obviously guiding the whole thing towards something on the 16th. But what was it?

He decided to have a fresh look at the Order's websites to see if he could find answers to these questions. He opened up his laptop. Mark was right. Things had gone nuts. The social media numbers were well over half a million. A counter that one of the two Fs had put on the main website said the cult had over one hundred thousand members. Could that really be true? One hundred thousand members at $50 each? That was an absolute fortune. Whose bank account would be holding that kind of money? Nastashya's?

Adam saw that there was a livestream starting in two minutes. The latest piece of the puzzle. He got up and grabbed a glass of water from the kitchen and returned to the couch. The steam auto-started from the cult's website. He saw the familiar meeting room at the syndicate and the familiar image of Nastashya.

This time Adam didn't need to squint to see that she was naked. She was still wearing the lace thing over the top but there was no ambiguity about it this time. Perhaps it was the way the lights interacted with the video camera that made it clearer to the eye. She was standing in a simple, everyday pose with arms by her side. Her long black hair hung down almost to her hips. The ends sprung up and outwards in small curls like flowers hanging over the edge of a pot. Her blue eyes shone brightly through the screen as did her red lips.

Adam allowed himself a moment to appreciate her beauty. Her body. He realised this was the first time he'd seen her on screen as opposed to in the flesh. She seemed even more beautiful this way. Perhaps it was the lighting and the camera angles.

She began to speak. The familiar heavy Russian accent rang out through the speakers of his laptop like a church sermon.

"Today we begin final preparation for the glorious 16th. At 9.43am Australian Eastern Daylight Savings time on 16th December, the culmination of our mission will come to pass. To achieve our design we require concentration and focus of enormous amounts of energy. Sex energy.

"I have taught you to realise your sex energy. I have taught you to harness it. Now, I will teach you to focus it. On left hand of screen is timer."

A digital timer overlay appeared at the bottom left of the screen. It was white text that read: 5.00.

"At the end of five minutes, you must focus all your sex energy. You must ejaculate."

The camera, which until now had been a close up on Madame Orlova, panned back. The other women were in the room. This time there was no S&M lingerie. There was no anything.

"Stare at women.

"Take us with your eyes.

"Pull down your pants.

"Rub your manhood.

"Say ohm."

The timer began to count down from five minutes. Madame Orlova remained standing in her initial position. The other women did not. The other women began to make use of the space around them to contort their bodies into a variety of sexual shapes. They touched themselves. The camera panned in and out maximising the sexiness on offer. It was an extravaganza of lips, hips, tits, hair, fingers and more. Despite his mood and despite his personal attachment to the matter, the video was starting to have the desired effect on Adam.

"Two minutes to ejaculation. Feel your sex energy. Let it grow. Let it build."

The camera panned to Madame Orlova. Adam felt his cock harden as he imagined kissing those full red lips, stroking that long black hair.

"Thirty seconds to ejaculation," announced Madame Orlova. The clock at the bottom of the screen reflected her timing. The camera had panned back to show all five women.

"Focus your energy. Focus on us. Give us your power.

"Ten seconds to ejaculation.

"Five seconds.

"Ejaculate."

Adam had never thought there was anything remotely sexy about the word ejaculate. But there was something about that Russian accent that did it. Or maybe it was just the fact that five naked women were on screen.

There was a pause. The five women stood perfectly still for about half a minute. Perhaps giving viewers the chance to reach for a box of tissues.

Eventually, Nastashya spoke.

"At 9.43am Australian Eastern Daylight Savings Time on the 16th of December, there will be a simultaneous ejaculation around globe. It will be greatest concentration of sex energy the world has ever seen. You must prepare. You must train yourself against a timer. New homework assignments are being sent. Do your homework and join us for final livestream Saturday morning."

The video ended.

Adam sat back in his chair, then reached for his phone.

CHAPTER 24

"A simultaneous ejaculation?"

Liam Love leaned back on his bar stool and stroked his chin. This stroking went on for some time. Adam waited for a while but impatience got the better of him.

"So, what do you think?"

"I think it could work. It could be one of the most brilliant ideas ever conceived."

"How? How can a bunch of guys jerking off around the world do anything?"

Liam turned to face Adam.

"If you're thinking purely on the physical plane, it can't do anything. All that's gonna happen is there'll be a sudden spike in the sales of tissues and a lot of angry mothers throwing old gym socks into rubbish bins. But if you allow for the possibility that there are other realms beyond the physical, then you can absolutely get something to happen."

"What realms?"

"The etheric, the astral and the mental. Those are the standard occult categories. They exist simultaneously with the physical. On the physical plane, a guy jerking off is just applying friction to his cock to achieve a physiological outcome. But there could be an etheric, an astral and a mental component at play too."

"Could be?"

"Well, I don't know enough about this stuff to say for sure. I only dabbled briefly in the occult. But it seems likely to me. And if there is and Madame Orlova knows how to harness it, she could do something with it."

"How can she harness it?"

"Again, that's a question for an experienced occultist. But you said she was always going on about *focusing*, right? That's a big part of occult practice. You take energy and you focus it. So it does sound like she knows what she's talking about. The big question is, where does she plan to focus it? What does she want to do with it? You said she keeps mentioning the 16th. That was the original date for the end of the world. Maybe that's her goal."

"Nonsense! A bunch of guys jerking off at the same time is not going to bring about the end of the world."

Adam took a big drink of his beer.

"The more I think about it, the more I think it's just the money," Adam continued. "All this bullshit was just so she could make some money. And that's what she's done. Millions, in fact."

"You don't know if she's the one receiving the money," Liam reminded Adam.

"Who else would be?"

"At the risk of saying I told you so again... ok, fuck it, *I told you so,* Sampson."

"Told me what?"

"There's a common thread here."

"What?"

"The common thread is that you still know *nothing* about this woman. You don't know why she joined the group. You don't know if she knows anything about the occult or she's just making it all up. You don't know if she's receiving the money. You don't know what she hopes to achieve. She ran rings around you because you didn't bother to find out the smallest detail about her. You don't even know if she's Russian."

"She sounds Russian."

"I can sound Russian too," said Liam in what Adam had to admit was a very convincing Russian accent.

"Y'know, Sampson, I'm afraid I'm starting to see a pattern."

"What's that?"

"You have a woman problem. First it was Jackie and now it's Miss Orlova."

"It's *Madame* Orlova. And my girlfriend's name is Julie. At least I can remember the names of women."

"Anybody can remember names. Your problem is you don't go any deeper than that."

"That's not true."

"Really? Let's test that statement. Now, we've established that you know absolutely nothing about our Russian friend, so let's find out what you know about Jackie."

"It's Julie! *Jool-e,*" said Adam. His cheeks were starting to go red.

"Alright. What's her favourite food?"

"Indian."

"Where does she work?"

"She's a uni student who works part-time behind the counter at a pharmacy."

"Where did she go to high school?"

"Ivanhoe Grammar."

"What is her number one dream?"

"She wants to become a pharmacist."

Liam waved his hand like he was swatting a fly.

"No. What is her *dream*?"

"That is her dream."

Liam looked at Adam like a carpenter might look at an apprentice trying to hammer a screw into a wall.

"Was it your dream to become a network marketer, Sampson?"

Adam had to think about this.

"No."

"What was your dream? What *is* your dream?"

Again, Adam had to think. This was proving difficult for some reason.

"I dunno."

"Yes, you do. You told me last time we met."

Adam racked his brain but couldn't think of anything.

"Freedom. That's your dream. You want to be free. That's why you're doing network marketing. Make sense?"

"I suppose so."

"So, let me ask you again. What is Julie's dream?"

Adam had nothing. Not only was his mind blank, it had seemingly ceased to function. He couldn't even imagine what a possible answer might be.

Liam waited a little while for this to sink in before continuing.

"Why does Julie work at the pharmacy?"

"To get experience at pharmaceutical work."

"Did she tell you that?"

"She didn't have to. It's obvious."

Liam nodded his head but it wasn't a nod of agreement. Adam was feeling very stupid all of a sudden.

"Ok, last question. Why is Julie going out with you?"

"Because we like each other."

"Do you?"

"Of course."

"*Do you?*"

Adam turned to face Liam who looked him squarely in the eyes.

"Do you like her, Sampson. Do you *really* like her?"

Adam looked away.

Fuck. Liam had him pincered on this one. He let out a long sigh.

"No, I don't. In fact, I've been thinking about breaking up with her."

"So, if *you* don't like *her,* it's certainly possible that *she* doesn't like *you* and there's some totally different reason why she's going out with you."

"Such as?"

"If I had to guess, I'd say social status."

Adam let out an involuntary snort.

"What? That's ridiculous."

"Ivanhoe Grammar," said Liam knowingly.

"What about it?"

"Ivanhoe Grammar costs money, my friend. Lots of money."

Liam rubbed his fingers over his thumb as he spoke.

"And what people are buying at Ivanhoe Grammar is status. Let me guess. Her parents are rich and they work in high profile jobs."

"Yeah, so what?"

"So, they have to keep up appearances. She wants a boyfriend that will make mummy and daddy happy. That's why she's going out with you. Hard working, dedicated, rule abiding, financially secure. A nice, clean-cut young man in a suit."

Adam's cheeks were burning again. It seemed to him that they'd been burning for three day's straight. He realised that Liam was right. It all made perfect sense. Julie had always been super sensitive about how he presented himself in public. She was constantly concerned with how they came across as a couple. There was one time when they were going to meet Julie's sister and they had argued for fifteen minutes because she insisted on choosing the clothes Adam would wear. And, of course, he had been supposed to meet the parents several times now and each time it didn't happen Julie got a little more hysterical.

Liam grasped him on the shoulder.

"Look, mate. Don't feel bad. I do this for a living."

Adam didn't respond to this. He took another drink of his beer. Liam turned back to his whisky. There was a long silence. A silence that went for several minutes.

Finally, Adam spoke.

"I need your help, Liam."

"With what?"

"I need to stop The Order of the Secret Chiefs."

"Why?"

"What do you mean, *why*? Isn't it obvious?"

"No."

"Because, because, the whole thing is a fraud."

"So what? There's plenty of fraud around. Half the economy is fraud."

"But this fraud is being run out of the syndicate."

"You said yourself that the syndicate has given them permission to be there. It's a business transaction. They're taking a cut."

"Yeah, but….that's half the problem. Those pricks didn't do anything. Mark," Adam all but spat his name, "Mark did nothing and now he's taking the credit."

"For a fraud?"

Adam was struggling to keep his thoughts in order.

"You should be happy, mate. You could have been the one perpetrating a fraud. Now the syndicate has taken that problem off your hands."

"But they think I'm still involved."

"Who?"

"Mark and the other mentors."

"Why do they think that?"

Again Adam had to give an answer he didn't want to give.

"Because I let them believe that I *was* still involved."

Liam looked long and hard at him.

"I think I can see what's going on, Sampson. You want me to waltz in and put everything right. Somehow, I ride in and save the day and make The Order of the Secret Chiefs problem go away so you can keep your reputation at the syndicate. You know, I'm starting to think you, Julie and her parents might actually be a good fit for each other."

"That's not true. I don't care about my reputation at the syndicate. I'm worried there really might be something to all this. What if people are in danger?"

"Now you're worried about that? Five minutes ago you acted like I was crazy to say there might be something to this occult business."

"Well, you convinced me. I'm especially worried because Cameron is still involved."

"Who's Cameron?"

"He's my partner at the syndicate. He was helping me run the cult. When I told him I was leaving he said he wanted to take over. I haven't seen him since. And he hasn't answered his phone in three days."

"Maybe he doesn't want to talk to you. You did try and sabotage his cult."

"It's not *his* cult. He could never run it. He was never any use at running anything. I got a weird vibe from him. Like he was infatuated with Madame Orlova. Like she was manipulating him."

"She was manipulating you too."

"Yeah, but Cameron didn't know it."

"And you did?"

Adam sighed.

"No. I guess I didn't."

There was another long silence.

Liam appeared to be mulling over an idea in his mind. He took several glances at Adam before eventually turning to him to speak.

"Y'know, Sampson, one of the reasons I wanted to learn about the occult was because they say that you can't do magic, proper magic, until you have achieved a level of self-understanding. That resonated with me because I had realised the same thing with seduction. It seems counter intuitive, but the only way you can seduce a woman is if you know why you like her and what you want from her. Most men are afraid to admit what they really want. Most of my students are either angry or amazed when I tell them they don't know what they want from women and they don't know what they want from life. Some of them don't want to hear it and they piss off and ask for their money back. Most of them can be convinced but it's a hard pill to swallow.

"So, let me ask you the most difficult question I've asked you today. Are you ready for it?"

"Probably not," said Adam trying to be light-hearted.

"Why do you like Madame Orlova and what do you want from her?"

The question caught Adam completely unawares. Once again, his mind wasn't able to process it.

"What's that got to do with anything?" he objected.

"Do you want me to help or not, Sampson? This is the last time I'll ask."

Adam sighed loudly. Why did it have to be this hard?

"Yes, I want you to help."

"Good. Then answer the question, why do you like Madame Orlova and what do you want from her?"

Since thinking hadn't done him any good so far, Adam decided to start speaking. He was surprised when the words started to flow.

"I like her because she's beautiful. She's the most beautiful woman I've ever seen. As for what I want from her. Well, originally I wanted her to run the cult meetings. She seemed to know what she was doing and she was getting results. I didn't know anything. She was helping me to beat Kenneth and I let her do it."

"And what do you want from her now?"

"I want her to stop."

"Why?"

Again, Adam's mind was empty. Again, he started to speak. It was as if the words came from deep down and flowed out of his mouth without first going through his head.

"I want her to stop because I don't know what she's doing. I don't understand what's going on. And she's embarrassing me and making a fool of me. And she's making a fool of Cameron and all the other men."

His shoulders sagged and Adam felt drained like his energy had emptied out of him with the words. Yet, somehow, he also felt like a burden had been removed. He felt lighter and the feeling of lightness increased and seemed to spread through his body. It was the first time he'd ever felt that way. It was a good feeling.

Liam grasped Adam on the shoulder again.

"That's good, mate. Really good."

Liam waved to Sharon.

"Shazz, we need two more of the same, please."

He turned back to Adam.

"Above the Temple of Apollo at Delphi is written: *gnōthi seauton.* Know thyself. You've just taken the first and most important step, my friend."

They toasted with the last dregs of their drinks while waiting for Sharon to bring the replacements.

"Ok," said Liam putting his glass down. "Now that we know why we want to stop Nastashya, the next question is how. And before we can know that, we need to get to know her. More precisely, *you* need to get to know her."

"What do you mean?"

"You have to talk to her."

"Why?"

"So you can find out all the answers to the questions we need answered like, what the hell is she trying to achieve."

"As if she's just gonna tell me."

"Why wouldn't she?"

"Because she's been deliberately screwing me over."

"You don't know that? Has she ever told you that she was targeting you directly?"

"She called me a traitor."

"You *were* being a traitor."

"And that's why she's screwing me."

"You don't know that. It's just a little story you've made up in your head."

Liam reached over and lightly tapped the top of Adam's head.

"You've got all these little stories in your head that you don't know are true. You need to stop assuming, Sampson. You've got to clear your mind and start to see the real world. You need to start dealing with the big, wide world instead of the tiny little world you created in your mind."

"How?"

"Stop assuming and start looking. Start listening. Start asking questions. You assume Julie works at the pharmacy to get experience but you never bothered to find out. You never bothered to ask her."

"It doesn't matter why Julie works at the pharmacy."

"Maybe not. But it absolutely does matter why Nastashya is running The Order of the Secret Chiefs. You can't stop her if you don't know her reasons and the only way you're going to find out is to ask her."

"So, I'm just gonna go up to her and start a conversation?"

"That's the way these things normally work."

"Where?"

"You tell me. Do you know where she lives?"

"No."

"Works?"

"No."

"Studies?"

"No."

"Is there anywhere you know that she will be at a particular time so you can talk to her?"

Adam thought about it.

"There's one more livestream. Tomorrow morning at the syndicate office."

"Perfect. That's where you have to talk to her."

"But I can't get inside. They've locked me out."

"You can wait for her outside and start a conversation there."

"I suppose so."

Sharon reached over and placed the drinks in front of Adam and Liam.

"Shazz, perfect timing. We need to borrow you for a minute. Mr Sampson needs a little conversation practice."

"Oh, yeah?" said Sharon with a cheeky grin.

"Can you do a Russian accent?"

"Not really."

"Ok. Doesn't matter. But for the next little while, your name is Madame Orlova."

"Or-lova?"

"It's Russian for *my lover*."

Sharon blushed ever so slightly.

"Now, Mr Sampson here is going to ask you some questions and you're going to answer as Madame Orlova. Got it?"

"Got it." Sharon smiled already enjoying the game.

Liam looked over at Adam who didn't seem to understand what was happening.

"Sampson, what do you want to ask Madame Orlova here?"

Finally, Adam cottoned on. He thought about it for a couple of seconds.

"What are you trying to do to me?"

"Woah, timeout."

Liam held up his hands.

"What the hell is that?"

"I'm asking a question."

"That wasn't a question. It was an accusation. Look, your job here is to get to know *her*. Ok?"

Liam pointed to Sharon.

"You must find out about Nastashya. It doesn't have to be about the Order of the Secret Chiefs. Just ask her questions about herself. Ok? Continue."

"Hi, Nastashya," said Adam feeling like he was back in year seven drama class.

"Hi," said Sharon.

"How was the livestream?"

"It was good. Good livestream today. Better than yesterday."

"Did you get many new memberships?"

"Timeout," said Liam. "Ok, that was a little bit better. The first question was good but now you're getting onto boring stuff about memberships. You need to keep the conversation about her. Ask her questions about herself."

"What, like what's your age and where do you live?"

"You can start there but you want to get into questions of how she's feeling, what's she thinking, what she believes in. All the interesting stuff."

Adam sighed with frustration.

"Ok."

He turned back to Sharon.

"So, I've been wondering, Nastashya, how does it feel to do the livestream? I mean, you've got all these men watching you. That must be pretty weird?"

"I'm a woman. We're used to having men watch us."

"Do you like it?"

"Sometimes."

"What's an example of when you like it?"

"When I'm on a date or I've been talking to a guy at a bar for a while. When we both know that there's a spark between us. I like to see him staring at me out of the corner of my eye. Like he can't stop looking. Like he can't take his eyes off me."

This time it was Adam who blushed a little.

"Excellent," said Liam thumping the bar. "That's what I'm talking about."

Liam took a celebratory drink and gave Sharon a wink.

"Are we done?" she asked.

"Shazz, you can be my Russian lover any day of the week."

Sharon smiled and went over to serve another customer.

Liam turned back to Adam.

"How did that feel?"

"Good," said Adam. He did not sound convincing.

"You feeling confident to talk to Nastashya tomorrow?"

"Not really."

"You'll be fine. Here's a little homework exercise to help you get some practice. Have you got a picture of Nastashya? Preferably one where she's fully dressed."

"Yeah. I think I've still got a photo that Cameron took at our very first meeting. It's of the whole group but she's in it."

"Perfect. Here's what you do. Look at the picture and just formulate questions about her. Where did she grow up? Who are her friends? What are her dreams? You can get a little dirty with it if you want. Is she into S&M? Just formulate as many questions as you can about her. Everything that might interest you about her. Everything that you would actually want to know the answer to. Do that for five minutes at a time and do it at least five times between now and tomorrow. Then you just have to walk up to her and ask those questions."

"Alright. I'll give it a shot."

"Good luck, mate. We'll meet back here tomorrow to debrief, ok?"

"Ok."

CHAPTER 25

If Adam was going to meet Nastashya at the syndicate, he'd have to be discreet so as not to bump into a Fritz or a Frank. Fortunately, he knew the perfect hiding place.

About six months ago, he had been accosted in the lobby of the ground floor. One of his marks had been driving his family nuts by insisting that all household groceries be purchased through him and, by extension, through the syndicate. The mother had grown so tired of every shopping trip becoming a domestic dispute that she had come after Adam directly.

Adam had been walking into the lobby on his way to the elevator when the woman had jumped out from a closet and clubbed him over the head with her handbag before demanding her son be removed from the syndicate. Adam never knew the cupboard was even there. Its front was wood panelled in the exact same materials as the walls. There were three horizontal gaps to give the space some kind of airflow but it was otherwise camouflaged. It was the perfect hiding place.

It was in that very cupboard where Adam now crouched on the Saturday morning of the final livestream. He had newfound respect for the mother with the handbag. The cupboard was small and cramped. He wasn't able to stand up straight and there was barely enough room to get into a comfortable posture for leaning against wall.

It was 6am. He'd wanted to be early but he was starting to think he was too early and might do some permanent damage to his posture if he stayed in the cupboard for too long.

As he crouched there, he realised that he had never actually seen Nastashya either enter or leave any of the cult's meetings. He didn't know if she came with the four other woman. He didn't know how she got there. There was a very good chance she wouldn't be alone. If she wasn't alone, he wouldn't be able to talk to her. There was no point even trying with one of the other cult members present. Especially if it was Cameron.

The time ticked by. Seven o'clock. Seven-thirty. Finally, there was some movement. The two Fs waddled past with their laptop bags and their coffees.

Robert arrived. Then Darrell. Then Francis. It was eight o'clock. Then eight-thirty.

Just when Adam thought his hamstrings were about to give up the ghost, he saw her walk up the front steps of the building. The glass doors buzzed open and she came inside. She was wearing the long black coat again. She was alone.

He saw her stop in the foyer and turn to a mirror that hung on the wall. Adam watched while she checked her appearance including a furtive look beneath the coat to make sure the lace thing was in order. It occurred to Adam that this was the first time he had ever seen Nastashya do anything 'normal'. She was a real person after all.

Satisfied with her appearance, Nastashya turned and headed for the elevator. Adam saw the blue eyes and the red lips through the three horizontal slots in the front of the cupboard as she walked past.

He had no idea what he was going to say. All Liam's homework he had done since yesterday, the exercise with Sharon at the bar, all that preparation was for nothing. His mind was blank. But he slid open the cupboard door and stepped out.

"Hi, Nastashya."

She spun around. Her high heels sliding smoothly one eighty degrees over the black tiles of the foyer floor. There was a hint of surprise in her face. Just a hint and then it was gone. Replaced by her familiar expressionless mask.

"How are you?"

She said nothing.

Adam felt a lump in his throat and a tightness in his chest. He had a bad feeling he was about to make a fool of himself. Again.

"I was, uhh, I was thinking that you and I have never really gotten to know each other and, in fact, I don't really know anything about you at all."

Still Nastashya gave him no sign. She neither spoke nor moved. She just remained there looking at him.

"I was wondering, do you have a boyfriend?"

The hint of surprise returned. This time it stayed longer. She hadn't been expecting this question.

Adam hadn't been expecting it either. His mouth was running on autopilot. Liam's exercise had worked after all. This was one of the questions Adam had thought up while doing his homework yesterday evening.

"Why you ask?" she said in a flat tone.

"Because, I..." Adam's heart was racing. "Because I think you're very beautiful."

For the first time since Adam had known her, Nastashya's face showed an emotion: she was flattered. Her right leg seemed to involuntarily raise at the knee. Just a little.

She re-gained control. The mask returned.

"No. I do not have boyfriend."

"Or a husband?"

Was that a smile? Did she smile!? Adam wasn't sure but the mask seemed to have cracked again for just half a second.

"No."

"Nastashya, what do you look for in a man?"

There was nothing in the history of their interaction that could have led Adam to believe that Nastashya would give him the time of day let alone answer such a question. He had realised this while standing in the cupboard for hours. The two of them had never really spoken at all. Their interaction until this moment had been completely abstract and business-like.

There were a few seconds of silence. It was difficult to read but Adam thought Nastashya was actually considering her answer.

"I like a man who knows what he wants. Who is confident. Who takes risks."

This time there was a smile. No question. A smile! He saw it clear as day. There was no doubt about it. He felt a wave of joy surge through his chest. But the wave quickly disappeared. The two Fs had appeared behind Nastashya.

Adam hadn't heard the elevator open or seen anything except those amazing red lips smiling at him. *For* him. But he saw something different now. Beauty and the beasts.

The two Fs said something but Adam wasn't sure what it was. What he did know was that he needed to leave the area very quickly.

He turned and ran. He ran outside and across Johnston St heading for Punt Road. After twenty metres or so he turned around and saw that they weren't following him. Running extended distances was not something the two Fs were much interested in. Fritz waved a fist at him from the top of the stairs then turned and went back inside.

That was it. That was all he was going to get. But what a get it was. His heart was still racing and it had nothing to do with the running. She had smiled at him. It was like every sunrise he had ever seen combined into one perfect moment.

Later on, much later on, Adam would also realise that this was the first time he had ever told a woman that he thought she was beautiful. This was a strange fact because he'd had several girlfriends in his life.

For now, though, he was simply elated. He turned and headed towards Brunswick St where he would meet Liam at the bar.

"Mr Sampson," came a shrill tone from over his shoulder.

Adam swung around and raised his fists in an instinctive fight response. He put them down when he saw who it was. It was Mrs Mitchell. The mother of Neil Mitchell. The woman he had cheated with to tie the sales competition.

"Mrs Mitchell. How nice to see you again," he said trying to remember his network marketing tone of voice.

"Don't give me that crap, Mr Sampson. You don't wish to see me again and when I'm through with you you'll wish you *had* never seen me again."

"Look, Mrs Mitchell. I understand fully. You're not happy with the syndicate, the syndicate's products or the syndicate's administration procedures. It's a common teething problem and I'm most certain we can work through it together."

"I don't give a shit about the syndicate. I'm here about this cult of yours."

"I'm sorry?"

"The Order of the Secret Chiefs."

"You know about that?"

"My idiot son, Neil, is a member. A gold member."

"Gold member?"

"$500 a month that moron is paying to watch your pornographic pixies prance around. I came home from a trip to the supermarket this morning to find him doing his 'homework' in the lounge room instead of being at work. He hasn't been to work all week. He's hooked on these videos of yours. This Russian tart you've got babbling nonsense about ejaculating all over the globe. I've seen some sick things in my time, Mr Sampson, but that takes the cake."

"Mrs Mitchell, I assure you that I share all your concerns. I myself am no longer associated with the cult."

"Then why did they tell me to speak to you when I phoned the syndicate?"

"It's a long story. But I assure you that I am no longer involved. In fact, I am actively trying to have the cult disbanded as we speak."

"And how are you doing that?"

"I...., I don't know. I'm not going to lie to you. I don't know. I'm still figuring it out."

"Well, you'd better figure it out soon, Mr Sampson. You've got exactly two days till the end of the world."

"The what?"

"The 'glorious' 16th. That's what this witch Orlova keeps talking about. She's trying to cause the apocalypse. And with enough fools like my son to help, she may just pull it off. Or rather, they'll pull it off for her."

"No, no. That stuff. Don't worry about that apocalypse stuff, Mrs Mitchell. That's all just a story. It's a front to make the money."

"I know a witch when I see one, Mr Sampson, and that Orlova is a witch."

Adam was not about to get into a conversation about who is or is not a witch.

"Ok, Mrs Mitchell. Fair enough. Look, I've gotta get going. It's been very nice to see you again, though."

Adam started to walk away.

"Do you have any help, Mr Sampson?"

"Help with what?"

"Disbanding The Order of the Secret Chiefs."

"I have a friend, a mate of mine. He's helping out."

"One man?"

"Yes."

"That's not enough. I'll help you."

"That's very kind…"

"Don't fob me off, Mr Sampson. I'm in need of some excitement and I'm sure as hell not going to sit around at home and watch my son watch your videos."

"Mrs Mitchell, I've already told you I don't really know what I'm doing so I don't know how you can help."

"Well, I can tell you now, two men alone are not going to solve this problem. You'll need a woman's help for this job."

"No, no. It's ok. My friend knows women. He's a professional pickup artist."

"A what?"

"A pickup artist. He picks up women for a living."

"So, it's you and a professional bullshit artist against a witch. I know who my money's on."

"She's not a witch."

"Mr Sampson. As I told you when we first met, I've been involved in more than one or two scams in my time and some of those scams were based in the occult. I know a little bit about these matters. What you're dealing with here is a classic case of sex magic and you need somebody with experience in that field. I am that somebody. As a matter of fact, Madame Orlova reminds me quite a lot of myself as a young woman. I was quite a looker back in the day, you know."

"You still are, Mrs Mitchell."

Adam gave her a cheeky smile. It was the first time he'd ever said anything like that too. It was turning out to be a morning of firsts.

"That's better, Mr Sampson. That's better," said Mrs Mitchell patting him on the right cheek.

"Keep that up and you and I will get along fine. Now, where are we off to?"

Adam gave in. It actually sounded like Mrs Mitchell might be able to help. It was crazy but nothing made sense any more. He would just have to go with it.

"A bar on Brunswick Street. My friend is waiting."

"Lead the way."

CHAPTER 26

It was not yet midday but the unicycle bar was open and Liam Love was in his usual position sitting in front of a glass of whisky at the counter. This time, there was nobody else around except for Sharon and a somewhat shady looking middle-aged guy in a suit who, from his demeanour, looked like he was the owner.

Adam walked over to Liam with Mrs Mitchell.

"Liam Love, this is Mrs Mitchell."

Liam turned around and grabbed Mrs Mitchell's hand.

"Delighted to make your acquaintance, m'lady," he said kissing the back of her hand in magnanimous fashion.

To Adam's surprise, Mrs Mitchell did not respond with a sharp riposte but simply allowed Liam his gesture and gave a small nod of greeting.

"Why don't we grab a booth," said Adam. "It'll be easier to talk."

"So, Mrs Mitchell will be joining us?" asked Liam as he spun around and followed them to a booth on the wall directly opposite the counter.

"Yes. She's, umm, she wants to be involved in the effort to bring down the Secret Chiefs."

"It's not the Secret Chiefs I'm worried about," said Mrs Mitchell, "it's the witch Orlova."

Adam sighed and threw his head back.

"She's not a witch, Mrs Mitchell."

"She most certainly is."

"Help me out here, Mr Love," said Adam looking imploringly at Liam.

"She might be a witch. We haven't established it either way. How did you go this morning? Did you get to speak to her?"

"I did. But only for a couple of minutes."

"So, what did you find out?" asked Liam.

"Nothing useful, I'm afraid," said Adam. "We were interrupted by the two Fs."

"The two whats?" asked Mrs Mitchell.

"Fritz and Frank. They run the IT side of the Secret Chiefs. They saw me talking to Nastashya and chased me off."

"Why don't you tell us exactly what was said," said Liam. "We might pick up something that you missed."

Adam sighed.

"It's gonna sound dumb."

"Dumber than starting an apocalypse cult?"

Liam had a point.

"I was hiding in a cupboard in the foyer of the syndicate office when she came in. I got out to talk to her but my mind went blank. I had no idea what to say. So, I asked her if she had a boyfriend. She asked me why I wanted to know. I told her it was because I thought she was beautiful. Then she said she didn't. So, I asked if she had a husband. She said no. Then I asked her what she looked for in a man."

Mrs Mitchell clucked her tongue disapprovingly.

"What did she say to that?" asked Liam holding up his hand to Mrs Mitchell to signal her to withhold judgement.

"She said she liked men who were confident and strong and who took risks."

"And then what happened?"

"That's all. The two Fs showed up and I had to split."

Liam leaned back against the soft red cushion of the booth seat.

"That's not much to go on," he said. "In fact, it's nothing to go on."

"Well, you asked me to find out something about her. And I did," said Adam defensively.

"I know. I know. I guess I had assumed you would keep the conversation subject on the Secret Chiefs so we could find out something that's actually useful."

"On the positive side, if I ever need to find her a husband I know where to start," said Adam attempting to make a joke.

"She doesn't need a husband. She needs a swift kick in the backside," said Mrs Mitchell.

"Excuse me, Mrs Mitchell," said Liam, "what's your interest in the Secret Chiefs?"

"My good-for-nothing son is a member. He plans to defile himself in public at the ceremony in two days' time."

"The ceremony is open to the public?"

"It will be held in a public venue somewhere in Melbourne. My understanding is the venue will be announced this morning on the internet."

"Of course, the livestream!" said Adam checking his watch. "It's on right now."

"Can we watch it?" asked Liam.

"Yep," said Adam pulling out his phone and navigating to the website.

Liam looked around the room. A couple of customers had wandered in since they had started talking and were having a drink by the window.

"I think it would be better to do this in private."

He turned to Sharon at the bar.

"Hey, Shazz. Is there anywhere here we can watch something in private just for fifteen minutes or so?"

Sharon shot a look at the man in the suit who was seated a couple of booths away. He glanced over at Liam and then flicked his head in the direction of a door that led to the back of the bar.

"C'mon. I'll show you," said Sharon.

The three got up and followed Sharon through a couple of swinging doors. They walked down a dimly lit corridor. Sharon opened the second door on the right which led into a small office that had a desk and a couple of chairs as well as some other office furniture.

"You can use this," said Sharon.

"Thanks, babe," said Liam giving her a wink.

Adam placed his phone on the table and pressed the screen a couple of times. A few seconds later a video appeared. It was the usual scene at the syndicate's meeting room.

"Ten seconds to ejaculation.

"Five seconds.

"Ejaculate."

The timer at the bottom of the screen hit 0.00.

"Outrageous," said Mrs Mitchell shaking her head.

Once again, the women on the screen did not move for about thirty seconds. Then Nastashya spoke.

"This concludes final preparation for glorious 16th. In two days, all secret chiefs around the globe will unite in final ceremony. The ceremony will begin at 9.13am Australian Eastern Time. Details are being sent to members. Non-members can still join and complete training prior to event. Members in Melbourne can join us at a venue that will be revealed by email soon. Until then, goodbye, my Secret Chiefs."

The screen went black.

"Well that wasn't very informative," said Liam. "We still don't know where the venue is."

"They must be doing it somewhere other than the syndicate if they're inviting a crowd," said Adam.

"We need to find out," said Liam.

Adam slumped down in one of the office chairs.

"We're screwed. We don't know where the final ceremony is going to take place. We don't know what they're going to do. We don't know how they're going to do it. We don't know why they're doing it."

"Hang on, hang on," said Liam.

"We do know some of those things. We can be very sure that the final ceremony is going to be similar to all the other ceremonies. Nastashya hasn't been training the men for no reason. We know they're going to livestream the whole thing. And we know it's going to end in a simultaneous ejaculation at 9.43am."

"Do you have any contacts at the syndicate who can tell us where the venue is, Mr Sampson?" asked Mrs Mitchell.

"I doubt it," said Adam then had a brainwave. He grabbed his phone.

"But I'm pretty sure I'm still a member. Nobody bothered to delete my details from the database. Which means I might have received the email containing the venue."

Adam pressed his phone a few times then leapt out of his chair.

"Hah! It's the masonic hall in East Melbourne!"

"You know it?" asked Liam.

"Yeah, we had the syndicate's end of year meeting there."

"Alright. Now we're getting somewhere. How well do you know the building, Sampson?"

"Very well. I've been backstage and everything."

Adam walked over to a small whiteboard that hung on the wall and drew a large square.

"There's a foyer here at the front. The main hall is here and there's a second level which has a gallery that runs all the way around. The stage runs all the way across the front of the main room and there's a large backstage area which is one big room but subdivided into smaller spaces."

Liam got up and took the marker from Adam.

"Ok. So, the girls will obviously be on the stage in the usual formation."

He drew five dots to mark the likely placement of Nastashya and the four other women.

"The secret chiefs will be out front on the floor. Maybe they'll put them up on the second level as well."

Liam drew in some squiggly lines to mark out the probable location of the secret chiefs.

"Who else do we think will be there?"

"The crew," said Adam. "The original crew have become the operations team. They do all the work to organise the livestream."

Adam took the marker off Liam.

"Richard handles the cameras so he will need to be somewhere in front of the stage around here. Fritz and Frank will need to be monitoring the livestream and other IT stuff. I'm guessing they'll do that backstage. There's Pavlos, Francis, Darrell and Cameron also. They might be backstage doing social media or whatever but they could also be wandering around making sure everything is running ok."

Adam made a mark of each of the names he had mentioned and where they might be.

"Is that all?" asked Liam.

"I think so," said Adam. "Oh, wait. The mentors will probably be there too. It sounds like the syndicate is fully involved now so they will probably show up to count their money or something."

"A VIP area?" said Liam.

"Probably the gallery."

Adam drew the mentors in a space to denote the second level of the hall.

"Good enough," said Liam clapping his hands together.

"Alright, we have a map. Next step is a strategy."

"We burn the whole building to the ground," said Mrs Mitchell.

Liam tapped her lightly on the shoulder.

"Little extreme, Mrs M."

"What can we do?" said Adam waving his hands around. "There's three of us and hundreds of them. I doubt we can even get through the front door."

"They're not selling tickets for this thing, Sampson. I'd be surprised if we can't just walk in with the rest of them."

"And what if they do have security?"

"We'll just have to deal with that on the day. Now, let's assume that we can get in without hassle. Mrs M and I should be fine. Nobody knows us. But they know you."

"Yeah, I'll be out on my arse in no time."

"But, if we look at the map, I think you should be able to get into the main room. The only people that know you are likely to be backstage or wandering around. If you hide yourself among the secret chiefs you should be right."

"Hang on," said Adam pointing to the gallery on the map. "The mentors. They still think I'm involved in the cult. If I can get in with them, I might be safe."

"Interesting. Could work. So, let's assume Sampson is up here on level two."

Liam marked the spot on the whiteboard.

"I can pass for a secret chief down here in the hall."

Liam marked himself on the board.

"That just leaves Mrs M."

The three of them stood looking at the drawing of the hall for a while.

"It would be really good to have somebody backstage," said Liam. "Mrs M, can you do a Russian accent?"

"Nyet," said Mrs Mitchell without missing a beat.

She waited for the two men to show some appreciation for her joke but was greeted only with blank faces.

"Mr Love, I'm disappointed in you," she said. "Mr Sampson, I can understand, but I expected you would be worldly enough to appreciate this demonstration of linguistic wit."

"Well, no Russian woman has ever said *nyet* to me, Mrs M," said Liam shrugging his shoulders and giving Mrs Mitchell a wink.

Mrs Mitchell groaned.

"Now, how would you feel about pretending to be Madame Orlova's grandmother for the ceremony?" asked Liam.

"Sounds interesting."

"Why do we want Mrs Mitchell to be Nastashya's grandmother?" asked Adam.

"We can safely assume that Nastashya is going to spend most of the time on stage. At least half an hour. Mrs M can go backstage and pretend to be Nastashya's grandmother who has come to watch her granddaughter perform. It will require some acting skills but I get the impression Mrs M is up for it. The question is, would anybody back-stage be likely to call her bluff?"

"I doubt it," said Adam. "Darrell, Francis, Pavlos, Cameron. They're all pushovers. Fritz and Frank might cause some trouble but I reckon Mrs M has their number."

"I eat little boys for breakfast," said Mrs Mitchell in Russian charac-ter.

"There's nothing little about these boys," said Adam.

"Good. More meat for me."

"Alright, alright," said Liam rubbing his hands together. "I think we have a plan."

"What plan?" said Adam. "We haven't even started to talk about what we're going to do when we get in."

"Look, Sampson, this whole map, this whole drawing of yours could be complete bullshit. For all we know, everything might be different on the day. So, there's no point coming up with a big plan when we don't know what we're talking about."

"I think we should at least identify the primary objectives," said Adam pressing the point.

"The main objective is to stop the ceremony," said Liam.

"The secondary objective is to stop the livestream," added Mrs Mitchell.

"Happy now, Sampson?"

"No. How are we going to stop the ceremony? There's literally hundreds of people in the hall who will stop us."

"The best way would be to get to Nastashya. If we can get her off stage or at least away from the cameras that might end the whole thing straight away."

"Where would we take her? She'll be surrounded by hundreds of se-cret chiefs blocking the exits."

"Backstage maybe?"

"Where all the rest of the crew are?"

"Look. We're not gonna get the answer to this today. We have to get in and get the lay of the land before we can know what we're dealing with. What we will need is a way to communicate on the day. Now, if Sampson is upstairs, I'm downstairs and Mrs M is backstage, that's gonna be hard."

"We could use our mobile phones?" suggested Mrs Mitchell.

"Too conspicuous," said Liam.

"Walkie-talkies," said Adam.

"Also too conspicuous," said Liam.

"Not any more. These days you can get wireless ones that are hands-free. There's an electronics shop near my place. I'll pick up three of them. Leave it to me."

"Ok. If you say so."

Liam took one last look at the whiteboard and let out a long exhale.

"I think that's about as much planning as we can do. Happy, Sampson?"

"I guess so."

"Happy, Mrs M?"

"I still say a few sticks of dynamite would be a better solution."

"Don't forget, your son will be in the building."

"I haven't forgotten."

CHAPTER 27

It was the morning of the end of the world.

Adam stood at a fountain on the easternmost side of the Fitzroy Gardens. From his vantage point he had an unimpeded view across the road to the masonic hall which was about fifty metres to the east. He had been there since before 6am having woken up early and not been able to get back to sleep.

He'd spent part of the previous day checking out the building and the surroundings to get the lay of the land. The hall was on a standalone block. There was a carpark at the rear and a driveway to that carpark down both sides of the building. Nearby was a small hospital.

Other than that, the area was quite sparsely populated. Pretty much all of East Melbourne was a relic of the art deco days. The street on which the hall stood was full of large estates featuring mansions with extravagant gardens where the ultra-rich of Melbourne had their abodes. It was a busy area on a workday and there was already a fair bit of traffic on the road that separated Adam from the hall.

Adam looked around for a sign of Mrs Mitchell or Liam Love. He couldn't see them. That was ok. It was still five minutes to seven.

He checked the batteries in the walkie talkies for the fifth or sixth time. They were small units. Much smaller than the one he'd had as a young boy. Each one consisted of a receiver that was about the size of a packet of cigarettes, a single wireless bud headphone and a small clip-on microphone.

He looked over at the hall. The crew were already there. He'd seen them arrive in a large van driven by Frank. Robert showed up in a separate van that contained all the audio-visual gear. The women had gone into the hall accompanied by Cameron. The three Fs (Fritz, Frank and Francis), Pavlos, Robert and Darrell had started to load in the gear. It took them a good fifteen minutes to do so. Whatever they were planning, it was going to be quite a production.

"Shouldn't you be keeping yourself hidden?" asked a voice from behind him. It was Liam.

Adam turned around.

"I am hidden."

"Not very well. Don't forget, one of our few advantages here is the element of surprise. They won't be expecting us and we should try and keep it that way as long as we can."

"Are you two gentlemen ready to save world?"

Mrs Mitchell was doing her Russian accent. They turned to see her walking up the footpath from the south.

"What the..." started Liam.

She was wearing what, to the two uneducated men before her, looked like a little red riding hood costume. It was a bright red Russian peasant's dress accompanied by a coat and a headscarf in the same colour.

"I think we've got a problem."

"You want me to be babushka. I be babushka."

"Babushka or not, this is *not* gonna work."

He gestured to her outfit.

"What is problem?"

"The problem is you're about to walk into a hall full of men," said Liam.

"And you're going to stick out like Stalin at a peace rally," said Adam.

"You said you wanted me to be Grandma Orlova," said Mrs Mitchell.

"True. We didn't think this through properly."

The three of them stood there for a while trying to think of a solution. Eventually Liam spoke.

"Does that coat turn inside out?"

Mrs Mitchell opened one side of the coat to have a look. The lining was black satin. She removed the coat, turned it inside out and held it up for inspection.

"I think we might be in luck," said Liam. "Let's see how it looks when you're wearing it."

Mrs Mitchell put the coat back on. The lining was not properly joined but it did cover the whole garment. It looked a bit like a rain coat.

Adam took the headscarf from Mrs Mitchell and turned it inside out. It was also black on the inside. He placed it on her head and wrangled it around a few different ways before taking a couple of steps back apparently satisfied with his work.

"Almost looks like a hoodie. That should do the trick. Now you look like a man with something to hide. You'll fit right in."

Mrs Mitchell grumbled reluctant acceptance of her new outfit.

"Ok. Let's get these fitted," said Adam stepping forward and handing Liam and Mrs Mitchell their walkie-talkies.

He helped them fit the receivers. The earphones were straightforward and the microphones clipped easily into place on their collars.

"Now, in order to speak, you need to press the button on the outside of the receiver," said Adam holding his up so the other two could see.

"Testing, testing. Did you get that?"

The other two nodded. They each tested their own microphone and verified that they were working.

Now that they were fully equipped, they turned back to the hall.

There were some secret chiefs already showing up. They were easy to spot. They spent some time loitering around in front of the hall and, when they thought the coast was clear, scurried up the steps and into the venue.

"What time do you think we should go in?" asked Adam.

"We'll want to wait until it's pretty full," replied Liam. "As I said, our main advantage is that they aren't expecting us. It'll be easier to take cover in a full room."

They waited.

Men came in dribs and drabs. It wasn't until half past eight that things started to pick up and a steady stream of secret chiefs flowed down the footpath and into the building. They waited and watched. Eventually Liam turned to Adam.

"Sampson, you know the size of the hall best. Do you think it's time?"

"I reckon it's about three quarters full," said Adam.

"Alright. Let's do this."

They approached the hall in an arc rather than a straight line. This gave them the benefit of blending into the stream of men that were walking to the hall. They crossed the road about fifty metres from the hall and slotted in behind a tall skinny man who looked like he was dressed for work. Adam thought that if the world didn't actually end at 9.43am the man could probably still arrive at the office in time for the morning coffee run.

The front steps of the hall were just ahead. As they got to there, Adam ducked down sharply and in a crouched position hurried towards the cover afforded by a big concrete ledge that ran across the front of the hall in between the two sets of stairs that ran either side.

Liam and Mrs Mitchell stopped to see what had happened. Adam furiously waved for them to keep going into the hall. They cottoned on quickly and continued up the stairs. Adam pretended to tie his shoelace then glanced up at the doors to ensure he wasn't seen.

"*What's the problem, Sampson?*" Liam's voice crackled in Adam and Mrs Mitchell's earphones.

"*One of the crew is standing on the door. Francis. The short blonde guy. He'll recognise me if I try and walk in.*"

"*10 4. Got him.*"

Liam and Mrs Mitchell walked past Francis and into the foyer of the hall. Liam placed his hand on Mrs Mitchell's back and led her over to the wall near the men's toilets.

"*What are we gonna do?*" asked Adam.

"*I'll distract him while you come through the door,*" said Liam. "*You ready?*"

"Ready."

"Start walking in 5, 4, 3, 2…"

Liam walked up to Francis ensuring that the latter turned towards him to face the inside of the foyer thus giving Adam a clear run through the door.

"Excuse me, mate. This is, ummm, this is a little awkward. But I, I forgot to bring a box of tissues for the, y'know, for the, ummm, *completion* of the ceremony. If you know what I mean? The *end*. The big finale. The simultaneous ending. So, I was just, umm, wondering, if you know, I mean, if there's any chance I can pick up a box here somewhere."

Adam entered the foyer using two taller men who were entering at the same time for cover.

"Just get some from the toilets," said Francis as if the answer was the most obvious thing in the world.

"The toilets. Of course. Why didn't I think of that? I think I'm just a little nervous. Y'know. Big occasion and everything. Ok. Thanks, mate."

Liam walked away and Francis turned back to his duties on the door.

The three of them reunited on the wall where Mrs Mitchell was desperately trying not to break out laughing.

"Enough jokes," said Adam. "We've got work to do."

"Quite right, Sampson. Let's go and have a look at what we're working with."

They walked through the extra-large double doors that led into the hall proper. Adam had guessed right. It was now more than three quarters full of men. It was standing room only. On the stage was a single microphone on a stand. Right in front of the stage, on a raised platform that had been placed there especially for the occasion, was Robert who was looking through a large video camera that was sitting on a heavy duty tripod.

To the right of the stage about level with the second-floor gallery was a huge projector screen that was currently black except for the timer in the bottom left which read *5.00*.

"Looks like they're going to broadcast the livestream up there," said Adam pointing to the screen.

"This is like the worst swingers party I've ever been to," said Liam surveying the room and shaking his head.

Adam turned around and looked up to the gallery.

"I was right," he said to the other two who followed his gaze upwards.

"Who's that?" asked Mrs Mitchell.

"The mentors. Looks like there's some other syndicate associates up there too."

"There's not many people up there. They must have blocked it off to the general audience."

"You should head up there now, Sampson."

Adam turned Liam.

"Why?"

"What do you mean why? It was your idea. You said they still think you're running the show."

"Well, I've changed my mind."

"You might be able to find out something useful."

"I don't want to talk to those pricks."

"Just go up for a couple of minutes and see what you can find out. We need to gather as much information as we can get. Mrs M, you go down the front and watch the door that leads backstage. It looks like they're keeping it shut but it would be good to see who's coming and going. I'll wander around the room for a while and see what I can learn. Let's keep in touch over the radio."

They each went their separate ways. Adam reluctantly turned back towards the foyer. He took up a position behind a couple of men to check that Francis wasn't hanging around. When he saw the coast was clear he made as if going to the men's toilets then turned and went and stood by the wall. From this vantage point he had a clear view up the staircase that led to the gallery. There was somebody standing on the door at the top. Adam vaguely recognised him as a syndicate associate. There didn't seem to be any crew members around.

Checking once again for Francis, Adam turned and walked quickly up the stairs. He slowed as he approached the top trying to look confident.

"Hey, Max, wasn't it?" he said to the guy at the door who looked unconvinced by this display of familiarity.

"Adam Sampson. I'm running the show here today. Just wanted to say hello to Mark and the others quickly."

The door guy was unmoved. Adam was about to trying another tack with him when Mark waved and called out from inside.

"Marty, you can let him in. He's kosher."

Marty gave a gruff nod and stood aside. Adam walked through the red velvet curtains that had been pulled aside in the doorway and over to Mark who was standing with Marco.

"Adam," said Mark reaching to shake his hand. Adam took it and then shook Marco's.

"Marco was just saying that we hadn't seen you yet. We were wondering where you were."

"Oh, just busy with the organisation and things. Big event. Lot of stuff to get through."

"I'll bet."

"Adam, I just want to say that what you've accomplished here is mind boggling," said Marco with a level of sycophancy that took Adam by surprise. He was used to sucking up to the mentors not having the mentors suck up to him.

"It really is amazing," added Mark. "The numbers are out of this world. We picked up more than a thousand more gold members over the last twenty-four hours. I mean, you did. You did, Adam. Of course, the syndicate's cut for a gold member is also not insubstantial."

The mention of the syndicate receiving money and Mark's insufferable smile caused a flash of anger somewhere down in Adam's stomach like lighting signalling the coming of a storm. He tried to ignore it.

Adam looked around to see who was present in the gallery. There were about fifteen people. Most he recognised as associates. Trevor was over near the railing that looked down onto the main hall. He was talking to a couple of syndicate people. Mark noticed that Adam had spotted him.

"Trevor is super keen to speak to you, Adam. In fact, I'll go and get him now. I know you're going to be very busy later."

Adam was about to object but Mark was already on his way. He and Trevor returned with big smiles on their faces. Adam felt like a school of fish might feel at the approach of a great white shark.

"Adam. So good to see you again," said Trevor in his familiar drawl.

"Adam, this is great. Incredible. What a buzz. And early on a Monday morning. You couldn't get this kind of crowd for a rock band on a Saturday night these days."

Adam could feel something stirring in him. Like the tide changing. These men he had once revered suddenly seemed ridiculous. Imagine heaping praise on a room full of masturbating men who were trying to cause the end of the world. What was there to praise? Were they that dumb? Or were they that greedy that they didn't even care?

"Now, Adam," said Trevor putting his arm around Adam's shoulder. "I've had a chat with Singh back the US. I've gone all the way to the top with this and I can tell you that we want to be involved. The syndicate is super impressed with your efforts and we're happy to back you. Now, we will need to re-negotiate that agreement that you made with Mark. We'll need a slightly higher share of the revenues due to the increased administrative costs that we'll incur and we'll want a share of the IP rights. But we can discuss that further another time. Congratulations, buddy. This is your lucky day."

Adam grabbed Trevor's arm and threw it away. In doing so, he accidentally knocked the button on his walky-talky receiver to the on position. The conversation beamed into the ears of Liam and Mrs Mitchell.

"You want a higher share, do you?" said Adam backing a couple of feet away from Trevor and the other two like he was bracing himself for a brawl.

"For doing what exactly?"

They could see the anger in his face. Trevor put his hands up in a gesture of conciliation.

"It's just for our higher administrative costs. In order to grow this thing, you'll need our support."

"We don't need your support," Adam spat. "This thing has been growing astronomically without a single shred of input from you."

"*Sampson, keep your cool up there. You don't want to blow your cover,*" Liam's voice crackled through Adam's earpiece.

"*Give 'em hell, boyo!*" said Mrs Mitchell.

"We're paying for this venue here today. Don't forget that, Adam," said Mark in the tone of a father talking to a rebellious teenage child.

"I'll be sure to take it out of the commission that you're receiving for doing jackshit, Mark," said Adam turning to his mentor.

"In fact, Mark, name me one single thing you've done to get us to where we are today," Adam gestured around the hall.

"That's not the point, Adam. The point is we set the framework in which you operate. Without us you'd be nothing. You've been standing on the shoulders of giants, son."

"Yeah, a giant pile of shit. That's what I've been standing on." Adam's face was now well truly red.

He watched the mentors exchange glances. In any normal syndicate interaction this gross insubordination would have meant instant dismissal. But this was not a normal interaction. Adam realised that he had the power now. The tables had turned. They were not trying to discipline him. They were trying to persuade him.

"The only reason you're standing here today is because of the syndicate, Adam," said Marco doing his usual trick of parroting Mark.

Adam threw his arms out and looked around him in conspicuous disgust.

"And what a glorious place it is to stand. Up high, looking down on all our good works. Looking down on a room full of grown men jerking off together. Does that make you proud, Marco? Trevor? Mark? Do you even care why we're here today or do you just care about the money?"

The three mentors were speechless. Adam realised it was because they didn't understand the question rather than any moral qualms they might have had.

"You know what I think?"

He pointed his finger at the three of them.

"I think you three are right at home here. Right where you belong. In your element. A big wank fest. That's where you belong."

Adam dropped his arm and took a moment to saviour the dumbfounded looks on the faces of those around him. Then he turned and headed for the door.

"Enjoy the show. Wankers."

"*Ata boy!*" shouted Mrs Mitchell over the radio.

Adam stormed down the stairs and back into the main hall forgetting to look out for Francis. The room was now very full. He came to a stop just inside the entrance doors. The main room lights went out. They were replaced by a similar kind of reddish light that Adam remembered Robert using for the livestream in the meeting room at the syndicate's office. The effect was like being in a nightclub.

"*It's game time,*" crackled Liam over the radio.

"*Where are you two?*" asked Adam.

"*I'm just behind the camera guy at the front of stage,*" said Liam.

"*I'm over the to the left of the front of stage near the door that leads to backstage area,*" said Mrs Mitchell.

"*What's the status with that door, Mrs M?*"

"*I've seen two different men come and go through it so far. They don't lock it after they leave. I'm pretty sure I can get inside.*"

"*Ok. You'll have to wait for Nastashya to come on stage. Otherwise, she'll blow your story about being her grandma.*"

"*10 4.*"

"*What can Mrs Mitchell do backstage?*" asked Adam.

"*Find out what's going on. We need to see what they've got set up back there.*"

"*I think we need to start to doing something.*"

"*Patience. We need to gather as much information as we can before we act. Once our cover's blown they'll be all over us and we won't have much time. Sampson, go and have a look around in the foyer for the electricity meter or fuse box or whatever. If we can kill the power that might stop the ceremony in its tracks."*

"Alright."

All of a sudden, the men in the hall pushed towards the stage. A white spotlight shone on Madame Orlova who was in her lace outfit. Adam couldn't tell from the back of the hall whether she was wearing anything underneath. His curiosity was answered as the giant projector screen flashed into life and a close up from Robert's camera confirmed that she was indeed naked.

The four other women joined her, each illuminated by their own spotlight. Adam looked around to see who was moving the lights but they seemed to be operated by remote control.

Nastashya spoke into the microphone.

"Welcome, my secret chiefs here and around the world. Today is the glorious 16th. The culmination of all we have prepared for will arrive in thirty minutes. We begin with ohm."

The ceremony with which Adam was now so familiar got underway. He turned and headed into the foyer.

"Mrs M, now's the time to make a beeline for backstage."

"10 4, Mr Love. On my way."

Mrs Mitchell pushed her way past a couple of ohm-ing men and walked up the several steps on the left-hand side of the stage that led to a black wooden door. She swung it open and stepped inside.

Ahead was a long, straight hallway that was lit with harsh fluorescent lights. She saw another black wooden door at the end of the corridor which faced out from the right-hand side. She headed towards it. This must be the door that led back stage. She opened it and walked into the room.

It was the same room that Adam had been ushered into on the awards night but Mrs Mitchell was entering from the left. The area directly to her left contained the series of small changing rooms. In front of them, directly in front of her was the makeup area where a number of mirrors, tables and stools were placed.

About ten metres in front of her in the middle of the room was an area that had been set up as the IT operations. A large desk was placed in the middle. Fritz sat on one side, Pavlos and Darrell on the other. All three turned towards her as she walked in.

"Hey!" shouted Fritz in his big man's voice. "This is a private area."

Mrs Mitchell ignored him and removed her hood and her coat and threw them onto one of the make-up tables. She walked over to the desk in her bright red Russian peasant's dress.

"Who are you?" asked Pavlos.

"Babushka Orlova," said Mrs Mitchell in her Russian accent.

"What?"

"Or-loh-va," said Mrs Mitchell slowly like she was talking to a fool.

"Do you understand, idiot?"

She bent over and stuck her face in Pavlos' as she spoke. He recoiled in a mixture of confusion and obedience like a young boy who had just been scolded but didn't quite understand what for.

Mrs Mitchell began walking around the table like she owned the place.

"I am grandmother of Madame Orlova. I come to make sure you morons not make mistake."

The three men exchanged looks each hoping one of the others would deal with this unexpected problem.

"Excuse me, ma'am," said Darrell in an extra polite tone.

"Mrs Orlova," corrected Mrs Mitchell.

"Ok. Mrs Orlova. We are right in the middle of a livestream here and we can't have any interruptions."

"I not interrupt," said Mrs Mitchell. "I want to watch from here. Is too many men outside. Is not suitable for woman out there."

Mrs Mitchell continued to walk around like a general inspecting a barracks.

The men looked at each other again and silently agreed that this was too much hassle to deal with.

"Just don't touch anything," said Fritz.

Mrs Mitchell swung around and slowly walked over to Fritz.

"May I touch you? Big, strong boy." She leaned over and ran her hand down his chest lasciviously.

"I like big man."

Fritz's cheeks went bright red.

Mrs Mitchell wandered back over to the make-up area and pretended to look around. She clicked on her receiver.

"*There's three of them backstage.*"

"*Only three?*" asked Liam.

"*What do they look like?*" asked Adam.

"*There's a big fat bald one, another bald one with a huge beard and a skinny nerd.*"

"*That's probably Fritz, Pavlos and Darrell.*"

"*How many others are there, Sampson?*" asked Liam.

"*There's Frank and Cameron unaccounted for. Francis is still loitering around outside the front door. I almost got busted by him a minute ago.*"

"*Have you found the electricity box yet?*"

"*No.*"

"*Alright, it's time to start making a move,*" said Liam. "*I'm standing right on the camera cable. Let's just see what this does.*"

Liam was right behind the elevated platform where Robert was operating the camera. The camera cable had been run down the back of the platform and seemed to run underneath the stage itself. There was a connection where the shorter cable from the camera joined the longer one that went under the stage. Liam reached down and pulled the two cables apart.

The audience was currently on the rubbing part of the ceremony. A murmur went through the crowd as the giant projector screen went black. The counter still showed 5.00 at the bottom.

Nastashya turned her head from the stage noticing the problem but turned back and continued to lead the audience. She shot a glance at Robert who was frantically checking the camera for a problem.

"The camera's gone," yelled Fritz from the table backstage. Pavlos and Darrell jumped up and ran around the other side to see.

"Is it a software problem?" asked Pavlos.

"I don't think so. Check the cable."

Pavlos followed the cable from the computer back to the wall.

"Looks fine on this side. I'll check it out front."

He ran out through the side door that Mrs Mitchell had come in.

"*Watch out, Mr Love. They're sending somebody out to inspect that cable,*" said Mrs Mitchell over the radio.

"*10 4, Mrs M. I'll make myself scarce.*"

"I told them we needed more than one camera," said Fritz banging the table.

Out front, Liam watched Pavlos come out the side door and push his way through a bunch of men who were rubbing their chests furiously. He found the two cables and re-joined them. The projector screen flashed to life with a close up on Madame Orlova.

Liam saw Robert hand down a roll of gaffer tape to Pavlos who was beneath the camera platform. Pavlos took it and swung the tape around the cable connections half a dozen times. He bit off the end with his teeth then threw the roll back up to Robert before pushing his way back past the crowd and disappearing through the side door.

"*They've fixed it,*" said Liam over the radio. "*Pretty quick response. We've got some competent opponents.*"

"*We'll see about that,*" said Mrs Mitchell.

Pavlos came back into the room and returned to his seat.

"What was the problem?" asked Darrell.

"The cables were disconnected. Somebody must have accidentally kicked them. I taped them back together. They're not going anywhere now."

"Good work, bro," said Fritz.

Mrs Mitchell ran her eyes over the power jacks on the laptops and other gear which was situated on top of the table. They all led back to a single power point from which a giant power board with multiple outlets ran. The masonic hall had obviously not had an upgrade to its electricity infrastructure in a long time.

The power board was located on the wall behind where Fritz was sitting. Mrs Mitchell gave him a big smile as she approached. Fritz glanced at her briefly before gluing his eyes back to his monitor.

Mrs Mitchell strolled very casually behind him observing his monitor like a united nations weapons inspector looking for warheads. She hooked her ankle around the cable that ran from the power board to the wall socket and proceeded with a yanking motion that turned effortlessly into a tripping motion. Several monitors went black. Lights that had been flashing, didn't. Three men who had been seated became upstanding.

"Oooops," said Mrs Mitchell as she stumbled.

"Oh, shit."

Fritz jumped up out of his seat and flung the plug back in the socket in a surprising display of agility. Mrs Mitchell watched carefully for the results.

"Oh, so sorry. Is everything ok?"

Fritz frantically pressed several buttons on several devices. Lights came back on and several seconds later the camera feed re-appeared on his monitor. He spent another minute getting everything back to normal. When he was satisfied they were back online, he turned to Mrs Mitchell.

"Over there!" He pointed to the make-up area.

Mrs Mitchell, acting as though thoroughly ashamed, started to walk in that direction but Fritz blocked her path.

"You go round that way."

He pointed for her to go around the other side of the table.

Fritz watched her like a hawk and waited for her to arrive at the makeup area.

"Stay!" he said as if ordering a disobedient pet.

Mrs Mitchell, continuing her mock remorseful posture, slinked towards the dressing rooms at the back and out of sight.

"*What was that Mrs M?*"

"*I disconnected the power that's running all their machines back here. What happened?*"

"The big screen went black. Even the timer wasn't working. Which means, we can take this whole thing down if we can disconnect the mains power. Sampson, how are you going in the search for the electricity box?"

"Wait, I think I've found it!"

Adam had scoured the whole foyer. He'd checked the men's toilets. He'd even checked the women's toilets figuring they would be empty. In desperation, he crept outside the building when Francis wasn't looking and had a look around outside.

The one last place he thought to look was the gallery on level two. That would suck. That would mean going back for a second round with the mentors. Thankfully, that wasn't going to be necessary.

The electricity box was halfway up the staircase on the east side of the building. He pulled the front door of the box open.

"Alright. I'm in. What am I looking for?"

"There should be a big line of switches, right?"

"Yep."

"Just turn them all off."

Adam started flicking switches to the off position. Inside the hall, the giant screen went black. The microphone went silent. Eventually the lights themselves went out. Backstage, the computer monitors flicked off. The flashing lights went out.

Adam finished turning off all the switches. The staircase itself was now mostly dark. It was lit only by whatever sunlight made it up the steps from the foyer.

"How's that?" he asked.

"Perfect. Everything's dark in here," answered Liam.

Adam closed the door of the box and started to turn around to head back downstairs when one more set of lights got knocked out. His.

CHAPTER 28

"Sampson, are you there? Sampson!"

"The lights are back on here."

"Sampson, talk to me."

"The computers are on."

"Sampson, what's going on?"

"They're starting to broadcast again."

"Shit. I think something's happened to Sampson, Mrs M."

"What time is it?"

"9.30. We've got eight minutes until Madame Orlova gives the pull your pants down command."

"Oh, god."

"I do not want to be in this room when that happens, Mrs M."

"We've gotta think of something quick."

The voices of Liam and Mrs Mitchell crackled away in Adam's ear. The sound waves travelled down the back of his head to the base of his skull like an earthquake travels along a fault line.

Something was calling out. Something was in trouble. It was his chest. It seemed to say: "Hate to be a bother, old chap. I know the noggin's not exactly firing on all cylinders at the moment but it's not all peaches and cream down here either, let me tell you."

There was an extra sharp jolt of pain from his sternum. Adam tried to lift his head. That wasn't gonna happen. Perhaps he could start by lifting his eyelids and build up from there.

The dim fluorescent light of the staircase fell against his retinas like snowflakes. A large shape began to take form in front of him. It was big and bulbous. Maybe it was a snowman. That would be nice. He could ask the snowman to please get off his chest. Then they could throw snowballs at each other. In the snow.

Adam gave his head a couple of shakes. What was he thinking. It didn't snow in Melbourne. And it was summertime.

His eyes gradually attained focus. It wasn't a snowman. It was one of the three Fs. The biggest one: Frank. His rotund head looked like a bit fat, ugly, butternut pumpkin that had been dressed with black rimmed glasses. Like the worst Halloween you've ever had. Like a pumpkin soup that's been in the fridge too long.

"Wakey-wakey, rise and shine," grinned the ugly bastard.

Adam let out an involuntary groan as Frank transferred some of his ample bodyweight to a different part of his chest.

He realised there was somebody else present. Another of the three Fs, Francis was standing over him near his right arm.

"What should we do with him?"

"Let's lock him in the men's dunny," said Frank.

The two Fs pulled Adam off the floor and stuck a humerus under each armpit. They dragged him down the stairs and into the men's toilet where they dumped him beside the urinal.

"How are we going to lock it? There's no lock," said Francis as he at Frank surveyed the toilet door. There were two doors in fact. Swinging doors. A bit like an old saloon in the wild west. Each door had a large squarish handle that was a slice of steel that wrapped onto a flat metal plate that was stuck to the wood.

"We need a broom or something to stick between the handles," said Frank.

The doors swung shut and Adam could hear them both scurry off.

"Got something," Adam heard Francis say from a distance.

There was a scratching and knocking sound as they slid the broom through the handles. Adam saw the doors shake violently. There was still several inches of give. Just enough to see out of if the doors were pushed or pulled.

"That'll have to do," said Frank. "You go back outside. I'll stand guard here."

Adam heard Francis depart. He could just make out Frank's figure through the crack between the swinging doors.

He pressed the button on his receiver.

"*Is anybody there?*" he groaned.

"*Sampson, are you alright?*"

"*I've been better.*"

"*What happened?*"

"*I got knocked out by one of the crew. The big bastard. Frank. He found me switching off the power.*"

"*They've switched it back on. Everything's back up and running out here. Where are you?*"

"*In the men's toilets.*"

"*You couldn't wait?*"

"*No. They've locked me in here.*"

"*Gotcha. Alright, looks like it's up to you and me, Mrs M. Things are getting pretty hairy out here in the hall. Literally and figuratively.*"

"*How long have we got, Mr Love?*"

"*Five minutes till pants down.*"

"*I have an idea. Mr Love, you follow my lead.*"

Mrs Mitchell stood up from where she was sitting on one of the makeup stools backstage. She removed her earpiece and unclipped her microphone and her receiver. She placed them in the bundle that was her coat and headpiece which were resting on the table of the make-up stand. She began to undo the large white buttons that held the front of her Russian peasant's dress in place. One by one they popped out to reveal a white petticoat beneath. She slid out of the arms of the dress. It fell to the floor in a bright red heap. She stepped out from the dress and undid a buckle on her left boot, then her right boot. She slid the boots off. She slid her socks off. She slid her petticoat off.

In the mirror of the make-up stand, Mrs Mitchell took a moment to look at herself in her underwear.

"Still got it," she said under her breath.

She undid her bra.

***

At the desk, Fritz, Darrell and Pavlos were in the final preparations for the big moment. Fritz was getting ready to kick off the timer on the livestream. Pavlos and Darrell were handling social media and the forums where they were live posting the events for anybody who didn't have access to the stream.

"Four minutes til we start the countdown," announced Fritz like he was at NASA getting ready for a space shuttle launch.

"10 4," said Pavlos and Darrell simultaneously.

There was a shuffling at the end of the desk. Mrs Mitchell gave a not-so-discreet cough.

The three men turned their heads and dropped their jaws.

"How I look, boys?"

There was no response from the men who had the appearance of a herd of stoned cows on a hot summer's afternoon.

Mrs Mitchell walked over to the door that led out onto the stage and gave a final look back.

"Once an Orlova, always an Orlova," she said as she swung the door open.

Out in the hall, things were moving towards the crescendo.

"Harder. Harder. Feel the energy building inside you. Inside your groin. Rushing up from your toes like a tidal wave."

Madame Orlova's voice rang out over the PA speakers as the hall full of men, groins out and heads back, rubbed the outside of their pants. The four women stood either side of Nastashya and demonstrated the correct technique.

Liam Love saw movement. A shadowy figure emerged and stood in a doorway at the back of the stage. The light of the room from which it came lit it from behind and created a silhouette that shone out into the hall cutting like a knife against the reddish glow. It flashed forward into the spotlight. Madame Orlova's spotlight. The black lace that half hid Nastashya's nakedness was replaced by the pure white of Mrs Mitchell's skin. There was nothing hiding *her* nakedness.

Mrs Mitchell began to dance, if that was the correct word for it. She danced like a demented marionette. Liam thought she looked like a coked-up Cossack after a few too many vodkas. Her limbs were flying around in all directions. She extruded and protruded and protracted her groin in and out and side to side. It was a wild, untamed, Dionysian extravaganza. A one-woman Eleusinian mystery orgy.

Perhaps out of disbelief at what was happening, Robert had kept the camera close up on Mrs Mitchell. She was up on the big screen and up on the livestream. She was sticking her tongue out and raising her eyebrows. She held her wrist to her groin and swung it back and forth mimicking the masturbators in front of her. Her visage was of the most patent mockery and condemnation.

Liam grasped the intent behind Mrs Mitchell's manoeuvring. He looked around to see if her performance was having the desired effect on the men. To his surprise, to his unparalleled amazement, to his raging disbelief, the answer was: no. The men had not stopped rubbing.

To be sure, they had adapted themselves to the change that had happened onstage. The rhythmical, repetitive, disciplined rubbing that Madame Orlova had demanded of them had been replaced by sporadic, disjointed motion that seemed to match Mrs Mitchell's deranged movements. The timing had changed but the intent remained.

The man standing beside him noticed that Liam was looking at him. "Bit of granny action, eh?" he smiled as he continued to rub himself. "She's got some life in her yet, this one," said the man behind him.

Liam felt as if he was about to wretch. He turned back to the stage. Mrs Mitchell was starting to tire. She stared out desperately at the room of men. Her plan to derail the ceremony wasn't working out. The men were still rubbing furiously. She looked around for Liam Love and spotted him down the front. She motioned to him to come up on stage but he looked at her with a confused expression.

Mrs Mitchell turned around to the microphone. Madame Orlova had disappeared. She was nowhere on stage. The four other women were continuing the show apparently oblivious to what had taken place. Mrs Mitchell pulled the microphone over to her.

"Liam Love. Get your arse on stage. Pronto."

Finally, Liam understood. He pushed his way to the side of the stage and whipped off his shoes and socks. He pulled down his pants and flung off his shirt.

He sprinted up the stairs that led onto the stage. His tackle was flying in all directions like an over-excited toddler punching a balloon tied to a pole.

The men cheered. This was not the desired response. Liam Love joined Mrs Mitchell on stage and began to mimic her as best he could while she stood off to the side to catch her breath.

He pointed to his cock then pointed to the men and made the masturbation gesture with his hand. He mimed himself punching his balls then punching his head. He mimed having a pair of scissors and cutting it all off. None of this had the slightest effect on the men who were still apparently enjoying the show.

Finally, Mrs Mitchell joined Liam on stage for one last hurrah. It was the Punch and Judy Show adults-only version. It was Commercial Road on New Year's Eve. It was a St Kilda strip club during the football finals. They whirled and wheeled and, eventually wheezed, around the stage. They were out of breath, out of energy and out of time.

Liam stood with hands on his knees and looked out onto the hall. The men had not stopped rubbing. Nothing could stop the rubbing.

"What's going on, people? Liam? Mrs Mitchell? Anybody there?"

Adam clicked the button off on his receiver. He had heard the cheers from the main hall. That was unusual. That had not happened before. Something must be going on.

He got off the floor and went over to the doors of the toilet.

"Frank? Frank, you there?"

There was no response. Adam pushed against the doors. They opened a few inches. Just enough to see Frank's ugly mug on the other side.

"Don't make me come in there," said Frank menacingly.

Adam let the doors swing back.

"What's going on inside? Something's happening. You better go and have a look."

"That's the oldest trick in the book, mate. I'm not falling for that one."

Adam pushed hard against the doors. There was a creaking sound from the hinges on either side. The doors of the toilets of the masonic hall had not been replaced since it was originally built. Adam figured he would do a little testing for structural integrity.

He leaned back and put all his weight against the doors pushing each side with one hand. They flew forward several inches before the broom handle stopped the momentum. A loud crack came from the right-hand frame.

"Hey! Stop that," shouted Frank.

Adam stepped back and threw his foot with as much weight as he could to the left edge of the right door. More movement. Another crack. It sounded like one more would do it.

He took one step back and elongated his stride like an Olympic triple jumper at the start of the run. He threw his right knee as high as it would go and brought his leg down hard against the door. It flung open as the right hinges removed themselves from the frame.

Frank took the door right in the nose. If he was angry before, he was now livid with a side order of infuriation and an entrée of seething rage.

Adam slipped past him much like a runner avoids the tip of a horn at the Running of the Bulls in Spain. This time there was only one runner and only one bull. Adam ran.

He kept to the edges of the foyer. In the grander scheme of things, time was not on his side. But, in the short term, it was. Frank was not the healthiest specimen. Soon the eight-cylinder engine of anger would be replaced the two-stroke motor of morbid obesity and Adam could make his move.

It happened quicker than he thought. Frank started to slow then stopped slowing. He stopped. He was bent over like yesterday's spinach. So complete was the breakdown that Adam felt no need to do anything further. He gave him a couple of kicks then left him there like a dilapidated car on the side of the highway.

Adam started walking toward the power box on the eastern staircase and when Francis appeared from the front door and strode across to block his path. In this particular matchup, it was Adam who had the weight advantage and he knew it.

He strode forwards towards his enemy. All the anger, all the frustration, all the embarrassment and humiliation and regret coalesced in his right elbow. He drew the elbow back like a Mongol archer and fired his fist at Francis' nose.

Francis had never been punched before. Francis had never even been in a fight before. He fell backwards but not because Adam had hit him. In fact, Adam's fist had sailed past missing his jaw by several inches. Francis fell backwards from sheer terror and it was sheer terror that picked him up off the floor and lifted him straight out the front door, across the road and as far away from the masonic hall as his legs would carry him.

Adam sprinted to the electricity box and opened the door. He reached for the switches again, then stopped. He decided that something more permanent was warranted. He stepped back and looked around. On the wall was a big red thing. A big red metal thing. A big red metal red rag to a bull.

He pried the fire extinguisher loose and lifted it up. The energy in his right elbow had not dissipated. It had spread to his left elbow. To his legs, his back and his chest. He felt the energy surge as he smashed the fire extinguisher into the power box. Again and again he whirled the metal container against the wall.

The power box came lose. The frayed ends of the cables poked out in weird directions like broken bones. A few small sparks gave notice that the job was done. The lights went out and this time they weren't coming back on.

CHAPTER 29

Adam dropped the fire extinguisher on the ground and slowly walked down the stairs and into the foyer. The surge of energy he had felt just a moment ago was gone. It was replaced by a vacuum. He felt empty.

Frank was still *non compos corporis* although he looked a little better than before. He was down on one knee and hunched over like he was pleading with the oxygen to enter his lungs. Otherwise, the foyer was empty.

Adam waited off to the side near the bottom of the stairs. Something seemed wrong. By now there should at least be a commotion. Some signal that things had gone awry. He leaned against a wall and waited some more. Nothing happened.

He checked his watch. 9.35am. Three minutes til the countdown would have started. Three minutes til hundreds of men in a hall and thousands, maybe even millions of men around the world, would have started working towards a simultaneous ejaculation.

Adam couldn't hold back a smile. How ridiculous. How utterly absurd the whole thing was and yet it had almost happened. He had a feeling that he might even regret not letting it happen. One day, when the emotions had died down and the urgency was gone he would sit back and wonder what it would have been like. Would the world really have ended? Would anything at all have happened? Probably not. And if nothing happened it would really have been just the funniest thing ever. So funny that you might die laughing.

There was still no signal from the auditorium. Adam pushed himself off the wall and slowly walked over to the doors that led inside. He was about three metres away when Liam Love and Mrs Mitchell came bursting through. They were still naked.

"Sampson, we've got a problem."

"I can see that," said Adam holding his hand over his eyes to block the view.

"No. Inside."

Liam motioned for Adam to come into the auditorium. He entered. It was pitch black but he could make out the figures of the secret chiefs. They were no longer facing the stage. They were facing ninety degrees to the right towards the west wall. They were in their now familiar rubbing position but their necks were craned back further than usual, their chins up higher. He followed their gazes to the second level.

On the gallery, on the edge of the ledge of the gallery, was Nastashya. She no longer had the lace outfit on. She no longer had anything on. She was completely naked although the darkness made it possible only to see her silhouette. Her face was illuminated by a tiny white light that came from something in her right hand. Adam struggled to see what it was.

"It's her phone," said Liam Love over Adam's shoulder. "She's livestreaming from her phone."

A shuffling and a rustling broke out in the hall. The men reached into their pants.

"Oh, no. It's happening," cried Mrs Mitchell.

Liam checked his watch.

"It's still a bit early," he said.

Around the room, men began pulling out their mobile phones. One-by-one, a thousand tiny white lights lit up. The men held their phones out in front of them. On each phone was a picture of Madame Orlova beamed live from the camera of her phone only metres above their heads.

"They're watching the livestream," said Liam almost hissing with anger.

From up above, Madame Orlova began to speak:

"My secret chiefs, we begin our final countdown.

"Stare at Madame Orlova.

"Take her with your eyes.

"Pull down your pants.

"Rub your manhood.

"Say ohm."

The men in the hall dropped their pants with surprising ease considering they had only one hand free. That one free hand was soon occupied with the main task of the morning. There was less than five minutes to 9.43am.

"No!" shouted Liam Love.

He ran over to a man and knocked his phone out of his hand.

"Look at yourself!" he shouted.

The man didn't even seem to notice Liam. He reached down, picked up his phone and continued his work.

Mrs Mitchell accosted an older man who was standing next to her.

"Can't you see what she's doing to you!?"

There was no response. The man continued staring into his phone. So did all the other men. They were oblivious to all other stimuli. All around the room men stared into their phones and rubbed their manhood.

Adam ran his eye along the gallery.

"Come with me," he shouted to Liam and Mrs Mitchell.

They followed him out the doors and over to the staircase at the side of the foyer. They began running up the stairs that led to the gallery then came to an abrupt halt.

Ahead of them were two large doors on a small landing that divided the staircase into an upper and lower segment. Adam had not noticed them before when they were open. But now they were shut firm. In front of the doors stood Trevor, Mark and Marco.

"Out of my way," commanded Adam.

"You're not getting through, Adam," said Mark.

Adam's energy was back. He felt it coursing through his whole body. He put his head down and ran as hard as he could straight at Mark who just managed to jump out of the way at the last moment. Adam pushed against the doors but they were locked. He looked for a handle. There was none. He stepped back and kicked hard. This time there was no crack. This time the hinges would not give way.

Adam turned around.

"It's locked from the inside, Adam. You can't get in," said Trevor smiling.

"Give it up, Adam. You can't stop it," added Marco.

Adam let out a shriek. He ran back down the stairs, past Liam and Mrs Mitchell and into the foyer. He sprinted across to the other wall and up the stairs that led to the gallery on the other side of the building. It was the same story. The doors there were locked too.

He ran back down to foyer. Mrs Mitchell and Liam were there.

"You'll have to get up from inside the hall," shouted Liam.

Adam rushed through the doors and looked around. His eye caught the stage at the front of the hall. It seemed like the only option.

The men in the hall were now well into their preparations for the end of the world. Adam pressed himself against the east wall of the auditorium and squeezed past the men who were still facing west towards Madame Orlova. He manoeuvred to the front of the hall and ran up onto the stage.

There was a large pipe organ at the back of the stage. He tried to shimmy up the pipes but they were too smooth and their proximity to each other made it impossible to get a proper grip.

He could have tried to jump from the left side of the stage and grab onto the railing but the distance was about three metres and the height of the stage meant he faced a fall of several metres if he missed.

He turned to the right side of the stage. The projector screen! He rushed over. The bottom of the screen was just above his head. It was a big metal rod several inches in diameter that ran the length of the screen. It spanned practically the whole distance across to the gallery railing. He could try to swing across on the rod and grab the railing on the other side.

He gave the screen a shake. It flipped and flung around like a child's toy in a bathtub. He looked up to see how the screen was hung but it was too dark to see clearly. There was a cable at the top that seemed to be connected to the roof. It did not look to be especially heavy duty.

"Four minutes to ejaculation," announced Madame Orlova from over his right shoulder.

He had no choice.

Adam grabbed the rod and leant out as far as he dared over the edge of the stage. He pushed off with his tiptoes and swung out over the void. The projector screen lurched to the right. The end of the metal rod banged against the gallery railing and bounced backwards. The screen twisted and turned sending Adam into a confused spin.

He tried to balance and wait for the screen to come back to some kind of rest position but it was clear that this was not going to happen. There would be no equilibrium point. No stability.

He moved his right hand over an inch. The screen lurched again as his weight transferred to the left. Now he moved his left hand over an inch. The screen lurched right. Another inch. He was starting to get the hang of it. Starting to anticipate the lurch. Starting to work with rather than against it.

An inch at a time he moved himself along the rod.

"Three minutes to ejaculation."

What!? This was going too slow. He was still a couple of metres away. He upped the tempo.

The projector screen twisted and shook violently. Liam Love and Mrs Mitchell watched from below as Adam moved along the bottom of the projector screen like a drunk possum on a power line. Finally, he had reached the end. Getting off the rod and onto the railing was not going to be easy.

Adam hesitated wondering what was the best way to do it. He tried reaching out with his right hand but the projector screen dropped sharply and he almost fell. After regaining his composure he began to swing. Bit by bit, the whole projector screen moved a little back and then a little forward. The swings started to get longer and longer. The metal rod was almost hitting the railing on the westward swing. Adam braced himself and pulled himself up as high as he dared. He grasped the rod with all his strength. On the next swing he pulled as hard as he could trying to harness the sideways momentum.

That momentum wasn't much. He seemed to fall down faster than he fell sideways. He reached out both hands above his head and grabbed for whatever he could. Somehow, the very bottom of the railing fell into his hands. He swung for a second and steadied himself. His feet were dangling down into the auditorium. He swung them up to the railing and gained a foothold then pulled the rest of his body up. He reached his right hand to the top railing and stood up. He was on.

"Two minutes to ejaculation."

Adam flung himself over the rail. He was on the gallery proper now. He turned and headed towards Nastashya. She was about ten metres away. He ran straight towards her then stopped. He hadn't realised earlier but now he saw that she was on the other side of the railing. The side that faced into the hall. Her lower back rested against the handrail. She had her phone in her right hand. Her left hand was holding on to the structure.

Adam didn't know what to do. He didn't want to startle her and have her fall forwards. He considered rushing up and pulling her back over the rail but this was also high risk. What if she fought back? What if she slipped? He could snatch her phone but this would certainly frighten her and she might fall. Another idea came to his mind.

"Hi, Nastashya."

Adam had to admit this sounded a little trite given the gravity of the situation.

To his surprise, Nastashya turned. To his greater surprise, she smiled at him.

"Hello, Adam."

"I'm just gonna come over to the rail," he said putting his hands up and moving very slowly over to the railing about two metres away from her. He watched her carefully. She showed no sign of objection or anxiousness.

"I'd like to talk to you," said Adam.

"Ok," said Nastashya still smiling.

Then she turned back and addressed the auditorium in her Madame Orlova voice.

"One minute to ejaculation."

Adam's heart started pounding.

"Woah! No. Nastashya, you can't do this."

"Why not?"

"It's not right."

"No?"

"Of course, not. It's ridiculous. It's dumb. It's crazy."

"I don't see problem."

"You don't. Look at that."

Adam pointed down to the hall. Nastashya looked down at the men.

"Looks nice to me. Looks beautiful."

Adam looked over the rail and into the auditorium.

Nastashya was right. Seen from the gallery, it *was* kind of beautiful. It was soft and inviting and unthreatening. The thousand tiny white lights of the men's' phones looked like stars in the night sky. The men themselves were not visible. Only the slightest reflection of their faces, just the tips of their noses, could be made out. Considering what they were doing down there, Adam was grateful for this fact.

He turned back to Nastashya. He had only one chance left.

"Nastashya, do you remember what you told me the other day? I asked you what sort of man you like. You said you like a strong man, a confident man, a man who would take risks. Didn't you?"

"Yes."

"Do these look like that kind of man to you?"

Adam pointed down into the hall.

"These men. Hidden down there in the shadows. Sitting in their bedrooms on the internet? Is that the type of man you want?"

"I don't know," she said quietly.

Nastashya's blue eyes looked down at the top of the railing. She still had her phone in her right hand but she seemed to have forgotten about it. It was pointing down to the ground.

"I don't think you'll find your man here, Nastashya. Or there."

Adam pointed to her phone.

"The type of man you want is out there."

Adam pointed through the west wall to the outside of the hall.

"He's out there in the real world."

Adam watched for a reaction from Nastashya but there was none. She was still looking down. Still looking away from him.

He tried to think of something more to say but this time he was out of words. He leaned a little on the railing realising that time was almost up.

Nastashya slowly raised her head. Adam caught sight of it and turned his towards her. Her eyelashes fluttered like a butterfly as she lifted her blue eyes which shone brighter than he had ever seen.

"You're right."

She held her phone up, reached over with her thumb and switched off the livestream.

Adam took a long, deep breath.

Down below in the auditorium, the thousand tiny white lights went out. One-by-one the they blinked off until the entire hall was left in darkness. Then the darkness was extinguished by a ray of dazzling light as Liam Love and Mrs Mitchell wedged open the doors to the foyer. The sunlight flooded into the room and what had just a minute ago been tiny stars in the night sky turned back into men.

A shuffling sound began as the men turned towards the doors and walked out into the light of the morning.

"Can you pass my coat, Adam?"

Adam turned and followed Nastashya's gesture to a pile on the floor of the gallery a few metres back from the railing. He went over and picked up her big topcoat. As he went to return it to her he noticed for the first time since he had climbed to the gallery that she was still naked.

She gave him a shy smile and he averted his gaze as he handed her the coat. She put her phone down on the rail and gently slid into the coat.

"Can you help me?"

Nastashya reached out her hand and Adam held it while she swung her legs over the railing and made the small jump down to the floor of the gallery. She smiled at him and walked over to collect the rest of her things from the floor.

Adam took several deep breaths as he leaned over the edge of the rail. The room was already almost empty. Just the last few stragglers were making their way to the door. Liam Love gave a wave.

"Come downstairs, Sampson."

"We're on our way."

He looked over at Nastashya. She was looking at her phone.

"You're not going to start broadcasting again, are you?"

"No. Just checking my emails."

Adam felt a flush of anger.

"Checking your emails! At a time like this?"

"What you mean?"

"What do you mean what do I mean? Five seconds ago we were about to see the end of the world. Or at the very least a jizz fest of epic proportions."

"Jizz fest?"

"A jizz fest. A sperm explosion. An erection ejection. A semen outburst."

"You mean, a simultaneous ejaculation?"

"Yeah. That."

"But, we didn't."

"No thanks to you."

"If you wanted to see it you shouldn't have stopped me."

"I didn't want to see it!"

"Then you should be happy."

"I?....shou?....happy?"

Adam couldn't speak.

There was shouting down below. Adam and Nastashya rushed over to the rail to see Liam and Mrs Mitchell near the stage where several shadowy figures were moving around violently. Adam couldn't see well enough to make out who they were.

"Sampson, get down here," shouted Liam.

Adam and Nastashya ran down the stairs flinging open the doors on the landing and then down through the foyer into the main room. The morning sunlight was shining in from the front but the hall itself was still quite dark and got darker as they moved closer to the stage. There was a large and two smaller figures on stage. It was Fritz, Pavlos and Darrell.

"There she is," boomed Fritz. "The arch-deceiver. The temptress."

He pointed a finger directly at Nastashya.

"Little Miss Orlova," snarled Pavlos.

"What is problem?" asked Nastashya innocently.

"Oh, I don't know," said Fritz stomping around the stage. "Lies, deception, treachery."

"Treachery?"

"You promised us an ending," said Darrell. "At 9.43am on the 16th of December there was supposed to be an ending."

"But there was no ending," added Pavlos.

"No ending," echoed Fritz.

"Why don't you three idiots go and give each other an ending in the men's toilets and stop whining like a bunch of babies," said Mrs Mitchell from the front of the stage. She had regained her clothing. So had Liam.

"Hey, I thought you were a Russian," said Fritz noticing that Mrs Mitchell had not used her Russian accent.

"Of course I'm not bloody Russian, blubber-belly. Do I sound Russian to you?"

"I knew it! Lies. It was all a pack of lies," shouted Pavlos.

"Both of these two are to blame," said Darrell pointing at Adam and Nastashya.

"Hey, I tried to stop you," said Adam.

"If it wasn't for you, this never would have started," said Pavlos.

"He's got a point there, Sampson," said Liam Love.

Adam shot him an angry look.

"Just sayin'," said Liam holding up his hands.

"Look, I think you guys should relax," said Adam to the three on stage. "Come down off the stage and let's talk this through. I'm sure Nastashya would be happy to explain why she has put us all through this."

"What I put you through?" asked Nastashya.

"Let's see," said Adam holding up his hand to count the items. "There was the small group of men rubbing their bodies in public, then the large group of men rubbing their groins in public, a week of masturbation exercises sent to men around the world, and a roomful of men today with their pants down and their cocks out. How's that for a start?"

"Sounds like my kind of party," said Mrs Mitchell.

"It's manipulation, that's what it is," said Darrell.

Mrs Mitchell went and put her arm around Nastashya.

"You're being a bit hard on our girl here. It's not her fault if you men can't keep your pants on."

"She was literally giving the command to pull our pants down," objected Fritz.

"Is she the queen of this country, you big oaf? Is there a law that says you have to follow her every instruction like some primary school boy with a crush on his teacher?"

"She was using magic," said Pavlos.

"Nonsense," said Mrs Mitchell. "You blokes just don't want to take responsibility for your actions."

"I thought you said she was a witch," said Adam.

"I did. But now that I've met her I've changed my mind."

Mrs Mitchell gave Nastashya a hug. Nastashya smiled and hugged her back.

"This isn't getting us anywhere," said Liam. "I think we need to go outside and get some fresh air."

Liam turned towards the foyer and saw two figures standing quietly in the middle of the room about five metres away. They were both holding knives in one hand and some kind of photograph in the other.

"Uhhh, Sampson. I think you need to look at this," said Liam out of the corner of his mouth.

Adam looked over his shoulder then wheeled around to face the two. It was Cameron and Neil Mitchell.

"Cam, I was wondering where you were."

Adam saw what they were holding.

"What's with the knife, mate? You ok?"

"It's the glorious 16th," said Cameron with a crazed look in his eye.

"But it's past 9.43," said Neil sounding even more nuts than Cameron.

"There was no simultaneous ejaculation."

"The prophecy was wrong."

"But we know the right prophecy."

Both men raised the knives in front of their chests.

"Woah, just relax you two," said Adam. "It's all good. There's no need to do anything stupid."

"She was wrong," said Cameron pointing to Nastashya. "The right prophecy involves a little snip-snip."

"A little cut-cut," added Neil.

"There was no simultaneous ejaculation. But there will be a simultaneous castration."

"What!?"

The other men present instinctively took two steps backwards and moved their left leg in front of their groins.

Cameron and Neil undid their jeans which fell around by their ankles. They slid down their underpants and lowered their knives.

"Cameron, snap out of it, man. This is crazy," said Adam stepping forward while keeping a close eye on the knives.

Adam looked over at Mrs Mitchell.

"Talk to your son, Mrs Mitchell."

"What? He might as well chop them off. He hasn't done anything useful with them anyway."

"Nastashya, help," pleaded Adam.

Nastashya shrugged.

The two men held up their pictures to look at. Adam could see that they were photos of Madame Orlova.

"Madame Orlova, we love you," said Cameron.

"We are ready to sacrifice for you," said Neil.

They grasped the knives firmly and moved them into position to the right side of their genitals.

"Hey, Cam, Neil, Madame Orlova is right here."

Adam waved his arms above his head to get their attention. He motioned for Nastashya to join him.

"Hey! Look at me you two. Look here. It's Madame Orlova. You don't need a picture. She's right here."

Nastashya walked over to Adam's side. Cameron and Neil briefly looked away from their photographs and towards Nastashya then looked back.

"That is not the real Madame Orlova."

"Yes, it is."

"Say something," Adam whispered to Nastashya. "Order them to stop."

Nastashya stood upright and raised her chin.

"Cameron. Neil," she commanded in her best Madame Orlova voice.

The two men looked up.

"Look at Madame Orlova.

"Stare into her eyes.

"Put down your knives.

"Pull up your pants.

"Say ohm."

The men followed Nastashya's instructions as she spoke. When it was over, the knives were on the ground and their pants were securely fastened. They stood there like stunned mullets. Adam crept over, bent down and slid the knives away from the two men.

After several seconds, Cameron and Neil seemed to come to their senses. They rubbed their eyes and looked around the auditorium as if they had snapped out of a trance.

"Feeling better, boys?" asked Liam.

"Yeah, I think so," said Cameron groggily.

"Where are we?" asked Neil.

"You're about five seconds away from having my foot in your backside," said Mrs Mitchell.

"Well that was something you don't see every day," said Liam clapping his hands together. "Who would have thought starting an apocalypse cult could lead to this kind of thing."

Liam looked in Adam's direction.

"Again with the I-told-you-so?" groaned Adam.

"We still need answers," said Pavlos angrily from the stage.

"Somebody must be held accountable," said Fritz.

"Accountable for what?" snapped Mrs Mitchell. "Stopping the end of the world? Would you clowns have preferred that we were all dead now?"

"We were lied to," said Darrell.

"Ok, ok," said Adam addressing the group. "You're right. You were lied to. I lied to you. I accept responsibility for that and I apologise. I think we should go and find somewhere quiet to sit and we can go through the whole story from the start. In the meantime, I don't think it's helpful to assign blame. Mrs Mitchell's right. Everybody here is responsible in some way for what happened. We each have to accept our responsibility for it. But we should also be glad we've got out of it without any real damage done. Nobody's hurt. Everybody's got their family jewels intact. It could have been a lot worse."

Adam looked around. There were some chastened looks, some sceptical looks and some angry looks still in the room.

"How about one more, nice big ohm and then we leave this place and put all this behind us? All together. What do you reckon?"

Adam walked over to face Nastashya.

"Everybody ready?" he said looking around.

The others straightened up, put their shoulders back and lifted their chins.

Adam took Nastashya's hands in his and looked deep into her blue eyes.

"Everybody in on the count of three. One, two, three…"

"Ooooooohhhhhhhhhhmmmmmm."

They all vibrated the same tone. Fritz, Pavlos and Darrell. Mrs Mitchell. Liam Love. Cameron and Neil. Adam and Nastashya.

The masonic hall in East Melbourne resonated in a deep, sonorous hum and balance was restored to the universe.

For news on upcoming releases and semi-regular blog posts, check out Simon's website: http://simonsheridan.me